BY THE SAME AUTHOR

King Season

Vanishing

GOSHEN PUBLIC LIBRARY
601 SOUTH FIFTH STREET
GOSHEN, IN 46526-3994

DISCARDED
Goshen Public Library

QUAN
WI

KIRBY WILKINS

QUANTUM WEB

HENRY HOLT and COMPANY
New York

GOSHEN PUBLIC LIBRARY
601 SOUTH FIFTH STREET
GOSHEN, IN 46526-3994

Fic
WIL

Copyright © 1990 by Kirby Wilkins
All rights reserved, including the right to reproduce
this book or portions thereof in any form.
Published by Henry Holt and Company, Inc.,
115 West 18th Street, New York, New York 10011.
Published in Canada by Fitzhenry & Whiteside Limited,
195 Allstate Parkway, Markham, Ontario L3R 4T8.

Library of Congress Cataloging-in-Publication Data
Wilkins, Kirby L.
Quantum web / Kirby Wilkins. — 1st ed.
p. cm.
ISBN 0-8050-1260-5
I. Title.
PS3573.I4414Q84   1990
813'.54—dc20   89-24679
                                          CIP

Henry Holt books are available at special discounts
for bulk purchases for sales promotions, premiums,
fund-raising, or educational use. Special editions or
book excerpts can also be created to specification.

For details contact:
Special Sales Director
Henry Holt and Company, Inc.
115 West 18th Street
New York, New York 10011

First Edition

Designed by Katy Riegel

Printed in the United States of America
Recognizing the importance of preserving the written word,
Henry Holt and Company, Inc., by policy, prints all of its first editions
on acid-free paper.∞

1 3 5 7 9 10 8 6 4 2

For Jennifer
and in memory of my mother

I should say:
the overall number of minds is just one.

—ERWIN SCHRÖDINGER

ACKNOWLEDGMENTS

Thank you to all of you who read and commented on early versions of this book. Joan Zimmerman and Linda Fox were particularly helpful.

Special thanks to Bill Wiegand for his vision, and to Joseph McNeilly for his help at a crucial juncture.

My editor, Amy Hertz, has also been a true guide in the final shaping of this book.

QUANTUM
WEB

1

He jammed his walking staff into the snow and dragged himself up, wheezing with altitude and frowning with headache. A late spring snowfall made the way treacherous, and now he was exhausted. High mountains had always cleared his mind in the past, but this time they'd given him nothing but a skull full of mud, throbbing with pain. Licking blood from his chapped lips, Jack Malloy stabbed the snow and stepped up, lungs burning. The staff, made of Asian hardwood and heavy as steel pipe, came from the Kathmandu bazaar like everything else he was carrying—tent, parka, sleeping bag. Bought or stolen from foreign trekkers, even his socks and heavy wool trousers had been occupied by other bodies, and their ghostly odors were a constant reminder.

He pushed up another step and then another, looking through his Polaroid glasses at the ragged pieces of white cloth flickering in the black sky over Tibet—prayer flags tied to sticks and jammed into piles of stone at propitious points all over these mountains. Stone prayer walls, stone chortens, stone hermitages. It was amazing, really, the persistence of these people. Their faith lived on stone since there was nothing else. He heard the flags snapping in the vicious north wind, and then, at last, he was descending into the dry Tibetan borderland.

After ten days trekking with a Sherpa and porters, Jack was alone for the first time. There was no chance of losing his way on a track worn through the ocher-colored hills and rumpled canyons by centuries of trade with India. Despite the long days of walking, he was still surprised at his presence here, in the rainshadow of the Himalayas, on the edge of the Tibetan Plateau stretching across Asia like a three-mile-high roof.

He'd descended perhaps two miles into Inner Dolpo when the horsemen appeared, suddenly, as if conjured from the brilliant, empty landscape. It took a moment to realize that they had emerged from one of the dry gulleys—two horsemen trailing a third pony, saddled but riderless. Jack and his Sherpa and porters had encountered many such nomadic travelers and caravans during the last ten days, and at first there was nothing about these men to alarm him, except for the rifles carried alongside their saddles and Sherpa Pasang's dire warning about entering this forbidden region of Nepal.

"No allowed," he said.

"Only go one day," Jack had said. "Go first village. Sleep. Come back. One day."

"Bad men Dolpo. No go," Pasang insisted. "Permit no allow."

But Jack was damned if he would miss an opportunity to see the southern edge of Tibet, and he finally prevailed. The trekking permit forbade them to enter, but there was no one to enforce such prohibitions, and a day's travel and night spent at the nearest Tibetan-speaking village could do no harm.

But the dog worried him. Accompanying the horsemen was one of the huge, wild dogs that had attacked him in villages, and he'd driven them off with his staff, gingerly at first, more viciously when he saw how roughly the dogs were treated by the villagers themselves. He took up a defensive stance, but the two horsemen called the dog back and talked with each other. Although Jack understood nothing they said, the language of the dog—snarling, hair ruffed along its spine—was clear: bad-smelling foreigner, tear his throat out. Now wary and a little frightened, Jack studied the riders. In Kathmandu, he had been warned about the Tibetan guerrillas fighting the Chinese along this border. Long tolerated by the Nepalese and armed by the CIA, they had turned to banditry and the area was closed to foreigners. One of the men dismounted and walked toward him, a squat, brutal-looking figure in rags.

Jack smiled as much as his cracked lips allowed. The man gestured toward the third pony. The dog snarled, quivering with readiness. Jack held his smile. The bandit pointed at his pack and then at the ground. Jack got the point. He was being robbed.

He tried to feign ignorance, shaking his head as if bewildered, but the man stepped closer, and the last remnants of Jack's smile vanished. He could capitulate and hope to be spared any further indignity (surely a foreigner's life was safe), or he could fight. It was an absurd alternative, but the man's gruff demand was infuriating, and since leaving India, Jack had been in an increasingly strange state of mind. His presence here, on the far side of the Himalayas, was so unlikely and perverse that he had lost any clear sense of his own actions. And now, blocked by this bandit, he felt all the rage he had kept bottled up since Bombay pour into his veins. He tightened his grip on the walking staff.

Again the man gestured to him to put down his pack.

Jack slipped the straps from his shoulders, shifting the staff from one hand to the other as he freed his arms. Slowly, he lowered the pack with one hand, holding the staff with the other. The horseman stooped toward the pack, reaching out a hand that looked like a club, swollen and cracked from exposure. As he leaned forward, his hairy face vanished from view and Jack was left staring at the coarse wool hat covering the top of his head. Jack stepped forward, the smooth wood sliding through his hands, arms locked for maximum force.

Although the wool cap cushioned the blow, he felt the man's skull crack. With an amazing roar, the dog lunged, as though released from compressed springs. Jack met the animal head-on with the staff held in both hands. It was like being struck with a boulder, but Jack recovered before the dog could leap again. Sliding both hands to one end of the stick, he swung it like an ax. The dog's foreleg snapped, and it went down screaming. The man on the ground had not moved.

3

Jack stood very still. The mounted horseman held a rifle pointed at his chest. A long clip of cartridges extending below the barrel announced an automatic weapon. They stared at each other, and Jack waited. Why didn't he fire? The dog screamed and scrambled up on three legs. The man on the ground was motionless. Jack and the armed horseman continued to stare as if neither knew what to do next, and for the first time, Jack noticed how badly disfigured the horseman was—his cheekbone crushed as if by a heavy blow, the still livid scar running from eye to chin. The face staring at him was slightly tilted, almost bemused. At last, Jack did the only thing he could think of: he reached for his pack. He crouched, keeping his face turned up toward the horseman and rifle, and dragged the orange pack toward him.

As he retreated, the horseman rode forward and dismounted, as though in a choreographed dance. The man put down his rifle and drew a knife from his belt. Staring at Jack with an angry face, he jerked back the dog's head and slit its throat. The screaming stopped as blood gushed onto the stones. Jack waited for the rifle to be picked up, for the burst of fire, and for more blood. At this range, the sound of the rifle and shock of the bullets would appear simultaneous, although the bullets would arrive first. He remembered stories in which people were shot before they knew they had been fired upon and was mildly surprised to find himself considering his own death with the same impartial interest he had accorded the dog's execution. These events seemed vaguely familiar, as if rehearsed for a play long since forgotten.

The rider put the knife back in his belt and began to drag his unconscious comrade to his horse. He had difficulty pushing him up over the saddle; Jack was inclined to help but thought the gesture might be misinterpreted. Swiftly and surely, the man ran a rope from his companion's feet under the horse and around his shoulders, as if he had performed this act many times. He hung the rifle in a rope sling beside his saddle and stared at Jack as if there had been some terrible misunderstanding. Then he mounted, and trailing the other two horses—the unconscious man tied over the saddle of one, the other still empty—he rode back toward the invisible ravine from which they had emerged.

4

The dog heaved convulsively and silently on the bloody ground. Finally it lay still, tongue lolling in blood, teeth exposed in protest. Wind whipped its fur and wuthered on the stones, but otherwise the country was still and silent in the brilliant late light of the high plateau. Long shadows stretched from the stones.

Jack dropped the staff beside his pack, and then sat down himself, his heart flickering. His dreamlike flight from India had terminated here. The dog was dead. The man also, perhaps. He should be dead himself.

Twelve days fleeing from Bombay had ended. By now Mukerjee had returned to Berkeley without any explanation for Jack's absence. But he'd lost the ability to think sequentially about the last two weeks. His mind was like a shattered mirror, and the splinters were cutting through his skull. It was the altitude. He had to get down from the pass. Even a thousand feet would relieve the pressure. He had to get down to the village.

But he remained among the lengthening shadows of individual stones. The dog's blood blackened like tar and was covered with grit. Small flies drank from the filmy eyes. When a quick shadow moved across the upper slope, Jack was slow to understand its significance. He looked up. An enormous Himalayan vulture was working the updrafts above his head, waiting for him to abandon the dog.

His hands still vibrated with the collapse of a human skull. Bone had burst into the man's brain like the brilliant shards of pain glittering in his own mind.

He'd figure it out in a minute, the reason he was sitting on the Tibetan border with a dead dog. Bombay was the reason. The First International Congress of Nuclear Physics for the Future of the Third World was the reason. He and Mukerjee had been invited from Berkeley to Bombay to talk about the future of developing nations. Sitting at long hardwood tables inlaid with ivory in vast, marble lecture halls hung with brocades and silks, attended by swift, silent servants with white gloves who served pots of tea and flaky pastry, while air-conditioned currents carried the scent of cloves and incense to their nostrils, they had talked as if particle physics were the hope of these poor countries. A red carpet had been rolled down the steps of the hotel welcoming the new raj to India. The nuclear raj, the new masters of the universe: Soviet and French and German and American physicists, riding elephants together like maharajas and then reading their papers about high-energy physics, while outside the hotel bullocks pulled crude wooden carts and barefoot women gathered dung for fuel.

But what had that to do with a dead dog?

He looked back toward India but saw only bare rock and snow. A blasted landscape, denuded and debased by the humans clawing at the slopes like people trying to save themselves from drowning, clinging to the edge of these inhospitable mountains. A tide of Hindus and Moslems and Buddhists crashing out of the plains against the mountains, stripping vegetation, eroding the soil. And he'd fled Bombay over those blasted hills only to end here at the edge of Tibet. Beyond this frontier, the Chinese had obliterated one of the great spiritual centers of the world, denying Tibetans even that solace for their wretchedness. On the Indian side of the mountains, faith dragged humans deeper into poverty. On this side, a bleak rationalism denied any reason to live.

The shadow passed below him. He looked up. The bird was nearly at eye level and much closer. The tantalizing smell must be rising on the same currents of air that supported the bird. The river canyon far below was dark in shadow. It was much too late to return over the pass to where Pasang waited. He must go on to the village—Pasang had been adamant that he should not sleep alone and exposed in this desolate land.

"All right," Jack said to the bird, "he's yours."

He stood, staggered under the pack and balanced himself with the accursed walking staff. According to the Survey of India map, the village was down in the dark crease of the canyon. Only a whim of colonial mapmakers had included this fragment of Tibet in Nepal. Since the Chinese invasion, it was all that remained of Buddhist Tibet. And likely all the Tibet he would ever see.

Beneath a brilliant roof of sky, he descended into evening shadow.

The vulture landed. Once again he heard the dog scream and felt the skull give. In crossing this highest watershed in the world, he had crossed a watershed in himself. All his years of physics and Zen meditation to cultivate humility and an open mind had come to this. All because of the fucking Bombay conference where Indian technocrats wanted to hear about fusion and plasma, superconductivity, hydrogen power, and did not want to hear Malloy talk about frontiers of mind. "Particle Physics as Paradigm: An Exploration of Mind." Who needed it? The Hindus already understood the mind. They didn't need physics for that. And they expected better from a man well known for tracking the elusive quark.

Mukerjee had commiserated with him. But Mukerjee had behaved strangely in India. The moment they stepped off the plane in Bombay, the harsh, skeptical patina of the experimental physicist had dropped away, as if on returning home Mukerjee had entered a mysterious force field that made him soft, almost limpid in his manner, garrulous, and as naïve as an undergraduate. He blandly ignored India's dangerous scheme for plutonium self-sufficiency, its lack of safeguards, the whole haphazard mess. The very things that would have driven him crazy at the lab in Berkeley were now only quaint native folkways. The aloof Mukerjee even became a popular speaker at the conference, and an inebriated raconteur in the late evening, while Jack grew increasingly morose and isolated.

Finally, the technocratic buzz of plasma, accelerators and fusion had sent him wandering in the netherworld of Bombay slums, alone, where people in rags carried their filthy cardboard homes like precious treasures. They defecated in alleys, bathed in squalid puddles, lay dying in doorways, while his colleagues talked particle decay and superconductivity. He gave all his rupees to leprous beggars and deformed children, but when the rupees were gone, their fingers continued to pluck at his body as if to strip away his flesh. He seemed to draw these people as a corpse draws vultures, and he finally retreated to the hotel, frightened, sweating and stinking from the streets. He found Mukerjee vibrating with health and conspiratorial energy. He had a secret. "Not a word, Jack, to anyone."

7

Jack's eyes burned with the open sores and feces and twisted limbs and distended bellies and gaping mouths that had sucked him into a vortex of misery—Jack, the nuclear savior.

Mukerjee was insufferably insensitive to his state. "Jack, they have a device."

"A device?"

"They're going to detonate a device in the next few weeks."

"A device?"

"About ten kiloton."

This fat, complacent, lapsed Hindu bubbled with delight that his countrymen had succeeded in using their nuclear power capacity to devise an atomic bomb—in the birthplace of Buddha and Gandhi. Dazed from the heat and stink of the streets, Jack tried to comprehend.

"You dumb fucker!" Had he actually said that? "What are they going to *do* with a fucking bomb?"

"It's symbolic."

"Symbolic? You asshole. What do you think Pakistan will do? Iran? Iraq? Do you know what this means?"

Mukerjee's manner was very English, very Cambridge. To call him an asshole was unthinkable. But there it was. Mukerjee had flushed, stuttering, caught between his pride in conspiracy and this sudden anger from his friend, whom he had honored with the secret. Mukerjee remained enough of a Hindu to appreciate that the universe must self-destruct many more times before humans are enlightened (even lapsed Hindu physicists trained at Cambridge and Berkeley), so what was one nuke more or less?

Mukerjee's face decayed into confusion and hurt, and he was near tears when he left the room. About fifteen minutes later, Jack left the hotel carrying a suitcase, passport and traveler's checks. He left a terse note at the reception counter: "Go home without me. I'll be in touch."

He had to get away from this betrayal of physics, from the heat and poverty, and he headed north by instinct. North was cooler. North was mountains. He flew straight to Nepal as if following a radio homing beacon, but Kathmandu's lush spring at five thousand feet wasn't sufficient. The Himalayas pulled him forward like a magnet, and in only two days he'd arranged a trek into western Nepal, rather than along a popular route to Everest or Annapurna. He didn't want to see another foreigner. He wanted solitude. He wanted to push himself to the edge of the void and see what voices spoke to him there. He wanted to do penance for being a physicist. For being human. And so he had left the approved route behind Dhaulagiri massif and dropped right over the edge into the forbidden land called Dolpo.

Less than five miles from where he had left the dead dog, terraced fields appeared, and rough geometrical shapes of human habitation the same color as the bare land. Flat roofs, stone walls, a wisp of smoke. No dogs. It was the first village of the Tibetan frontier region. People appeared, as they had in other villages, but these were somber and unsmiling. And for the first time it occurred to him that he might be unwelcome here. Pasang's warnings rang in his ears: "Bad people Dolpo. No go."

He was alone without language among people who could no longer trade their wool with Tibet or winter their herds there, and whose animals had died as a result. Their monasteries had fallen into ruin, and bandit guerrillas armed by his own country roamed their desolate land. Debased by deprivation and a harsh environment, they stood stolid, unsmiling, filthy. And in their faces he saw himself reflected—a foreigner descending from another world.

Physics would serve no purpose here.

2

Jack had imagined that gestures, good intentions and common needs would be sufficient to let him travel on his own. But now he was bewildered and afraid. Even the children were wary of him, as if they had been warned about this murderer entering their village, and he was turning back toward the pass when men rushed forward to block the way. They shouted and pointed toward the dozen huts of the village. Their invitation wasn't friendly so much as insistent, and he was too exhausted and oppressed to resist.

The houses clinging to the steep valley walls were similar to others he'd seen in the barren Himalayan highlands, lacking chimneys or windows, the living spaces acrid and black with soot. But the people crowding into this room frightened him; they pressed on his mind like the lingering headache. Filthy clothes, greasy hair, barefoot—the room was full, and as the dung fire smoked and flickered, faces emerged and retreated from view. The smell was enormous. He yearned for morning light to guide him back over the mountains where Pasang would be waiting with new porters at the village of Tsharka.

He drank the awful salt-and-butter tea and ate the gritty roasted grain mush called tsampa with stoic endurance. When he offered money, the rupees were taken from his hand and replaced by several fire-blackened potatoes, withered by poor soil and altitude. He put them in his pocket for morning. When at last the room began to clear of voices and the rank oppression of packed bodies, one of the remaining men pointed at a smoky corner where he could sleep. Jack frantically opened his pack to display his down sleeping bag, pointing outside and yawning, holding his clasped hands under his face like a pillow. The man's fingers stroked the nylon as if it had been offered for sale, but he finally got the idea and escorted Jack into the starlight. He led him up the steep hill behind the hut onto the flat roof itself, one of the few flat spaces in the village, Jack realized. When he got down on his hands and knees, he found the dirt peppered with dung, mostly dry. From the goats, he supposed. He swept a space for his pad and sleeping bag, and when the last murky figure had vanished over the roof edge, he crawled fully clothed into his sleeping bag and lay looking east, waiting for the sun to release him from this dismal place.

Jangled by altitude and the hostility of these people, and by the sickening feel of a man's crushed skull, he couldn't sleep. The awful feeling inside him made the rumored Indian bomb that had triggered his flight seem remote—a theoretical problem. He looked up at a sky sprinkled with hard stars, unsoftened by atmosphere. Through these bright stones in the sky a dog's blood ran in a river, spreading into a dark lake against which the constellations defined themselves. This was the void in which flickered the transitory forms of human delusion: suffering and happiness. His heart beat shallowly as he stared at an unfamiliar night sky and the bizarre shapes his mind created there —like the absurd and monstrous figures of Tantric Buddhism in Kathmandu temples and on the frescoed walls of remote villages and monasteries. Or like the exotic particles created by his colleagues in Berkeley and caught on film as bright whirls of light. At least the Buddhists knew such phantasms were within the mind's power to create and extinguish. But physicists believed in the product of their own meditations. For a moment the brilliant void overhead seemed to be a bubble chamber that he was entering like an accelerated particle, and his buzzing headache felt like millions of electron volts surging into his body with each pass of the electromagnets.

He fell asleep with the taste of rancid butter in his mouth.

The constellations turned overhead. Moisture from his sleeping body seeped out through the nylon and froze. Frost glittered on his sleeping bag. Wind moved down the canyon. He heard the distant sound of water striking stone, and several times what seemed to be the rustlings of domestic animals.

What brought him wide awake finally was a rope around his shoulders, trapping him in the mummy bag. Faces loomed against the eastern sky, voices surged around him. He was being dragged to his feet. He was being carried off the roof into the street and stood up like a post, encased in his sleeping bag. Now he could make out figures standing in doorways, crouched on roofs, on the rude path between huts. He smelled horses before he saw them, swishing their tails and twisting their heads. The sky had turned metallic. He recognized his own pack tied behind the saddle of one of the horses. The rope was released from his shoulders and the sleeping bag peeled from his body. He emerged fully clothed into the freezing air. His arms were shoved into the sleeves of what he recognized as his own down parka, the desiccated lumps of potatoes still in the pockets. Other hands stuffed his sleeping bag into the pack on the horse.

He recognized the ugly scar and crushed cheek of the man who had not killed him. The villagers were backing away, leaving him alone with this man and a Buddhist monk in reddish homespun robes. His greasy hair was wound up on top of his head, and he was speaking slowly, emphatically to the horseman. The monk radiated such calmness that Jack's heart slowed its frenzy, and the constriction inside his chest opened. Even his hands stopped trembling when the monk touched him. He was being drawn toward a horse. He recognized the animal: it was the third horse, riderless, that he'd seen at the base of the pass. He pulled himself awkwardly into the saddle. The walking staff was thrust into his hands, and the monk led the horse forward. Jack looked behind at the horseman, rifle held in one hand.

Eyes watched from doorways and rooftops as their procession moved along the narrow path between buildings. These stone and mud houses of a primitive village of Inner Dolpo were the electromagnets accelerating him toward a target. That image of his restless sleep came back to him. But he wasn't dreaming now because his arms still hurt from rope and rough hands, and the wooden saddle banged his thighs.

Out beyond the village was the surreal emptiness of the Tibetan borderland, and as dawn brightened the stony slopes, he saw they were headed away from the canyon toward the mountains of the frontier itself. The monk no longer led the pony but glided ahead over the stony ridges with an effortless grace, as if his feet never touched the earth, and the horse followed him without direction. They climbed through the high desert wasteland beyond the Himalayas, crossing ridges and moving through eroded gulleys, and as Jack grew used to the motion of the horse, his grip on the saddle loosened. Grass, flowers, lichens vanished. Dolpo opened out behind them. And still the little figure in red appeared and disappeared in the distance.

In late afternoon they entered a south-facing canyon at the very base of the Tibetan border range. At the mouth of the canyon stood a low black tent—like those of the Tibetan nomads he'd seen in pictures. Horses grazed nearby, and as several men emerged to watch their approach, the horseman dismounted. The little monk led Jack's horse on toward the head of the canyon, a stone wall pocked with holes. The monk gestured for Jack to get off the horse, and he did, stumbling onto the sandy bottom of the valley.

He followed the monk into a cave at the base of the cliff where he saw a figure stretched on the stone floor. A man lay with his bandaged head propped on a rolled blanket as if in deep sleep. Jack felt the man's skull give beneath his blow. He saw the dog leap.

As his eyes adjusted to dim light, a ring of fire stones and several metal pots appeared. Ammunition boxes and rifles were stacked against a far wall. Someone spoke. Jack turned. The monk had leaned Jack's pack against a wall and was gesturing him back outside into the brilliant glare. Jack obeyed as if there were no alternative—he'd lost any will to resist. The monk pointed up steps hewn into the stone face.

Jack knew that hermitages such as these existed throughout the Himalaya and had been occupied for thousands of years, as legend would have it, by the most spiritually advanced men who ever lived. During his Zen studies, the magic and mystery of such tales had always annoyed him. And yet he now stood on the far side, staring up a rock wall at one of these hermitages. Instead of being killed, he had been brought here. The realization struck him as brilliantly incisive.

The monk began to climb, filthy bare toes gripping the stone, and Jack followed as though he were being drawn by a string up the hewn steps. When the monk entered the next highest cave, Jack followed and waited patiently for his eyes to adjust. Another monk sat in deep meditation. Arranged before him were a butter lamp and the ritual instruments of Tibetan Buddhism: the drum made of a human skull, trumpet of a human thighbone, vajra bell, scepter. Thankas hung on the walls. The air was close, smelling of the butter lamp and hundreds of years of unwashed occupancy. The meditating monk did not look up or acknowledge their arrival. Jack's guide sat down and indicated a woven pad beside him. Jack sat down. When he glanced again at the monks, both were in deep meditation.

He was alone, left to his own devices. Though it had been several years since he had practiced meditation himself, he instinctively folded his long, stiff, Western legs into a half lotus and let his breathing slow in the Zen way. He was captive, yet in the presence of the monks felt an odd elation. He was faint with altitude, and as he slipped deeper, he wondered if his mind had been dangerously deprived of oxygen. Above him, he felt the pressure from thousands of feet of stone forming the edge of the Tibetan Plateau. His headache vanished.

He woke to find himself covered by a yak-hair blanket; both monks were still meditating by the light of the butter lamp. When he woke again, there was faint light outside the cave entrance. The monks had evidently not slept. Wrapping himself in the blanket, he sat up in meditation once again. At midday, the monks brought a wooden bowl of roasted tsampa and butter tea. He had the impression that he had missed a day and thought back carefully: he had entered Inner Dolpo on the eighteenth of May. He had come to these caves on the nineteenth. This must be the twentieth. Pasang was in a very bad position now, having let his employer violate their permit by entering Dolpo in the first place, and then having lost his employer altogether. Yet Jack had no sense of urgency. He sat as though stunned by a blow from his own walking staff.

That evening both monks left the cave and indicated that he should follow. They led him down the valley to a rock outcropping jutting over the distant river gorge and the wild tangle of Dolpo hills. He could see halfway to India. The river below eventually became the Karnali, flowing into the Ganges and all the holy poverty that was India. A mile to the east, water ran to the Brahmaputra and flowed into the jungles of Burma. He stood on the greatest watershed in the world. Up here, a step or two could make all the difference.

And then he saw the body.

On the dome of the boulder lay the man he had struck. Naked. Dead. Beside him sat five men whom Jack took to be Tibetan guerrillas, one of whom he recognized by the awful scar and crushed cheekbone. And just as this man had drawn a knife and approached the screaming dog, the little monk now drew a knife and approached the corpse. The fight on the pass superimposed itself over this grisly scene, and Jack watched with horror as the monk began to peel the man's flesh from his bones, slicing away tendons, cutting ligaments and separating limbs from the body, disemboweling the corpse and spreading blood and slime. He was mesmerized. The other monk began to crush the bloody bones, beginning with the skull. He used a stone tied to a stick—Jack's walking staff—and brought the stone down as though chopping wood with a crude ax, splintering the bones and mushing the marrow into a dark ooze. A man was being reduced to bloody meat and fragments of bone. The two monks worked calmly, as if preparing a meal. Vultures gathered at a respectful distance, and when the monks finally sat back in their blood-spattered robes, the birds rushed forward, snapping at one another, beating their wings and ripping at the flesh. The monks began to chant, and their voices blended with the sound of wings and clack of jaws.

Jack sat, dazed, watching his victim being consumed. The slick intestines, the crushed skull, the sticky brains and smashed feet belonged to a man he had killed. He was paralyzed with horror at what a single blow of his walking staff had created. And he was grateful for the failing light and the monks' chant: for the human rhythm of strange syllables.

A bell rang in the mountain silence—a small sound but a comforting one. At dusk, the Tibetan warriors left the bloody rock, but Jack sat into the freezing night, hypnotized, half-awake. The horsemen had simply wanted to bring him back to this hermitage, and he had misunderstood. His own fear had killed a man. Never had he felt such despair.

A large animal came snuffling and snarling, and beneath the monks' voices, he heard its catlike chewing, teeth on bone, and against the dark sky, he saw its shape: the rare snow leopard had come to visit.

At dawn his own shivering had passed into a strange warmth. The corpse had vanished. Flecks of flesh and bone remained, and blood had darkened and coagulated on the stone, but the shape of a man had utterly vanished. The vultures were visible in the sky; somewhere a leopard was sleeping, satiated. He had witnessed a celestial burial that in books on Tibet had seemed so barbaric. But now he understood that flesh and bone had simply undergone a brief transition: from life to life via death. He even seemed to understand the monks' chant: they addressed the dead man as if he were still present in the universe —but in some new form. Jack had long studied the transformation of matter and energy, using quantum mechanics to describe the exchange in which nothing was ever lost. Now a human being had moved between two states, but for this event a wave equation did not exist. Quantum mechanics could describe the life and death of a particle with miraculous precision, but its mathematics were useless here. He had come a long way to see a man butchered and fed to the birds.

He had come a long way to kill the man. It was a bizarre accident. Yet here at sunrise, the events of the past three days no longer seemed accidental. The anger that had driven him all the way from Bombay to Dolpo had exploded with amazing force when he brought the staff down on a man's head. But it was no accident.

He listened carefully to the monks' chant, as if the answer lay in their words. While out beyond the bloody stone, morning sunlight struck the distant peaks and turned the sky a brilliant blue.

3

Thirty miles northwest of the cave where Jack sits meditating lie the ruins of another ghompa, a Tibetan temple complex. The whitened raw edges of stone suggest recent destruction, although constant wind, dust and freezing have already created a weathered brooding quality suggestive of ruins all over Asia. But unlike Angkor Watt or Annaratapura, no sudden jungle will obscure these walls, which likely will remain exposed until geological forces grind down the stone itself.

The ancient manuscripts of handmade paper and palm leaf from India, the silk wall hangings, some of which survived the Moslem destruction of temples in India, have been burned; the statues of gold have been melted back into indistinguishable bullion. An unexploded mortar shell, charred timbers and the dynamited fragments of a bronze Buddha scattered like shrapnel in the rubble tell a crude story. The monk who still lives in the broken stone like a feral animal could probably give a fuller account of what happened, but he says nothing that makes any sense at all, mumbling mantras, odd fragments of song, bits of Tantric scripture. His thumbs, which once counted 108 rough beads made from 108 separate human skulls, have been cut off. Lumpy scars suggest a blunt instrument like a dull ax or handsaw. Since the Tibet Area Military Command has driven all nomads from the immediate vicinity, he has no source of food except what he can beg from the military vehicles passing near the ruins. The Chinese soldiers once threw stones at him, but recently they have begun to toss him small sacks of cooked rice, which he carries back across the rocky plain toward the broken walls on the hilltop.

On the newly paved road, convoys of Chinese-made trucks travel from the plains of the Tsangpo and the main highway of western Tibet to the base of the mountains bordering Nepal. For a year now the rumble of high explosives has sounded like some monstrous storm chained to the mountains. Aircraft have begun to land and take off, and under certain wind conditions, they fly low over the ruins. The monk twists his head at the jets, babbling at what he sees through the Plexiglas cockpits. Human faces hang in the air above him like masks.

Inside the middle cave, Jack tries to focus his mind and gain control of his thoughts, but he's so exhausted from lack of sleep that he keeps drifting away, and whenever the trumpet blares or the cymbals crash, he wakes, his consciousness guttering like the butter lamp, sputtering, flaring up. He writes mechanically in his journal, trying to order his thoughts, but the words are nothing but ink marks on paper.

Finally, he wakes from a deep sleep to find a yak-hair blanket drawn over him and the monks gone from the cave. Silence. No chanting, no cymbals, drums, horns or bells. He's alone. But where? He tries to retrace his journey to this cave, to think his way back over the Himalayas to the village where Pasang must be waiting, but all the chanting, the meditation, the absence of language has blurred his thinking. He's alone with the rhythm of his own breath and blood; his eyelids open and close of their own accord. Saliva gathers and he swallows. His ears buzz with what he takes to be altitude, but after a while the sound seems to waver as if it's coming from nearby, and his head swivels, eyes searching the dim cave. Nothing. Then he leans over and presses his face to the stone floor, as if the mountain itself might be making the sound, and indeed it seems as if his ear is pressed to the taut skin of a drum. When he sits up, he knows where the sound is coming from. The cave above. The monks have gone up to the highest cave.

They've acquired names: Gyatsu brought him here from the village; Sonam speaks to no one, though he joins in the chanting. The monks have indicated there's another person in the highest cave above, a lama named Dorje. Now Jack is on his feet and moving toward the starlit entrance where the cold night air strikes his face. Without artificial light these past days, his eyes have become nocturnal, and he's learned to rely on the luminous night sky for vision. He looks up along the dim bulk of stone, his fingers touching the cold surface as he gropes for the first step cut into the rock. He swings onto the bare rock face, onto stone worn smooth by other hands and bodies, as if he's done this ten thousand times, reaching for the next step. The sound envelops him, wavers, flexes itself, is broken by the startling yowl of the bone trumpet and the beat of a drum. When the top of his head reaches the entrance of the highest cave, he looks in at floor level.

Against one wall a single butter lamp casts tall, distorted shadows of the two monks with their musical instruments. Opposite them in a kind of crib lined with grass sits a man, naked and skeletal. From his throat emanates a sound like a single vocal cord being scratched with broken glass. Eyes sunken in sockets, flesh wrinkled and dried, this ancient figure seems incapable of any sound, yet when his mouth closes, the sound stops. The drum claps once. Silence.

This emaciated figure is Lama Dorje, who sent the warriors to the pass and whose messenger Jack killed for want of understanding. In front of the lama sits a prayer rug—empty as the saddle of the third horse sent for him. As Jack raises his body into the cave entrance, a spectral appearance surely, none of the three men acknowledge him. Even as he crawls toward them, pulling himself forward as if still climbing the cliff, they don't look at him, not even when he sits up on the rug within arm's length of the lama.

There's a musty odor, neither human nor animal but familiar, and he feels faint. His mind thins out, like water evaporating, and leaves his body dry and clean. When the drum explodes behind him, he

20

doesn't flinch, because he isn't surprised. In the ancient mass of wrinkles the mouth is opening, shaping sound—a new sound that rustles and rattles around him like dry reeds, drawing him down inside it, snug, like hiding in tall grass; he seems to be vibrating right down the lama's spine, until he and the sound are one, and he is breaking the sound into syllables that seem familiar to him. As he gathers them into clusters, these pebbles of language grow translucent as diamonds. Later, writing in his journal, he tries to capture their meaning in crude hieroglyphs of English.

> *I have traveled.*
> *To the watchtowers of the north, I have traveled.*
> *To the underground cities, I have traveled.*
> *Beyond the salt flats, I have traveled.*
> *When the towers of dust arise, I am there.*
> *When clouds bloom from the earth, I am there.*
> *When the earth shakes and collapses, I am there.*
> *To the north, to the east, to the west,*
> *I am there.*
> *Now the circle closes*
> *To the south.*
> *Kali whirls and iron shutters close.*
> *To the south*
> *The earth shakes and rises.*
> *To the south*
> *The wrathful deities rise.*
> *From the light brighter than a thousand suns*
> *The wrathful deities rise.*
> *Such is the power of mind.*
> *Such is the power of delusion.*
> *With Mahakala the destroyer,*
> *I dance.*
> *In the white light*
> *I sing.*
> *For this is the chant of ten thousand ways.*

The voice stops. Sitting on a coarse woolen rug in a Himalayan cave, Jack knows the voice has stopped and that he is staring at a naked ascetic in a straw crib. Jack recognizes the images in his mind because he's witnessed the last surface atomic test in Nevada. He knows the Soviet test site at Semipalatinsk, the Chinese site at Lop Nor, the French site in the Sahara. But it doesn't seem possible that this hermit can know these things. He looks fragile as a reed, but a reed rooted in solid rock, quivering imperceptibly, like the needle of a seismograph. For a moment this new image blazes in his mind of the hermit registering the lonesome P waves and Love waves traveling around the earth from an underground nuclear blast, and of the scratchy sound of his voice engraving these movements on Jack's mind. As if Jack were the cylinder of a seismograph and the lama the needle, the two of them collaborating to create these words and images.

The thoughts seem transmitted from the lama, but Jack is certain the old man can know nothing of the test planned in India, so Jack himself must be the source. The flickering lamps, the chanting, the butchering of the dead man, the snuffling of the leopard, the vultures sitting like polite guests have made his thoughts crazy and unreliable. It's simply a matter of regaining control of his mind, but even as he tries to frame what might be happening here in logical terms, the words explode in his brain, scattering bright shards, and he winces with pain. Until now, the high-altitude headache had been absent in this hermitage.

The trumpet and drum explode behind him. The wrinkled mouth opens before him, and images once again begin to coalesce in his mind, emerging from the undifferentiated sound in his ears the way particles emerged from the undifferentiated flux of energy beyond his equations. But instead of establishing position or momentum, these particles of sound cast shadows in his mind. Later, in his journal, he tries to capture the reality behind these shadows in language which, lamentably, lacks the elegant precision of mathematics.

I see many trees. Dry hills ring the valley of trees. There is a great silence, except for the trees breathing in the breeze.

Beneath the trees are caverns. In the caverns, the people are listening. They cannot look at the sky; they cannot look at the earth; their caverns are dark. The people listen. The earth is carrying their valley in a great wheel through the night.

They hear a sound like distant drums. Drums coming into the trees. Drums outside their caverns. They are afraid. Why are they afraid? Because the drums have come inside their heads. Their heads have become drums. The caverns pulse with sound, in and out, with the sound inside their skulls. The beating outside is the beating inside. There is no difference. Now the people must leave the caverns.

They walk through the ten thousand trees. They walk toward the dead hills, and their sound lingers in the valley of ten thousand trees. It is like the sound of a brass gong that is struck once and no more, and the vibration follows them over the dead hills. There are no trees. There is no water. And their sound dries out in the great heat.

Now the empty caverns make a new sound. It is like wind blowing through an empty skull. The valley of ten thousand trees sings its emptiness. The sky is like a taut skin returning the sound.

The people have spread out like dry seeds on the wind that was their own sound. They can hear the lost valley of ten thousand trees in the distance, and they are frightened. The people move farther and farther away until they vanish from one another. They are alone. But in their feet, like an earthquake, is the sound of the lost valley.

This is the dream of ten thousand trees.

The voice stopped. A bell rang. Jack opened his eyes. The naked old man sat erect, eyes open but unfocused—the ancient figure had not yet acknowledged Jack's presence. Dorje's life had been spent meditating in remote hermitages like this cave, immune to the chaos of the world boiling beyond these mountains—to the north a Tibet ravaged by Chinese Red Guards, to the south India planning its nuclear betrayal, to the west the Soviet Union and its gulag, to the east Indochina and the last convulsions of an American war. For hundreds of years this cave had been occupied by monks—a still center in the violent mandala of the outer world. *There was no violence but the human heart.* Was that right? Or rather, wasn't it love that dwelled in the human heart? *No violence but the human mind.* Better. This man's voice had drawn him over the mountains for a simple truth. Hunkered in a Neolithic cave . . . what better place for a physicist in the twentieth century?

The trumpet sounded once, the bell jangled, the monks chanted behind him, and it seemed as if he were on the verge of understanding something vital once and for all. How long he sat, eyes lidded and at peace with himself, he never knew. But his life as a physicist vanished, and he could remember no reason to return to it. He was where he would always be and had always been.

When he felt a hand on his shoulder, Jack looked up. Gyatsu in his bloodstained robes gripped Jack's arm with fingers that terminated in blackened nails. The hand was pulling him. He couldn't believe it. This little bastard was pulling his arm. He looked to the ancient figure in his crib, but the lama was silent. He looked outside. The sky was a brilliant blue. The other monk, Sonam the silent, rang a bell, once, twice, clear as ice. Jack pulled his arm away angrily, but the hand clawed at him.

The lama made a sound.

"Why?" Jack shouted, his face contorted. It was the syllable that had dominated his life.

The answer was a shattering in his forehead.

The bell rang again.

The wrinkled mouth was making round, urgent shapes, the sound emerging, dry, thin, almost gargling. Jack stared with horror at the black hole in the man's face and felt his mind giving way like the surface crust of snow when your body plunges through. He was standing up, legs weak and uncertain after the long sitting, head swimming with lightness.

"Why?" he asked, wincing.

And sure enough, pain exploded in his head.

He stood wavering, unwilling to risk another question or even the thought itself. And seeing the lama's lips open once again to form that awful sound, he allowed Gyatsu to pull him toward the cave entrance, with his back turned to Dorje. The awful voice seemed to drive Jack from the cave like wind.

The monks led him down to the middle cave, where Jack stopped. At the base of the cliff were two horses, one mounted by Jack's old antagonist, the disfigured horseman, Aten. He scowled, gesturing angrily at the empty saddle of the second horse with Jack's pack tied behind the saddle. The monks pushed at him, indicating that he should descend to the valley, but Jack turned back as if there were some alternative to departure. He stared up at the highest cave occupied by Lama Dorje, and this time the sound struck him in the face like the shock wave from the Nevada test.

Dazed, clinging to the monks for support, he groped for the first step. The monks' faces peered down at him, but he kept his eyes averted, afraid that the next blinding flash would blow him away from the cliff face, launch him over the valley floor, spreadeagled, plunging down onto his own shadow. He descended until he felt sand underfoot, and when he turned away from the cliff, Aten was pointing sternly: Get on the horse!

"I prefer to walk," Jack said—rather than be bounced like a sack of grain.

Aten snarled and the two monks gesticulated wildly. Gyatsu emitted an alarming series of short, urgent syllables. He *must* ride. He clambered aboard the squat, quivering beast, which seemed even less enthusiastic about the project than Jack. Gyatsu handed him his walking staff, red with the dead man's blood. Jack risked a final glance at Dorje's cave, but it was only a dark hole in the rock. The crags and pinnacles above were struck with light. It was morning.

Aten rode ahead while Jack lurched forward, hanging on to the saddle and balancing his staff across his lap. As he relaxed into the movement of the animal carrying him out of Dolpo, he was soothed, as the chanting of the monks had soothed him, as his own breathing

25

had quieted him the past days. The sun rose and shadows shortened, and sometime early that afternoon they emerged from a ravine and stopped. He recognized the place—the solitary boulders and shattered rubble, the dog's lolling tongue, the man lying twisted, the vulture waiting for him to leave. Yes, here were scattered furry bones where a huge dog had died and left dried blood on the stones.

Aten dismounted and made a familiar, rude gesture. Jack slid from the horse, but his legs wouldn't hold him, and he dropped to his knees, the staff clattering to the stones beside him. His thighs had cramped from the short stirrups, his buttocks were knotted from the wooden saddle and his legs were numb. Kneeling beside the bloody stones, he tried to rise, staring up at a face twisted by some horrific blow. Aten pulled the knife from his belt, and Jack made no effort to pick up his staff. Passive, stunned by these past days, he was waiting for his throat to be slit. Instead Aten cut the cord holding his pack and threw it down on the stones. He rode away trailing the riderless horse.

When Jack checked inside the pack, it was all there, untouched, the sleeping bag and three days' supply of food. And something else— a peculiar metal object from the monks. Ten days later in Kathmandu, its use would be explained to him: a stylized bronze lotus that symbolized triumph over the illusionary world of the mind. The curving metal leaves could cut through pride, ignorance, aggression like a knife. To the enlightened man, it was like holding a handful of razor blades.

The ritual scepter was called a dorje.

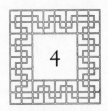

4

She was reading Jack's letter when Browny arrived from the campus. It was the third Thursday of June, meeting day of the Physics Consciousness Group at Lia's house in the Berkeley hills. Since the death of her mother, she had the house to herself and welcomed the company in the pleasant home overlooking San Francisco Bay. The garden gate slammed, the outer door opened, and Browny entered the living room, shambling along absentmindedly in his perpetual seersucker jacket stuffed with pipes, tobacco, scraps of paper.

"Hi," he said, and sat down in the brilliant summer light streaming through the open bay window along with the sound of distant traffic and the faint acrid odor of eucalyptus, geranium and ivy.

"I just got a letter," she said. "Guess who?"

Browny was already at work on his pipe, stuffing tobacco and staring out at the garden as if wondering where he could possibly be. "Nice day," he said.

"A letter, Browny," she said. "For all of us."

"Oh?" He was testing the draw on his pipe. "That's nice. Mail comes so late in the day, does it?"

"Guess who *from*?" She enunciated clearly as if to a slow-minded child.

"How would I know?"

"I'll give you a clue. The phantom of Bombay."

Now he was roasting the top of the tobacco with his first match. One of the many unbreakable rituals of Browny's life: two matches to light a pipe. Always. He shook the match out and dropped it into the ashtray. "Jack? Well, isn't that nice. Having a good time, is he?"

"Not exactly. He's killed a man."

Browny lit his second match, and she was amused watching him wrestle with the situation: whether to go ahead with the pipe or to acknowledge what she had said and risk using a third match.

"Oh?" he said, and looked up.

"Good for you, Browny," she said. This much interest in human affairs was uncommon in him.

"Killed a man?"

"Remember his Bushido phase?"

"Was that before or after the Zen?"

"During," she said. "When he took up the cudgel."

When Jack became enamored of wandering Zen monks and began striding about Berkeley with a six-foot walking staff, Lia had dubbed it his cudgel. Although the streets were dangerous in those days, he had never had any occasion to use the monk's weapon. It was the sort of affectation that annoyed you at first, like Browny's pipe rituals or Lia's own dramatic black cape, but one that you grew used to and then fond of. Since Jack didn't own a car at the time, he had walked all over town with his cudgel, arriving smugly ahead of those who drove and tried to find parking. He'd gotten terribly austere and almost dropped out of physics to retire to the woods. A lot of that sort of thing was going on at the time. He had left Ruth and moved in with that mystical girl and her dog, and soon they were all grateful to the girl because she was so far out of it herself that she frightened Jack back into the world. He could see where he was headed. The dog died. Jack returned to them, no less solitary, but more open and likable. Periodically, he disappeared into the High Sierra and walked alone for a week or so, reappearing one day among the Vietnam burnouts and raving saints of Berkeley, the psychopaths and perpetual students, striding along with his walking staff and burned black by the high mountain sun.

Only Lia understood his anguish during the Zen period, when he truly had sought enlightenment but found himself blocked by a physicist's mind. Of all the mystical disciplines circulating around Berkeley those days, Zen had been most suited to a man of Jack's temperament, but no matter how he struggled to let go, he couldn't.

"A physicist is *supposed* to use his mind," she consoled him. "That's what it's for."

"Sure, and look what we've done with it."

"Next time around you can be enlightened," she told him.

"Right. When our unenlightened minds have exterminated all other possibilities, we can come back as hydrogen gas and start all over again."

"Now, now," she said. "You've become righteous and introspective. You know what happens when you do that."

What happened, ultimately, was that other physicists began to share Jack's concern about weapons development, and the Physics Consciousness Group was formed. When Browny joined, they began to attract attention. The "old man" had worked at Los Alamos with Oppenheimer, at Princeton with Einstein, and had advised Truman and Eisenhower. Since consciousness was a word much abused in those days, Browny brought some respectability to the concept.

"Is this letter private," he asked, "or may I be apprised as to what exactly has befallen our colleague?"

"Why don't you get that damned thing incinerated, and I'll read it to you."

Browny—penny loafers, baggy grease-stained trousers, button-down striped shirt, wrinkled jacket—sat back and lit his unprecedented third match.

She read, "'I need one of you, Lia you're the most practical, to intervene with the lab. Surely a leave can be arranged, but it would be much easier if you softened them up in person. First, let me explain the situation. I apologize to Krishna, but I simply had to get away from

Bombay. To have come all the way to India only to find their nuclear technology producing a bomb, and knowing what that meant for reactors all over the world, for nonproliferation . . . well, it was too much. I had to escape. I suppose it doesn't surprise you that I went to the mountains, but it's not so easy to be alone out here. Not even in the mountains, as it turns out. I had to take a Sherpa and porters to carry my gear. It's geometric: the more porters the more gear, and the more gear the more porters. The only parameter is the size of my wallet. So I had five men to carry my stuff for three weeks. Imagine! And they were so *slow* that I had to drag my feet or range ahead and wait. It was the ranging ahead that got me in trouble.'"

"Ha." Browny exploded a cloud of smoke. "There's an understatement."

The garden gate slammed, and she stopped reading. Mukerjee entered the door in jogging attire. Since returning from Bombay, he'd been reported on various Berkeley back streets, jogging, and to everyone's astonishment had begun to lose his perpetual baby fat. He still looked cuddly, but his legs were vaguely muscular, and now there were vigorous wet spots at the armpits of his athletic shirt and his face was wet and rosy—damp hair stuck out in spikes above his ears. He'd made it across town in twenty-four minutes and was well pleased with himself, posing impressively on the threshold like his Hindu namesake, Lord Krishna, come to visit.

"Sit down," Lia said. "In the chair." Her sofa had just been reupholstered in white linen, and Mukerjee exuded street dirt and sweat. When he continued to stand, radiating virtue and breathing audibly, she added, "We're reading a letter from Jack."

That did it. He fell into the overstuffed chair like a sack.

"I was just reading to Browny. Do you want to hear?"

He emitted a satisfactorily plaintive groan, and she began the letter again with Jack's apology to Mukerjee, his flight to the mountains, and then the episode with the bandits.

"'This bandit came for me and I struck him down. But it was a mistake. I murdered an innocent man.'"

30

"Good Lord," Mukerjee said.

"'Came for me,'" Browny repeated, puffing on the pipe. "An uncharacteristic phrase."

"That's only the beginning," Lia said, and read Jack's account of being captured in the village and taken forcibly to the hermit. "'He sent for me, you see. He knew that I had entered Dolpo. I wouldn't admit this to anyone else, but I even wonder whether he didn't send for me in Bombay, because I went straight over the mountains and met his emissary. And killed him.'"

Mukerjee had been trying not to interrupt this fantastic tale, but now he couldn't help himself. "Jack, oh, Jack! What's wrong? I knew he was crazy. He went crazy in India. It does that to some people. But traveling a thousand miles to a hermit. Being called to a guru. Jack, what's become of you?"

"Let's hear this out," Browny said. "He's trying to tell us something. Let's listen."

But Lia had a hard time going on after Krishna's outburst. It was too much like mourning Jack's death and reminded her of her mother's death the previous summer. Reading Jack's account of the macabre funeral of his victim, she saw her mother's open casket. "'They butchered him and we sat all night at the banquet,'" she read, her voice quavering at the thought of her mother's body being dismembered.

"Butchered him!" Mukerjee was wiping sweat from his face and wiping his hands on the arms of the chair, but Lia didn't scold him because this second reading of the letter was sinking into her heart. Jack had crossed some void beyond them, this letter came from another world altogether, and her eyes reddened. Even when her mother had lost interest in food and television, she had still liked being wheeled through the garden. Her groans and eye blinks had told Lia as much, although by then she knew her mother's mind so well that no such signals were necessary to know her mother's faint pleasures.

"'You see the Indians exploded their bomb the day I killed him. The visions from Dorje told me that. He *knew* they had the bomb. It's

31

impossible, but he did. I sat for a day in his cave, at seventeen thousand feet on the Tibetan border, while he projected these visions into my mind. I've scribbled them in my journal. He *knew* I was a nuclear physicist. He couldn't know, but he did. He couldn't know I was coming to Dolpo, no one knew, but he did. He sent for me, you see. Me. My presence was no accident.'"

She stopped.

Browny's pipe had gone out, an unimaginable breach of decorum, and he was sucking distractedly. Mukerjee leaned forward, his already large eyes enormous dark pools, sweat pouring from his face.

"'The lama brought me *because* of the test. But then sent me away. This is the peculiar part of the story.'"

"Oh, I say," Mukerjee said. "Peculiar."

"'You know what they say out here, "When the chela is ready, the master will appear." The master has appeared. I felt that way about Oppenheimer. But why did Dorje force me to leave when I would have stayed forever? Now I can't control my thoughts, as though he and I are correlated photons and his polarization determines mine. I'll stay in Kathmandu until I have the tools to understand what happened back there, and then I'll return. Will you rent the house and get the money to me here?'"

She paused.

"Is that all?" Browny asked.

"Let's hope so." Mukerjee looked wildly disheveled.

"Oh, no," she said, "there's more. 'I killed a man the same day the Indians exploded their bomb. I went so far to escape it, only to do such a thing. Isn't that a remarkable coincidence? I can't get it out of my mind, as if the Indian explosion actually drove my arms and crushed his skull. I'm obsessed by what happened. I want to go back.'"

Then she put down the letter, and for a while the three of them avoided looking at one another, as if something obscene or embarrassing had occurred. Finally, Mukerjee said, "It casts a pall over our meeting. How can we go on in his absence, when this has happened?"

Lia had thought the same thing about her mother, but she had managed to go on until now. Tears poured down her face, and Mukerjee glanced at her in dismay.

Browny lowered his eyes to his pipe. "Perhaps," he said, "this is an opportunity rather than a loss."

Lia jumped to her feet and fled to the back of the house, her racking sobs still audible in the living room.

"What's wrong with her?" Mukerjee asked. "What's happening all of a sudden?"

"We're none of us getting any younger," Browny replied.

5

Kathmandu at dawn. Strange little city of the Himalaya, where Buddhists and Hindus mingle amiably. Woodsmoke on the cool air, mist off the Vishnumati; temple bells, clack of prayer wheels, a motor scooter in the distance. Medieval timber-and-brick buildings lean over narrow, cobbled streets. In the fetid alleys of the bazaar, the shops are closed at this hour. The steel and wooden shutters are still padlocked on the gold and silver bangles, the rough and colorful homespun blankets and jackets, the gaudy Korean and Chinese polyesters, the transistor radios, aluminum pots and pans from India, the burlap sacks of grain and tea from the hills—goods brought on the backs of men and women, on yaks, goats, bicycles and Chinese trucks. The cool air dampens the smell of the place—that basal odor of urine and excrement, incense and flowers, various spices, kerosene and diesel fumes—that rich humus of smell that will explode later in the day and let you know, absolutely, that you're not in London or Los Angeles. Half the reason for all these jets swooping into Tribhuvan these days is to bring deodorized Western noses out here for a good smell.

There is a new American in town, a tall figure with a walking staff like a pilgrim or holy man. Nothing remarkable, just another eccentric foreigner in Kathmandu. Certain things are known about him. He has been studying at the Tibet Institute all summer and is living with the Tibetan woman who translates for the lamas there. He's living in her house by the Vishnumati, one of those murky streams where women stand knee-deep doing laundry while sewage and ashes from the burning ghats drift past, and the occasional body part.

In the upper room of the crude-timbered stone house, Jack Malloy groans and turns over. She is watching him, still surprised that this arrangement has lasted so long—a month since the American left his hotel and moved in with her. He sits up in the half-light and rubs his eyes.

"You need more sleep," she says.

"No time for sleep."

"Your guru needs you so desperately?" She laughs, not a sympathetic laugh.

"He's very old."

She laughs again, mocking him, showing strong teeth. "You think you can swallow two thousand years of shamanism in a single bite?"

"I can try."

"And this too?" She opens her bare arms.

Her face and naked body speak of many centuries of migration and war in the racially jumbled center of Asia, home of warriors and swept by bloody savagery from Genghis Khan to the Maoists, a region so hostile to human life that it fosters survivors rather than inhabitants. Her face is Mongolian with high, prominent cheekbones, but her long neck and lithe muscular body hint of southern Asia, and her high breasts and narrow waist might have been the model for Indian erotic art.

She draws her nails down his back, hard enough to leave tracks, but he is thinking about the day ahead, the mantras and deities he must learn to visualize. Difficult enough for a Tibetan steeped in the tradition, almost impossible for a foreigner. But he is more determined than anyone she has seen at the institute.

She wrestles him down on the bed, and his body rolls with her, but his mind is someplace else, and finally she sits up on his thighs, staring down at this bearded stranger so desperate to enter the world she has left behind in Tibet. This abstracted expression of his she has come to dislike: intense and inward, obsessed with his own thoughts. Still their tussling has produced results. She raises her hips and guides his long, slender penis into her, but his face remains remote. Only when she begins to rock back and forth does his body turn pliant and his face soften. His eyes close. He is forgetting the hopeless task of learning Tantric mysticism; he is forgetting that she is just a means for his return to Dolpo. She can feel what is happening. When his eyes open again, they are blurred with desire. He sees her breasts hanging over his face and raises his lips, stretching his neck. He's alive now, and helpless beneath her. This brief submission excites her in a way she has never known before—because she retains the last remnants of control. And it gives her great pleasure to relinquish that control, slowly. His hands move down her body, and she begins to rotate her hips, watching his head drop back on the pillow.

Jack pulls clothes over his sweaty body: white cotton trousers, madras shirt, buffalo-hide sandals. His beard is flecked with gray, as is the hair pushed back in long strands along his head. His arms and legs are stringy-muscled, his chest is bony. He's gained no weight since his appearance at the institute, burned black from high-altitude sun, bearded, and mad to go back where he'd just come from.

They are always in a hurry, these Westerners who flock here for spiritual edification and leave behind their own bourgeois decadence like sewage, a stink over everything they touch. Their money, their drugs, their haste—Swedes, Dutch, Germans, Americans, Australians, now Japanese—a high standard of living breeds them like mosquitoes. But she's never seen one quite like Malloy.

He bends over and kisses her, then shuts the door and descends the stairs. The next hour will be spent meditating with the lama who lives on the floor below. How she could have brought this American into the same house as Gonpo still astonishes her.

Gonpo had thought the hippie children flocking to Kathmandu would carry his dying Tibetan faith back into the world, so he had simplified his practice in order to hold their interest, not understanding that their minds were too scattered and that they were too ill-disciplined ever to penetrate the Vajrayana. He did not understand that these spoiled Westerners would destroy what they touched. They looked poor, slept in squalid hotels, wore poor clothes, but would return to a life of luxury and sensuality unimaginable even to a maharaja. He never understood that they were playing at life. They needed immediate visions and immediate surcease from whatever real or imagined afflictions they suffered, and then rushed back to their mamas and papas. The trappings—trumpets made of human thighbones, necklaces of discs cut from human skulls, drums of more skulls, drinking cups of yet more skulls—held their interest. They liked the cute butter sculptures and smoky butter lamps, and the bizarre figures. They were intrigued by the magic and psychic events, the light shows inside their own poor skulls, and they happily wore the robes of the ascetic the way children dress up. But this monk, who had left fourteenth-century Tibet with the Dalai Lama, remained more naïve than these children.

Yes, it was true, Gonpo had lost his discipline just as he had lost his country to foreign invaders. He had begun to drink and wander around the city until Tsering intervened. She had cut through those self-indulgent Westerners like a knife. There was more than one Western child whose dope was confiscated and who was driven from his presence by the Tibetan Fury. It was she who took him in from wandering the streets cadging booze from Japanese or Americans in exchange for a photograph or mantra. It was she as much as anyone who made it increasingly hard for Westerners to study at the institute.

Then the head of the institute, Lama Z, had suggested that she tutor the new American who wanted to learn Tibetan.

"He's a physicist," Lama Z said. "A nuclear physicist."

This bit of information was supposed to intrigue her, but it annoyed her instead.

"And why is he here?"

"Because he seeks the white light. There are things more important than physics, Tsering."

Lama Z taunted her because she had nothing to do with Buddhism. One more Buddhist and the place would collapse. And the lamas knew that, too. What they needed was a Chinese-educated Marxist such as herself to run daily affairs. She could move in the secular world with the confidence of one who speaks many languages. Having worked as a cadre for the Chinese in Tibet, she knew only too well the modern Tibet to which the lamas wished to return, and her knowledge was useful to the institute. And the lamas, in turn, helped her, a former collaborator with the Chinese (what the Tibetans call "a two-headed one"), to regain a place in the Tibetan community.

But what possible interest could a nuclear physicist have in the magic and dogma and ritual that had kept Tibet in feudal bondage? What could a man trained to penetrate the very essence of the universe hope to learn from these shamans? During study sessions in her living room, she tried to probe him as delicately as she could, but he said little about his work in America and even less about his experience in Dolpo. His reticence was a challenge, and they spent long evenings together. But she had not expected to sleep with him. Nor had she expected Gonpo to like him so well that he would offer his services as Tantric guide—the first such offer he had made since leaving the institute. Lama Z was oddly approving of this arrangement, as if Tsering had married Jack and they were all part of the same family now. One day, as she complained about Jack's tendency to study in the middle of the night and her own inability to go back to sleep, she caught an amused smile on Lama Z's face.

"Very dedicated, our American," he said.

Our American. Then she realized why he had asked her to tutor Jack Malloy: in order to keep an eye on him.

Out the broad avenues toward the embassies and big hotels, the streets were empty, no taxis, no bicycle rickshas, only an oxcart plodding down the road, a flock of goats trailed by their herder wrapped in his blanket, and a foreign man in sandals, light cotton trousers, and one of those bright Indian madras shirts, hair and beard all tangled together. No native would walk the early morning streets at such a pace, planting his staff with determination and moving with terrific long strides.

Every morning he could be seen leaving the city. It was said that he was studying at the institute.

"Ah," the little Hindu asked, watching from the garden, "the institute? Which would that be?"

"The Tibetan."

"Toward Bodnath?"

"Yes."

"He walks all that way?"

"Yes. And back. It's said that he is preparing to climb some mountains."

"I see," the little Hindu said. "They are training mountaineers at the institute these days? I thought it was only the Dalai Lama's spies they trained out there."

"Or the CIA's spies."

"Really?"

"Who knows. Anything is possible these days. The buildings once belonged to the Americans."

"And this one is American?"

"Of course."

"CIA?"

"Oh, rather too eccentric, I should say. Most likely just another foreigner seeking the way. Imagine, leaving America to find the way."

"Ah, yes," the little Hindu replied, sipping his tea and watching Jack Malloy disappear.

The two government officials liked to begin their day over morning tea, watching the city wake and speculating on intrigues real and imagined. In the Ministry of Home Affairs it was this sort of rumor, swirling pleasantly beneath the ceiling fans, that helped to pass the long days.

The institute buildings of ugly unpainted concrete had been built by the Americans when they still believed that countries like Nepal needed to be taught how to do certain things, and that such enterprises required large concrete buildings. For a time the Americans had hired a watchman who kept most people out except for a few friends and acquaintances who lived there discreetly. Weeds grew over the parking lots, vines climbed the walls. In another ten years, it would have been a very picturesque ruin, but then the refugee Buddhists had come from Tibet.

Monks cleared the weeds, painted the concrete white and blue; and soon rooms that once housed fertilizer bags contained lamas and stacks of manuscripts. The American air-conditioning system kept the manuscripts from further deterioration and the rooms smelled of incense. A small stupa rose in the parking lot. The Dalai Lama gave his blessing. The Nepalese government, ever conscious of the Chinese building a road across the Himalayas and not wishing to offend their giant neighbor, kept a wary eye on these Tibetan developments at the institute and harassed the Tibetan refugees in petty ways. The lamas, in turn, were solicitous of the Nepalese authorities, who could terminate the relationship at any time.

For years foreigners had come here to study, but often for the wrong reasons. Around the flame of the Vajrayana, psychic phenomena accumulate as naturally as smoke around a fire. But such phenomena only distract from true spiritual practice and are disdained by a true lama. Ever since the bad time with the hippies, the lamas at the institute were wary of those interested in smoke. Smoke suffocates. It is the fire that burns. Even now a foreign scholar like Malloy was scrutinized for his true interest. And to his credit, he seemed entirely serious.

It was known that he was a professor of theoretical physics in a part of California where the Vajrayana was already thriving. These facts pleased the head of the institute, Lama Z. However, Malloy's illegal entrance to Dolpo did not square with his scholarly demeanor. And he was rumored to have seen Lama Dorje, who once had a large following in western Tibet and was thought to have died in Chinese captivity. Dorje disdained the formal Buddhist training of the monasteries; he was a powerful mystic linked to the ancient Bon religion predating Buddhism, a man connected to a long line of hermits and ascetics. In the eight years since the Red Guards invaded Tibet, little had been heard of Dorje except that he was associated with the Tibetan resistance forces and had been killed. That this foreigner should have contacted such a man troubled Lama Z and displeased the Nepalese authorities who were driving the Tibetan guerrillas from Nepal. When Malloy applied for another trekking permit to Dhaulagiri, the entrance to Dolpo, the authorities refused, and let Lama Z know they would not renew his student visa with the institute.

When Lama Z questioned Tsering about these rumors, she claimed to know little more than Lama Z himself. Jack had returned from his trek in "an exalted state and inspired with a sudden love of Tibetan Buddhism," she said. He had crossed the Kali Gandaki ascending behind great Dhaulagiri and returned by the same route; however, she neglected to mention Inner Dolpo or Dorje. So she was protecting the American, and Lama Z now questioned his wisdom in encouraging her relationship with him. His connection to Gonpo was a further annoyance.

Lama Z had been saddened by the loss of one of their most talented lamas. Gonpo had survived the Chinese but not the world. That he still wore the robes was a constant annoyance; that he dined in the major hotels on flesh, drank with foreigners, sold himself as a refugee Tibetan lama of great personal charm were several of the less happy circumstances of recent years. Corrupted, the qualities that had made Gonpo an adept now made him an attractive figure in the Kathmandu social world. And Tsering, who distrusted Westerners and sheltered Gonpo from them, had now taken in this American that he had intended for her to tutor only. She had been a collaborator in Tibet with the Chinese—*gonyipa*, a two-headed one—and no matter how much she did for the institute, Lama Z could not put this from his mind.

When Jack arrived from his customary five-mile walk across the valley, Lama Z sent for him. Jack prostrated himself and then sat facing the lama.

"Your progress is exemplary," the lama said, studying the American, who looked drawn and a little gray in the cheeks. His beard was streaked with gray. The eyes, too, were a smoky blue-gray. It was diffi-

41

cult to tell what life with Tsering was doing to him, but in recent weeks the man had changed appreciably, as if he were waging war with himself.

"Thank you."

The American sat with difficulty; his long legs were not adapted to a full lotus, and he managed a graceless half lotus, looking faintly uncomfortable on his cushion. "I have had several inquiries about you that I thought I should mention."

Malloy's expression did not change.

"Your own embassy has inquired whether you were, in fact, studying here."

Malloy's eyes flickered. He was annoyed. "And am I?"

Lama Z ignored the sarcasm. "They wished to know how long you intend to stay."

"Did they?"

Malloy was irritable. Good. Lama Z pushed forward. "I told them we had arranged a six-month visa. They also wished to know whether Tsering worked here." This time Malloy couldn't conceal his alarm. "They wished to know in what capacity we employ her."

"And what was your explanation?"

Lama Z smiled engagingly. "It is not possible to recapitulate my explanation."

Truly, an explanation of an unrepentant Marxist's relationship to the institute was not easy and had been a matter of some delicacy with the Nepalese. But the very qualities that had made her a star of the Beijing Institute of National Minorities and an outstanding cadre for the Chinese in Lhasa also enabled her to run the worldly affairs of the Tibet Institute. Her languages, Chinese, Russian and English, had been of great assistance. "But they were satisfied with it," he said.

"Was this the end of your discussion with my embassy?"

"Almost. The gentleman was kind enough to offer me some advice."

Malloy waited.

"He was a very sincere gentleman. 'Did you know,' he asked me, 'that she is a Communist?' I laughed."

But Malloy did not laugh. "So *that's* why I was refused a trekking permit."

"Refused a trekking permit?" the lama asked ingenuously. "You wish to leave us so soon?"

"While the weather allows."

"Ahh . . . This fascination with high places has always seemed curious to me. However, it does remind me that the Ministry of Home Affairs called some weeks ago. Did we know whether you had been into Dolpo?" The lama watched carefully as Jack's annoyance hardened to hostility.

"You told them?"

"That I knew nothing specific, but I was under the impression that the Dolpo border area was closed." The lama waited a moment. "However, I understood that you had walked into the region *near* Dolpo."

"And from which of your informants do you understand this?"

"Tsering told me about your trek, of course. It's no secret."

"Did she tell you anything else?"

"Was there more I should have asked her?"

Malloy was better at this kind of lie than Tsering, who too quickly denied knowledge. One would have thought the Chinese would have cured her of the habit. While this American . . . a formidable mind . . . if he were harnessed to Buddhism, a great force could be released into the world. Tsering was right about that, he was a true seeker. And yet his mind was so abstracted by training as a scientist that it could not relax. It was like a great muscle in his head, like the large muscular foreigners that descended on Nepal these days, so rigid that they pushed aside what they sought, like a plow in soft soil. And for some reason he was fighting a great war inside his mind. He was no decadent bourgeois of the sort Tsering despised. But what *was* he? And what had happened in Dolpo?

"What else do you know?" Malloy asked.

"Certain rumors."

Malloy waited.

"It is said that you visited Dolpo last May."

"By whom?"

"By my monks. You employed porters. These folk may be illiterate, but they talk. Your presence in those regions is not unknown. The Nepalese authorities may not extend your visa."

Malloy's face hardened. "They told you this?"

"Yes. It is precisely the sort of trouble the institute must avoid. We are here on sufferance."

"I was refused a permit because of these rumors?"

"Very probably."

"Does your network of informants suggest anything else about me?"

"There is rumored to be a famous naljorpa in Dolpo."

"Naljorpa?"

"An ascetic. Magician. Outside the strict Buddhist tradition."

Malloy's face made it clear that he had seen this man and intended to see him again. So he was using the institute solely for a visa and for sufficient language and mastery of the rituals to return on his own, without translators. It was well known that he walked prodigiously. Other Westerners jogged the streets of Kathmandu in preparation for their treks and climbing expeditions. But this man walked like the wind, as if no other mode of conveyance occurred to him. The porters had never seen anyone like him in the high mountains. And now he was trapped without a permit and without an extension of his visa.

What had happened in Dolpo was for the moment unknown. Tsering would lie for him. If she wanted to lie, nothing would stop her. But Malloy himself, oddly, had revealed his intentions in a way they both understood. The interview could be terminated.

"Is there something wrong with such men?" Malloy asked.

Lama Z smiled. "They have inhabited these mountains since before the Buddha. There are many legends about them and much fascination among your people. Some have succumbed to their own delusions; others have simply lost the way. Some may be dangerous. Without sufficient wisdom they are capable of great harm."

"And this naljorpa?"

"He is said to have great powers, even as one of the ancient Siddhi.

But it is also said that he practices black arts." Lama Z watched Malloy carefully.

"Black arts. What the hell does that mean?"

"Psychic arts that may be malevolent."

"Malevolent?"

"An adept may, for example, send messages on the wind."

"Messages on the wind?"

"The Tibetan expression for what you call telepathy. A common means for a lama to communicate with a disciple. But such a naljorpa, how to say it, he may take more firm control of a person's mind. Even with the admirable intent of the great liberation, this is a very dangerous procedure. And wholly unnecessary. A mind is enlightened under its own volition."

Malloy was agitated now, restless, wanting to ask more and restraining himself with difficulty. So Lama Z helped him along. "These techniques were known in Tibet long ago. There are few practitioners left. But mysterious deaths have been attributed to him."

Normally, this sort of thing disgusted Lama Z, and he did everything in his power to suppress any unhealthy interest in the psychic phenomena of Tibetan Buddhism. But an exception was required in this case, and already Lama Z's intuition was paying off: Malloy's composure was broken.

Was it possible the naljorpa had really taken control of this man's mind? Of course it was possible. But why would he bother to infiltrate a foreigner who lacked the language or tradition? If Dorje had done so, however, the mystery of this American gained great complexity and interest.

Malloy was breathing deeply, attempting to calm himself. "That's superstitious bullshit!" he said.

Lama Z watched his eyes. They were bright and confused, and his words were too emphatic for the occasion; he was trying to protect his master. "That may be," Lama Z said, "but there is some evidence that he is also one of the Khampa guerrilla leaders, and since the Nepalese are now wiping out these men, I should say Dorje's days are numbered. I'm truly surprised he escaped from Tibet."

Lama Z watched Malloy's face tighten with anger and something else—despair, injury? Good. It was sufficient for the time being to plant this doubt about Dorje's intentions in Malloy's mind, and Lama Z was satisfied with the interview. Malloy prostrated himself and left. These doubts would better allow Lama Z to control this politically delicate situation. And he'd said nothing that was not true. Except one thing. No Tibetan, especially a man like Dorje, would use a foreigner in the black arts. In fact, there was no one capable of doing so unless —and this thought troubled Lama Z—unless Dorje was, as long rumored, in direct lineage to the Siddhi. The satisfied smile left his face. In which case Dorje might not be employing the black arts but rather the opposite. In which case Lama Z himself might be practicing the black arts by poisoning Malloy's mind.

Yet Lama Z had to intervene. Malloy's presence at the institute was causing unwelcome scrutiny from the Nepalese. And since relations with China were shifting and the guerrillas were being eliminated, Tibetans were less welcome than ever in Kathmandu. The safest course was to cooperate with the authorities and drive Malloy from Nepal. But his connection with Dorje was so puzzling. The ascetic had once had enormous influence in western Tibet, and, distasteful as he was to some of the lamas, he'd been tolerated as part of the resistance. But now—Lama Z brought his fingers together beneath his chin, as he did when pondering spiritual matters of the most exquisite delicacy—now Dorje had come to them in the form of this American. Such a tantalizing opportunity could not be ignored.

The return walk to town that evening was not so pleasant for Jack. The Americans and Nepalese, the institute, Tsering, all observed his activities. Why the Americans should have an interest in him he couldn't imagine, unless inquiries had come from home. That Tsering might pose a problem because of her Chinese-Marxist affiliations had never occurred to him. Or that Lama Z, who knew far more than he was saying, would nose into his affairs. In these few hours the city had become a web and his every step sent tremors to a band of waiting spiders. He felt as if each step were destined to prevent his return to Dolpo.

Of course Lama Z's absurd suggestion of psychic mind control was a transparent attempt to poison his mind. He glared at the bicycle rickshas and wandering cows, stabbed the pavement with his walking staff and veered angrily off his usual route. He had an overwhelming urge for drink. There were several hotels where he was likely to find Gonpo—bar/restaurants too expensive for any but foreigners who thought nothing of spending a day's Nepalese wages on a single drink, and who were quite prepared to entertain an authentic Tibetan lama in exile.

Gonpo wore Western clothes with a kind of eccentric abandon, in this case yellow cotton trousers, an electric-blue shirt, and some Italian cloth slippers. He wore his hair up in a lama's topknot—at odds with both the milieu and his clothes. "Come meet my new friends," he said when Jack appeared, but he was in no mood for any of Gonpo's wealthy acquaintances, so he rudely ignored the invitation and went to the bar. But Gonpo wasn't offended for long.

"Jack, you must come to the table, one of these men knows you." Jack glanced at the table. Three men sat there, Indians he would guess. "But leave your club at the coat rack, or you'll frighten them."

Jack's "club" was leaning against the bar—a Westerner could be forgiven these eccentricities—and his immediate instinct was to bolt. But his first drink had already hit bottom and blurred his irritability; so he went with Gonpo, taking his club with him.

Gonpo had affected a gold chain and medallion that showed through his carefully unbuttoned rayon shirt. It was his latest man-about-town garb.

"You are colleagues," Gonpo said exuberantly. "Jack, this is Mr. Ghose, a physicist at Trombay, you may know that facility."

"I do."

Mr. Ghose, in blazer, tie and gold-rimmed glasses, held out his hand. "I'm so pleased to meet you, Mr. Malloy. I heard you speak at Bombay."

Christ, it all came back, his humiliating speech about the physics of consciousness; this was one of the Indians in the audience. The sticky strands of web wrapped him up on all sides. He delayed extending his own hand just long enough to make his mood apparent. The man spoke the mellifluous Indian English of the Oxford-educated.

Gonpo introduced the other two men, who seemed, in the Indian caste system, to be distinctly servile to Mr. Ghose. Gonpo sat back with a pleased smile, waiting for an instant friendship to form. The Indians tried to be polite, but Jack's sullenness threw a cloud over the gathering.

"Well," Gonpo said brightly, "we've just been discussing the recent Indian triumph."

Mr. Ghose smiled modestly and the other two Indians shuffled their feet. Trombay, where he worked, was the Indian nuclear center designed around a Canadian-built research reactor, Cirus, that had provided the plutonium for the "device." Since the explosion, the Americans had cut off further heavy-water deliveries and the Canadians further assistance. But too late. The Indians were developing their own heavy-water facilities and had stored plenty of spent fuel for reprocessing. Since their device now made them the sixth nuclear power, they were feeling comfortably independent of further Western or even Russian assistance. And that smug satisfaction showed in Mr. Ghose.

It was too much for Jack. "Let me congratulate you on your triumph, Mr. Ghose, the Mahatma would have been proud of you."

The sarcasm was not lost on Mr. Ghose. His smile waned. "I see. It is permissible for your country and others to hold the world hostage. But if India explodes a peaceful device, you condemn it."

"There is no such thing as a peaceful nuclear explosion, as you well know. One looks to India for moral guidance in these matters. One does not expect a country with millions of starving people to waste resources on yet another bomb and to squander its moral authority."

"This is a very righteous attitude, Mr. Malloy. But entirely unacceptable from a country that has squandered its moral authority by incinerating hundreds of thousands of Asians."

"Please," Gonpo said, distressed at the sudden turn of conversation. "Let us be friends here and not let petty national concerns distract us from present comradeship."

It seemed to Jack that, once again, the more he tried to leave behind events in Dolpo, the more insistent they became. Now they had followed him across town to this very table. It seemed utterly unbelievable, but in all of Kathmandu he had found these nuclear technocrats reeking with nationalistic pride.

"I understand that the Buddha himself smiled on your endeavor," Jack said.

Mr. Ghose managed a cautious smile. "Ah, yes, you know the code, Mr. Malloy."

"Code?" Gonpo asked.

"It has become somewhat famous," the Indian said. "The code sent to Mrs. Gandhi when our device was successfully detonated."

Now Gonpo looked troubled. "'The Buddha is smiling'?"

"Yes," the Indian replied. "Without entirely peaceful intent, can you imagine any country using such a code word?"

Jack stood up. Jerking his stick from under the table, he said, "Of course I can imagine such hypocrisy. We called our first bomb a "gadget" and our first test Trinity."

He looked around the table at the drunken lama and the three eager Indian scientists. He slammed his walking staff to the floor and heard voices stop all over the bar. "I am become Death, the shatterer of worlds," Jack roared, quoting Oppenheimer at Los Alamos, who was himself quoting the Bhagavad Gita. The Hindu and Buddhist faces before him were alarmed and fearful, and Nepalese officials and other foreigners watched warily from all over the bar.

He snatched his glass from the table and addressed Gonpo and his companions in a voice that carried throughout the bar: "A toast, then, to a smiling Buddha."

No one moved. Finally, in an attempt to defuse the hostility, Gonpo raised his glass. The three Indians reluctantly followed him. They banged their glasses together with Jack's and drank. Then, to the obvious relief of everyone in the bar, Jack turned and stepped into the

Kathmandu night, carrying his club. Outside, he felt oddly liberated, as if he'd torn through the surrounding sticky web.

Of course, he hadn't mentioned Oppie's initial response to the Trinity test: "If the radiance of a thousand suns were to burst into the sky," he had said, also quoting the Gita, "that would be like the splendor of the Mighty One."

Jack strode toward Tsering's house full of a new resolve that he didn't yet understand. Truly, the Buddha must be smiling. Jack Malloy was. Of course, he was drunk. So far as is known, the Buddha was not.

6

Tsering waits in the mushy low-wattage light of Kathmandu, wearing the French-style silk blouse, the flared jeans, and the high-heeled sandals that reveal her amputated toes. That first night she had held out her foot to Jack. "See this." The middle toes were missing. "Frostbite when we crossed the mountains in the winter of 1969." She was not complaining. Others had remained behind as corpses. Her long black hair is swept up on top of her head, accenting her long neck, her broad cheekbones and wide-set eyes.

The door closes below, and she hears Jack lean his walking staff against the stone wall. She knows Gonpo has left on a drinking spree and can guess that Jack has helped him debauch. He comes upstairs toward the light, the room where they spend their evenings. She is surrounded by newspapers: *Izvestia*, *The People's Daily*, *The Wall Street Journal*, but this evening she is not reading. She is waiting. This moment has been coming for weeks, like the first snow sealing off the passes and isolating a winter encampment. He steps inside the room and crosses to the rattan chair where he reads the Book of the Dead or other Buddhist nonsense. Light crosses his face, casting shadows. He leans forward and she can smell alcohol, but his eyes blaze with another kind of light. For a moment she is afraid of what will happen.

51

And then not. She has no fear any longer. No one can touch the dead place inside her.

"You're working with Lama Z, aren't you?" he says.

"Of course."

"You know what I mean. To keep me out of Dolpo."

Whether he goes to Dolpo is little interest to her but, for some reason, of great interest to Lama Z.

"No," she says, crossing her legs.

"*You* approached me as a tutor. *You* invited me to live here. But you're his spy."

"Ah," she said, "he's summoned you to an audience, I see."

"The American embassy has talked to him; the Nepalese have talked to him. And *you've* talked to him. Why? If I want to walk back into the mountains and study with a lama, why are so many obstructions being raised?"

"Obstructions?"

"The Nepalese won't extend my visa; they won't grant a trekking permit; the Americans are suspicious about my affiliations with you; Lama Z is probing about Dorje. Why? Or aren't you free to give an honest answer?"

She feels a familiar pinch in her chest—a pain that has accompanied her ever since she was sent to Beijing to study—the pain of surviving in a world far more complex and hostile than she had ever known as a nomad's daughter. "Just what are you saying?"

"I am living with a fink."

"Please . . . ?" It is a reflex, this inquiry of hers whenever he uses a word she does not understand.

"A fink. A mole. A fifth columnist."

A collaborator. So Lama Z has told him that she collaborated with the Chinese, and that's why he is so angry. For a moment, the shame keeps her silent. But not for long because his face, righteous with privilege and alcohol, is the face of a man whose country has never been occupied, who has never had to worry about betrayals of friends and family, torture or reeducation. Her voice is quiet, but tight with anger: "It is not I who betray."

"Meaning?"

"How long have you lived in my house?"

"Six weeks."

"And you have told me everything about your trip to Dolpo?"

"Everything I wished to tell."

"Was there perhaps something of crucial importance that you have omitted?" His eyes give him away, he knows what she is about to say. "You killed one of my countrymen, who fought the Chinese for years."

He leans toward her, reeking of the expensive Scotch foreigners drink. He spits words at her: "Who told you?"

His face is strange and misshapen. A stranger in her house. She waits calmly for the rest of his accusation.

"Lama Z told you, didn't he? Then it's finished. I'll never get back to Dolpo."

And finally she can stand no more: "Is that all that worries you about killing a Tibetan, whether you can go back and play with your guru?"

To her surprise his contorted face shifts in a way she doesn't recognize at first—from anger to grief and the verge of tears.

"It was an accident, Tsering. I killed the man by accident. But it's driving me back."

"And if you can't go back?" She is thinking of her own exile in Nepal.

"But I must."

"Ah," she says, "you think your personal will removes you from historical necessity?"

"I'm simply returning to Dolpo," he says. "Your Marxist bullshit notwithstanding."

The shadow of grief has passed from his face and been replaced by the familiar obstinate willfulness of an American who thinks he can bend events to his desire. But she knows better. She was dragged from medieval Tibet to the Beijing Institute for National Minorities and then brought back to Lhasa as translator and cadre for the Chinese. Such historical forces cannot be disdained. What does he understand

53

of her humiliation at collaborating with the Chinese while the Red Guards betrayed the revolution? The images are burned in her mind: of Chinese hoodlums cutting the nomad girls' long hair, stripping them naked in winter and leaving them bound on the ice; of their forcing Karma Sherab and his daughter to make love in the square and making the upper-class families stand in the river, wearing dunce caps and strapped to stones, until their legs weakened and they sank; raping the woodcutter's daughters and bringing them into the city in sacks; torturing the lamas and driving them through the streets, bent under the heavy stone and metal images of their faith, and staggering to their execution. While she, from the security of her fervent belief in socialism and Mao, watched. She watched her culture excised like a scab. And when she fled, it was not only from the Red Guards. She fled her own humiliation.

But his pain makes no sense to her: how the Indian nuclear explosion shattered his faith in physics makes no sense because his solution, turning back to magic and shamanism, makes no sense. It's a bourgeois indulgence—a nuclear physicist drawn by some vague mystical magnetism to an ignorant shaman! And this familiar contempt of hers wells toward harsh words, except that he is dropping to his knees beside her, lowering his face to her lap.

"I need help," he says. "Can't you understand?"

She looks down at his tangled hair, at the gray that has seemed to appear in these recent weeks of struggle. He wants to abandon the world and go back to innocence and mystical oneness. She knows better. She's left the chanting monks, the offerings, the wail of the bone trumpet and patter of stones on a human skull drum, the robes and flags and prayer wheels, the ignorant nomads, feudal serfs, and corrupt lamas in monasteries of enormous wealth. Buddha will never end human suffering, and this man, possessed of the knowledge to truly end suffering, should know better. Yet he renounces his science. Incredible! And now he's on his knees asking *her* help. She feels his coarse beard on her thighs and strokes his head—her physicist, reduced to this yearning rack of bone and flesh.

She knows where they are headed now. In a country where

brothers share children by the same wife, sisters by the same husband, and conceptions occur in crowded tents or rooms, sex is like breathing or eating. Or like a walk on the sparse grassland of the Chang Tang under a sky larger than anything conceivable, where distance is stretched out of proportion and the mind is stretched by oxygen deprivation, among the black tents of the nomads and their yak and goat flocks, on a day before winter locks up all of central Asia.

A place she will never see again.

He is pulling her down toward him, but she feels another presence surrounding them like water, holding them up, tossing their bodies in a current. She feels herself caught and turning out of her own control, as if she were a child once again lying in a warm tent, submerged in the voices of nomads talking of weather and fate. Tears are streaming down her face, wetting his beard, and his cry sounds vaguely familiar, like a cry once heard echoing over the high Tibetan Plateau.

That night he has a dream: high mountains, snow—familiar but strange—an enormous sky over bare stone and sparse grassland. A tremendous yearning, for what it is not clear. A sense of loss, of mourning. The landscape is empty, the sky is empty. He wakes with a tremendous jerk as though falling. Outside the open windows, moonlight. Beside him, Tsering. Her eyes are glittering, wide open, and he has the impression that she is staring at his dream landscape: the fantastic rupture in the earth's surface known as Tibet, an ancient seafloor bulged three miles into the sky. The tiny specks wandering across the grassland are her father's yaks carrying bags of salt; the black tents are her fellow nomads, flecks of human consciousness warping the topography as a gravitational field does space-time.

It is Tibet: her lost home.

Light and dark swirl together. Her life in Tibet and his in America are locked together in a Tantric *yab-yum*, the father and mother copulating, joined in an endless transference of energy. But what does medieval Tibet have to do with the particle accelerators of the United States?

There is no answer from Tsering. She is staring straight up at the whitewashed timbers supporting the roof. The terror of waking from her dream freezes him; she no longer seems human—more like one of the dakinis he has been studying: Vajra Varahi, the indestructible sow, dancing on a cringing male figure with her upraised knife in one hand and skull cup of blood in the other—the wild, sexual and lethal feminine principle so integral to the Vajrayana, so difficult to absorb.

The fifteen- to twenty-thousand-foot rupture in the earth's surface burns in her mind like pure fire. Tibet. Those spaces are forever denied her, daughter of nomads, except at night like this. Then he hears it, less actual hearing than awareness of sound from the room below: Gonpo has returned from his debauch and is chanting the Bardo Thodol—the Tibetan Book of the Dead. He usually sleeps through the night like a Westerner, drugged with food and wine and loss of purpose, but now he is chanting the text that he and Jack have been studying because of Jack's obsessive interest in Tibetan funeral customs. Spoken over a dead body, these words guide the departing consciousness through that confusing time between death and rebirth known as the Bardo; they guide the dead toward the white light. These were the words spoken over the butchered corpse of the man he killed, sounds that have echoed in his mind since Dolpo.

Gonpo is reciting the Chonyid Bardo although no one is dead in this house. It is the eighth day after death when the peaceful visions of the heart leave the dead person's consciousness and are replaced by the wrathful deities of the head. The words from below, which he has only begun to learn, trigger his dreaming mind. A door is opening. It is like the door beyond death through which no living person can look; it is the door to the subatomic world forever closed to physicists; it's the mathematical door of quantum probability, locked by Heisenberg. Yet it's opening, and Jack is sliding toward it as if on a capsized vessel.

"So we have begun at last."

The voice is not Tsering's. Her eyes are closed, and she is breathing deeply and regularly. But when he touches her, reaching for help, he feels her sow's head at his throat. He hears animal grunts, feels the curved knife at his throat, tastes the skull cup of blood at his lips. Then the sharp, triple-tipped trident, around which she writhes and dances, touches his groin.

And he is lost. Because it is not her voice. It is not his own. It is Dorje speaking from the edge of Tibet, in this same moonlight flooding Kathmandu. The wizened figure of the lama beckons from the other side of the quantum door.

"Now," the voice says. "It is time to return."

But it is impossible. The mathematics are absolutely clear and irrefutable. Yet the mouth opens and shapes a sound. From the skeleton covered with leathery skin, a hand rises, gesturing for him to approach. And then, like that first shock wave across the New Mexico desert, the voice strikes him like a fist. As if all his years studying quantum theory and relativity had slapped shut like a book. Wake up!

But he is asleep on a moonlit night in September.

7

Near moonset, Jack slipped from bed and went into the small corner study where he worked, leaning his head out into the moonlight: a quiet night, a few distant dogs. Gonpo's words still droned from below, and now half asleep and mesmerized by the sound, Jack turned on the light. On his desk was the Tibetan woodblock print of the Chonyid Bardo, which he had been studying with Gonpo. Open beside it, and held open by the scepter he had brought from Dolpo, was the Evans-Wentz translation of the Book of the Dead, turned to the eighth day after death. Here began the terrifying descent into the illusions of mind: the monstrous deities holding intestine nooses, skull cups of blood, decapitated heads, swords. But the dead person, descending toward rebirth into samsara and the world of human suffering, was always comforted: "Fear . . . not. Be not awed. Know it to be the embodiment of your own intellect." The words repeated through the text like a mantra. The cause of all human suffering was individual consciousness that created the world of suffering from an ocean of bliss.

The unfamiliar ink scratches of the block print blurred into differential equations, matrix arrays and the elegant von Neumann formulation of quantum mechanics—the very mathematical symbols swimming beyond the quantum door that had opened in his sleep. He was asleep again, sitting in the chair.

When he woke, it was daylight. He heard Tsering's voice in the courtyard below his open window. The answering voice was American, Midwestern dry. Dazed and unsettled by the night's dreams, he looked down from the window.

The man looked like a fundamentalist preacher or Bible salesman, very tidy and wiry, wearing horn-rims and hair that had been cut and styled in one of those new salons that passed for barbershops in the States. He wore baggy, multipocketed, military-looking khakis, a loud print shirt, white tennis shoes and an orange Denver Bronco cap. He saw Jack at the window. Tsering looked up: "He wants to see you."

From her attitude he could tell that she didn't like this man. Jack's head was still full of confused images and the voice from beyond the quantum door saying, "It is time to return." But the words coming from the lama's mouth were equations. Jack blinked his sleepy eyes.

"Send him up," he said, and remained seated when the man entered and surveyed the room through thick glasses. He quickly took in the prayer wheel, bone apron, skull, thanka, and crudely printed Book of the Dead open on the desk. Jack picked up the bronze dorje worn smooth by Dorje's hands. The stylized lotus blossom felt heavy as brass knuckles, and to Jack it had actually begun to seem like a weapon. His fingers closed around it.

"Let me explain my presence," the man said. "The head lama at the Tibet Institute sent me to you. He says you are a physicist studying the Vajrayana."

Since his talk with Lama Z and the Indian scientists, his night's dreams and Gonpo's odd chanting of the Bardo, Jack's mind was as disordered as it had been in Dolpo. The curving prongs of the scepter in his hand were the legs of a spider; fine filaments were squeezing through his fingers and spinning this stranger into the web. Jack dropped the dorje on the desk.

"That's right," he said.

"I, too, am a student of Buddhist methodology."

Methodology grated but explained a lot. He wasn't a missionary of the Christian type but some kind of half-assed academic studying the heathens. The man, whose name was Wilson, asked if he could sit down in the only other chair available in the small room. Behind thick glasses, Wilson's eyes looked peculiar, slightly lunatic.

He represented something called the Institute for Psychic Research at Boulder, Colorado. They were studying Eastern approaches to psychic phenomena and since he happened to be in Kathmandu and had discovered that a well-known physicist was out here, he'd wanted to meet him.

Jack blinked. From beyond the quantum door an ancient figure was beckoning—burning with light. Dorje reached toward him, speaking. Jack saw the orange cap, the magnified eyes, the gaudy shirt of the man seated in his study. It was Wilson, the American psychic, who had spoken. But what had he said? Jack had no idea. "Is psychic research prospering these days?" he asked lamely.

"Oh, you bet. Lots of interest. Foundation money, government grants."

"And what is it you want?"

Wilson blinked at the blunt question, and his expression changed slightly, becoming less guileless and demented.

"It occurs to me that as a scientist, with an interest in Buddhism, you might be interested in our protocol. Our methodology is beyond reproach. And you would be a perfect contact here—"

"Just what are you saying, Mr. Wilson?"

From beyond the quantum door a gnarled hand emerged from the brilliant mist of equations. The hand burned with a radioactive glow, and a single syllable unfolded in his mind.

Wilson sat obstinately. "We've heard the most amazing tales out here. I expect you have, too."

"Who hasn't. Levitation, trance walking, thought transference, monks copulating with dakinis in remote caves and turning semen into moonjuice. You've come to the right place. But the wrong person."

Wilson's eyes became shallower, more glittery behind the thick lenses.

"Or how about breathing through your anus, Mr. Wilson?"

"Just what have I done to annoy you, Mr. Malloy?"

"It's not anything you *do*," Malloy said.

Now the syllable in his mind became a harsh pain, sharp as a migraine. Jack had never been susceptible to migraines, but this pain was driving him back over the crest of the Himalayas on the day the Indians exploded their device, driving him back into the cave where he sat before Lama Dorje—pain exploding between his eyes.

He detested this man before him—his jargon, his appearance, his bureaucratic stench—everything he had left behind in physics labs and universities had just entered his Buddhist study. But instead of driving the man out, he was being more polite than he felt because of the blinding pain between his eyes. "Perhaps I *can* be of some assistance, however. Downstairs is a genuine lama from Tibet, who speaks excellent English."

But Wilson's feelings had been hurt and he was standing. "I really can't accept anything from you, Mr. Malloy. I've done nothing to deserve rudeness."

And now, as though he were being physically pulled to his feet, Jack was standing. He took Wilson's arm and emitted a single syllable: "Please."

Wilson allowed himself to be steered downstairs to Gonpo's chamber, where Tsering was waiting outside the door.

"Where are you going?" she asked.

"I'm taking Mr. Wilson to meet Gonpo."

"Why?"

"You explain," he told Wilson, who reluctantly explained about the Institute for Psychic Research in Boulder, Colorado.

"Then come to the Tibet Institute," she said. "We can give you information."

"I've been there," Wilson replied.

"Then go to the tourist board," she snapped. "But not my house." Once again, Wilson looked injured, but before any further complications could arise, Jack opened the door.

The stone-floored room was lit by a flickering butter lamp, and there was a strong, rancid smell of alcohol and cigarette smoke. The window shutters were drawn, and on a small raised area surrounded by his drum, bell, trumpet, scepter, was Gonpo, sound asleep—an overweight middle-aged man, stretched out on his back with his mouth open. Jack was embarrassed, but before he could back out of the room, Gonpo groaned and opened his eyes with an apologetic smile. When he saw Wilson, the gentle, slightly sad and pudgy face composed itself instantly, and he snapped wide awake.

"Who is this man?"

"He wants to ask you some questions."

"Who is he?" Gonpo asked with unusual sharpness.

Now Jack was feeling almost sorry for Wilson, who once again had to explain his quest for psychic phenomena in the name of science. Perhaps they could continue their conversation over lunch, Wilson said, since he did not seem welcome in this house. He named a restaurant, and Gonpo lowered his eyes bashfully. "That would be quite acceptable," he said.

Jack demurred from joining them and was stabbed with pain between his eyes.

"I hope you'll reconsider," Wilson told him.

"I'll think about it," Jack said.

Wilson looked nervously out the door, but Tsering was nowhere to be seen. After he'd left, Gonpo said enthusiastically, "I imagine he'll feed us handsomely. I shall order the veal, borscht, that vinaigrette salad, and a decent Bordeaux. And you should come, Jack. Never turn down a free meal."

Jack winced like one of Pavlov's dogs shocked by electricity, but it was only Gonpo, red-eyed and hung over, saying, "I feel it is important for you to come, Jack. It is difficult to say with certainty, but there is a tangling here, an intertwining . . ."

"You may have certain intuitive powers," Jack replied, "but there is no intertwining, believe me."

He winced again, but was spared the jab of pain. It was more than a bad night's sleep or yesterday's disastrous interview with Lama Z befuddling his mind. Perhaps he was coming down with fever. Or dysentery. Or hepatitis. Or worms. The list of possible Asian maladies multiplied in his mind.

Gonpo was grinning at him. "Good, Jack. You won't regret this. There is an intertwining. Believe me, I haven't felt anything like this for years."

When had he agreed to lunch?

The smiling Buddha face before her was almost more than she could bear. Two thousand years of benign paternalism condensed in a single face. Had the Chinese been anything but Chinese, she could have lived quite happily in lama-free Tibet.

"Our friend is attracting quite a bit of interest," Lama Z said to her.

"Not from me."

"Is there something wrong?"

"Your American and I have come to a parting."

On the spiritual mask drawn over the politician's face, the little upturned lips quivered with sympathy. "I'm sorry to hear that."

"Are you?"

"And what is the nature of the problem?"

"At this moment? A certain reptile you sent to my house."

"Ah, the other American?"

"Yes, the other American. You know I dislike these people."

"He seems a well-meaning man," the lama replied, "granted that he is only superficially interested in Buddhism. But he confesses a lively interest in the black arts."

"So why did you send him to my house?"

"It's no secret where Mr. Malloy is living, is it? He would have found you in any case. And surely Gonpo is beyond any further corruption." Aside from his official compassion for all living things, Lama Z had little sympathy for Gonpo.

Tsering smelled some new political game. All kinds of currents were in the air since the criminal Nixon had gone to China. Her colleagues in Kathmandu had been put under surveillance, as she supposed she was. The Khampa had left the border areas and turned in their weapons or gone to Sikkim. The Dalai Lama himself had asked them to lay down the arms provided by the CIA. There were political shifts, and this lama was a conduit. She knew that. The Americans were playing their China card. And when the great powers shifted in their sleep, tiny Nepal was shaken by an avalanche. Lama Z was manipulating a delicate balance between the government of Nepal, the Dalai Lama in Dharmsala, and his own aspirations to spread Buddhism to the West. And he would use her any way he could. The arrival of this new American at her house was no coincidence.

"Of course it's no secret," she said, "but nothing *you* do is accidental. You sent him to my house. Why?"

His lips curled like the petals of a lotus. Hands clasped like a bodhisattva and eyes radiating compassion, Lama Z watched her shrewdly. She stared back, drilling holes in him.

"It's true that I sent Mr. Wilson as a kind of test. Since your Malloy professes no interest in the black arts, I am curious what he will do with this man. You must tell me."

"They are going to lunch today."

"Ah. Very interesting. There is something about this man that intrigues me. If you should observe anything . . ."

"I think . . ." Tsering paused to be certain of what she would say next. "I think that I will live my own life from now on." Lama Z's expression became even more compassionate and loving as he reached his hand out toward her, but she refused it. "First," she said, "you send me Malloy because you wish to know more about him. Now Wilson. I'm no longer interested in your plots."

The lama continued to offer his hand. "Tsering, you are the most sophisticated politician at the institute. Your reading of foreign papers is invaluable to us. You must understand better than anyone that there is a certain global delicacy just now. Political realities are changing, and our future depends on intangibles. I wish to be certain of these Americans."

"Your Buddhist future may depend on these Americans, but my

future does not. If you find this inconvenient, I will resign immediately."

Lama Z withdrew his hand and broadened his smile, which became less enigmatic and more warmly human. "If we had ten Buddhists like you, our future would be assured."

She maintained her scowl.

"If you care to take vows . . ."

The idea of taking vows was so absurd that even Tsering was forced to smile.

"Please forgive me," Lama Z said. "I have been distracted. I won't impose on you further." She stood up to leave. "And what of our friend Gonpo?" the lama asked. "Is he still carousing about the streets?"

"As a matter of fact," she said bitterly, "thanks to you, he is also carousing with this reptile—at lunch today."

"Really?" the lama said. "How very interesting." And he brought his fingers together in a small tent under his chin.

"If it were not for Gonpo, I'd leave Kathmandu," she said.

His eyes slipped half-closed, lidded, as if directing his attention inward. "Would you? As a matter of fact, since our friend Malloy has moved in with you, I have felt certain emanations. I believe there is a dramatic change for you coming soon. I feel it."

Despite her contempt for such divination of the lamas, she asked, "Soon?"

The lama was still meditating. "Yes," he said. "I begin to see it now. Only a matter of days perhaps."

She caught herself leaning forward. A matter of days! She remembered her dream of the previous night: flying over the crest of the mountains, out over Tibet, like a big bird, a vulture perhaps, and seeing small specks below, and knowing that they were humans scattered like grains of sand. She had swooped down toward them, while beside her was another shadow, another bird perhaps, a presence of some kind. It had been a restless night, the moon shining through the window, the fight with Jack. Even sex had seemed lonesome, as though they were both far away and a dry voice were describing their activities. A dry, harsh voice out of stony Tibet.

Leaving the lama, she passed a group of monks arguing a fine point of theology; she passed the Swiss couple, very sweet and dedicated. It was lunchtime. Classes were letting out. But when she stepped outside, she saw Jack striding through the bullock carts and mopeds and bicycles of the crowded street, planting his stick vigorously with each step. He was leaving the institute for lunch with Gonpo and Wilson.

Her heart constricted. After years of collaboration and survival, she knew conspiracy when she saw it. She wanted to run after him, humiliated, and beg him to stop—or else beg to go with him. But she turned dutifully back into the institute. Today, she was translating for a Soviet scholar.

8

Wilson is dapper as a golf pro in Sta-Prest trousers and athletic shirt. After the borscht and first bottle of Bordeaux, when Gonpo begins recounting his flight with the Dalai Lama in 1959, Wilson turns on his tape recorder. Jack, uninterested in this man Wilson and still annoyed by the odd pressure he feels to be here, swirls the dark wine and looks sourly at the tape recorder, half-listening.

"The Chinese are very thorough," Gonpo is saying. "They cleaned up lamaism the way you might clean the kitchen floor. And they use stiff brushes." He holds the long-stemmed wineglass up to the light. "Very sad. Our practice is like this wine, a product of place. Delicate. No Bordeaux outside of France, no Vajrayana outside Tibet. If you could have talked to me up there, our conversation would be very different. Even your tape recorder would be different."

"Different?" Wilson asks.

"Yes. Hard to describe at a fine meal like this. In such . . . sophisticated surroundings." Gonpo waves his hand generously around the restaurant: an ancient palace of the Nepali royalty converted by a Russian émigré to a restaurant much frequented by the new international clientele of Kathmandu—Russians, Japanese, Indians, even Chinese since the completion of the highway—new royalty for the old palace.

Dressed in English country-gentleman style for this lunch, Gonpo waves a ringed finger at the other diners, hushed in the vaulted stone room of the old palace, at the crusty bread, the empty bowls, the wine-glasses and table linen. Then he points between his eyes. "In here," he says. "In here it is different. In Tibet the mind knows things."

Wilson looks eager. "Telepathy?" he asks.

"In your terms. In ours, meaning simply travels ahead of words, and the words become ornaments, jewels, a pleasant addition to the truth." Gonpo swirls the wine, stares into the glass for a long moment as if considering his next words. He sips, rolling the wine in his mouth, and makes a small, satisfied gurgling sound.

"Mr. Wilson, I must thank you. This is more than delightful."

"You were saying," Wilson interrupts him.

Gonpo looks puzzled as if unable to remember any experience other than this wine.

"About the Vajrayana on the high plateau," Wilson prods him.

"Ah, yes. That. It is lost, dissipated." Gonpo's face changes as nakedly as a child's, remembering the loss, the descent from fourteenth-century Lhasa into nineteenth-century Kathmandu, and how in the last fifteen years he and the city have traveled together into the latter part of the twentieth century.

"But refugee monks have scattered all over the world. We have them in Colorado, in New Zealand, Scotland, Switzerland. If anything, your practice is spreading. Look, it has brought me all the way here."

"Yes," Gonpo replies, his eyes still distant. "It has brought you here. But in Tibet, we lived at the center of the universe. I think it is different in Colorado. Perhaps you can tell me."

"We too have high mountains," Wilson says.

"I see."

Annoyed at how easily Gonpo is being sucked into the black box with the spinning tape, Jack snorts rudely: "The Rockies wouldn't make decent foothills out here."

This turn of the conversation disquiets him. Until now, he hadn't considered his Tibetan visions a product of place, like the wine they are drinking. But if that is true, what is happening to his mind here in Kathmandu? Under Wilson's prodding, Gonpo is now relating his own psychic experiences on the high plateau. Yes, he *had* practiced the yoga of heat, tum-mo. Training in the dead of winter, he *had* dried wet sheets wrapped around his body. But that was many years ago.

Jack remembers sitting on the exposed rock beside the remnants of the corpse, all night, without any sensation of being cold.

Yes, Gonpo had known lung-gom-pa, the trance walkers, to cover vast distances at extraordinary speeds.

And Jack remembers the slight monk, Gyatsu, floating ahead of the horses.

"Yes," Gonpo says, he knew cases in which lamas had projected their thoughts visibly.

"Like holograms?" Wilson looks to Jack for approval of this scientific metaphor, but Jack is reseeing the visions projected inside his brain in a remote Himalayan cave.

It is quite common for a lama and disciple to communicate telepathically, Gonpo says, but so do a mother and child, or a husband and wife. So what? Such things were simply more difficult outside of Tibet. Rarer perhaps.

And Jack remembers dreaming the Tibetan landscape inside Tsering's head while her glittery eyes stared upward in the moonlight.

Now Wilson is inquiring whether lamas can see what is happening many miles away.

"*Of course*," Gonpo replies. "But this is scarcely worth discussing. There are very few who are good at it, but a few ancient practitioners exist in remote hermitages."

And Jack is thinking of a fragile figure almost mummified by altitude and dry air, by age and asceticism, who at that very moment is sitting naked in a wooden crib.

"And you, Mr. Malloy, do you have an opinion on these matters? I'd be interested in your opinion, as a physicist."

It was difficult for Jack to leave the granite cave of Dorje. "As a physicist? What we believe is stranger than anything Gonpo has told you. But in order to function as human beings, we simply ignore the craziness. It's a form of schizophrenia required by modern physics."

But with a well-lubricated Tibetan lama in his presence, Wilson is not much interested in the philosophy of modern science, so he turns back to Gonpo.

That suits Jack, who gazes around the former palace, which must have seen its share of intrigue and political machination. He begins to brood on the machinations of his own breed who are pushing the doomsday clock ever nearer midnight. Like Nepal, he and his colleagues live on a crucial border without any effective means of resistance except skillful capitulation to power.

What in the hell is he doing in a Nepalese palace owned by a Russian émigré listening to a petty researcher like Wilson question a drunken Tibetan lama who is drinking astronomically expensive French wine?

He stands up. "I'll be leaving."

"Must you?" Wilson is startled. "I was hoping we would have a chance to speak further about the scientific aspects of these matters."

"Another time. I need to walk off the meal now."

Gonpo laughs. "Don't try to prevent him from walking, Mr. Wilson. By the time you've paid the bill, he'll have reached Bodnath."

With a minimum of handshaking and protestation of further meetings, Jack takes his leave of the earnest American psychic with the thick glasses, whose eyes swim in and out of view, and who has made Gonpo talkative with wine. Jack plunges into the press of an Asian city, the cows, bullock carts and pushcarts, the humans struggling under enormous burdens carried on their backs, on their heads, on bicycles; he wades through automobiles, motorcycles, holy men and throngs of residents and tourists clad in a stupefying mix of traditional clothes and Western wear. And always there are temples, and the strange painted stupas with the eyes of Buddha watching one's progress.

Perhaps three miles out of town he feels the car slowing behind him and knows who it is even as he turns. Inside the Mercedes, Wilson is alone. He rolls down his window. Could they take a little drive? he asks.

The alcohol, the August heat, the sudden inrush of memory blur his hostility to this disagreeable and persistent man. Almost as if bowing to his fate, he lets himself enter the air-conditioned interior of the automobile. He shoves the walking stick in back and climbs in beside Wilson, who raises the window beside him electronically.

"Where to?" Wilson asks.

"You tell me."

"I assume you're returning to the institute. I'll take you back after we've had a chance to talk."

One-handed, Wilson swerves around an ox cart and brushes back a bicyclist—it's the kind of driving, just a fraction this side of mayhem, that takes years to learn in Asia. But Wilson seems unaware of the near collisions.

"Have you ever heard of a region called Dolpo?" he asks.

Naturally, a man like Wilson in a Mercedes will ask about the very place dominating his thoughts. The Mercedes plunges honking into a herd of goats, the herder trying frantically to save his animals. Wilson touches the brakes at the last minute, bumping the animals, driving one frightened kid ahead of the flock, legs kicking wildly. The kid darts wildly into a field and the herder is left in the dust waving his staff.

"Yes, I know Dolpo," Jack replies.

The cool air inside the car circulates around his face, making him more aware of the befuddled, overheated state of his brain.

"Interesting region."

Jack waits.

"Hardly any foreigners have visited . . ."

"Snellgrove, the Englishman; Corneille Jeste, the Frenchman; Toni Hagen was Swiss; Furer-Haimendorf was German." Jack lists the foreign scholars who had made it back there over the years.

There's the faintest trace of a smile on Wilson's face. "But that was before these recent problems with the Khampa. Now it's totally isolated, I hear. Lots of monasteries gone to wrack and ruin. Sold off the relics, or stolen by the Khampa more likely. Not much left there, I hear."

71

So Wilson had done his reading. Beyond the tinted windows of the Mercedes, Jack sees the institute pass as though it were a distant phase of his life.

"The lamas have gone to Pokhara or Dharmsala," Wilson continues.

"Or Denver."

"Yes. Well, as a matter of fact, we do have a manuscript from Dolpo, probably illegal as hell. It's written in sandhyabhasa, you know about that."

"The twilight language of the ancient Siddhi," Jack says.

"It's pretty arcane. The Tibetans in Colorado are reluctant to translate, or else can't. But it seems to be connected to a lama in Dolpo, rumored to be the eighty-fifth Siddha."

Dorje's web is jiggling again, and Jack dangles, helpless as one of the goats in front of the Mercedes. They are approaching the hills near the Royal Game Sanctuary, where the road ends and dirt cart tracks begin.

"We're thinking of going out there to talk with him. I have financial support. The logistics can be arranged locally. They tell me you've been back that way."

"Do they?" He's no longer concerned by the identity of this "they." It no longer makes a difference.

"Hear you're quite the walker. And now that you're getting some Tibetan studies under your belt—"

"I'm not even a novice yet."

"Still, you *are* the only physicist in this part of the world with this kind of experience, with this knowledge and interest. You could be indispensable on an expedition like this."

"Could I?"

The road has narrowed to dirt, and Wilson, as he looks up to meet Jack's eyes, is heading full tilt for a muddy stream. Once the sheets of water subside and the windshield clears, Jack hears water gurgling under the car. Wilson looks astonished that a mud puddle like this could have stopped the Mercedes. He begins spinning the wheels, digging into the streambed.

"You'd better ease up," Jack says. "Or you'll be afoot. Or afloat."

But Wilson isn't listening and races the engine, sliding the car sideways, downstream. He whips the wheel, trying to head the car back upstream, but there's no traction.

"Too bad," Jack says. "We'll have to walk." He opens his door, stepping into knee-deep water, and Wilson gets out on his side, swearing.

As Jack wades back the way they've come, Wilson says, "Where are you going?" His voice sounds panicky.

"For a short walk."

"Are there leeches in this water?"

"Probably."

He hears Wilson splashing for shore. The air is hot and humid in the aftermath of the monsoons. The farmer turning over the paddy field with a brace of water buffalo seems to understand the problem despite Jack's primitive Nepali. He'd seen the Mercedes roar past, and he detaches the buffalo from his plow and leads them down the road. Wilson is sitting under a rhododendron bush, barefoot, his muddy trousers rolled to the knee. He watches in silence as the farmer yokes his buffalo to the Mercedes and begins dragging it backward out of the stream.

"What do you suppose this is worth?" Wilson asks.

"Let your heart speak."

Wilson reaches for his wallet and extricates a ten-rupee note. "I should think this would be quite handsome."

"What did one bottle of Bordeaux cost?"

"For Christ's sake! What's that got to do with it? This took him half an hour. Ten rupees is half a day's wages."

The animals drag the car's back wheels onto the main road, and the farmer squats, dhoti drawn up between his knees, untying the rope. The buffalo switch their tails at flies, anxious to get back down into the stream with the Mercedes, where they can sink into the mud with only their backs and noses showing.

The farmer ignores the money and climbs onto one of his animals. Wilson takes out another ten-rupee note and glances at Jack. It's still a long way to that first bottle of Bordeaux. Finally, he pulls out a hundred-rupee note. The farmer clasps his hands together in a gesture of blessing, shaking his head.

"He doesn't want it," Jack says.

"Oh, horseshit, they all want it." And barefoot, wincing at the stones on the road, Wilson walks toward the two buffalo, who watch him approach. The near one twitches its skin and blows through its black nose.

"Here," Wilson holds up the bright hundred-rupee note, but the farmer won't extend his hand. "Goddamn it, I'm not giving you any more. This is all you get." He stuffs the note under the yoke, and the animal twitches its shoulders and whips its tail as if it had been stung.

Jack clasps his hands together in farewell, the farmer does the same and bangs his buffalo with a stick. When the Mercedes passes, the half-bottle of Bordeaux is gone from beneath the buffalo's yoke.

Wilson is trying to regain his composure, while Jack suppresses a grin. He's actually beginning to enjoy this outing.

"You know what?" Wilson asks.

No need for any response from Jack. Unlike the Mercedes, there's no stopping Wilson.

"I'd like to mount an expedition into Dolpo."

"You told me the area's closed." At least it was to Jack Malloy.

"Oh, I wouldn't worry about that. There are ways around those things. Out here." He looks significantly at Jack, as a fellow Westerner wise in the ways of the East.

"And what would you be looking for?"

"I told you. The lama from western Tibet."

"And what do you want with him?"

"Evidence. If he's any good, he'll demonstrate the psychic forces we're studying. Gonpo says these things are common up there."

"Who cares?"

The bluntness of the question stops Wilson for a moment. "I *told* you there's a lot of current interest, has been for years."

"But what difference does proof make? People have believed in these phenomena for years. Who cares about proof?"

74

"You ask this?"

"I do."

"Because proof extends our knowledge, it turns theories into facts."

"And then what?"

"They are applied, of course."

"And what application of psychic powers?"

"Well, if you're a gambler, of course . . ."

"If you're not a gambler?"

"There are possibilities for medical diagnosis; faster-than-light communication. Who knows? The real uses never manifest themselves at first."

There's an odd scratching sound as though something left by their plunge into the river were dragging underneath the car. Jack glances around the interior. The dry, scratching sound is familiar, and his chest tightens. It's Dorje, and the question emanating from his own throat surprises him as much as Wilson:

"Any military uses?"

Wilson's head jerks around to face him. "Military?"

"Just asking." But Jack already knows the answer.

"Well," Wilson hesitates. "The Russians are very interested in psychic control. They're putting quite a bit of money into the area, and some of their best people have been studying psychic phenomena for years."

"I see," Jack says. And suddenly he does see. Wilson is no research drone from Denver. "So first those sneaky Russians beat us with Sputnik and now they're beating us with psychics."

Wilson is not amused. "There's a good deal of interest in the Pentagon. In fact the Defense Department is helping to fund our study."

"Are they?"

Jack glances at the man driving the Mercedes. Jack is sitting here because he wants to return to Dolpo. And he went to Dolpo because the Indians were going to explode a bomb. And the Indians were going to explode a bomb because the Chinese had done so ten years earlier, after first defeating the Indian army in the Himalayas. And now the Pakistanis, having been defeated by the Indians ... The sound inside the car sharpens like the faint after-ring of a small bell rung at seventeen thousand feet in the Himalayas, over the remains of a dead man. Wilson is repugnant, yet he's here because of Jack. And suddenly Jack understands that his departure from the lab has had serious repercussions—namely this man from Denver. CIA no doubt.

"I'd hoped you'd accompany us," Wilson says.

Jack reaches for the door handle. "This will do."

"I thought you were going back to the institute."

"I was. But this will do."

"You're miles away."

"I know it."

Wilson pulls to the side of the road, trying to compose his face. "If I arrange an expedition, will you accompany us?"

Jack reaches into the backseat for his walking staff. "Thanks. But I'd prefer to go on my own." It's an instinctive resistance to Wilson and Dorje's ever-expanding web, but this time there's no warning pain between the eyes or scratchy gargling voice. It's good to keep Wilson off balance. And besides, in Asia one always bargains.

"Thanks for the ride. And lunch."

"You know where to reach me, if you change your mind."

The tinted window slides up and Wilson guns the muddy Mercedes straight into a flock of sheep. Bicycles swerve out of the way, people dive for the side of the road.

If it was necessary for people like Wilson to exist, then it was probably better to know who they were and who was paying them. And after this encounter with the psychic recruiter, Jack found himself smiling. The way to Dolpo lay open before him.

9

Gonpo hears him come in but remains in silent meditation as Jack sits on his cushion. Jack's tension and lack of concentration are palpable. He's like a restless animal. Gonpo picks up the big drum and slams it with his hand.

Jack is staring at him. "What the hell did you do that for?"

"Get out of your head!"

Jack is thinner and bonier than ever—the cotton trousers and shirt hang off him. He wants to speak. Words shouldn't be necessary for Gonpo to understand his need, but Gonpo's mind is blurred by Bordeaux, and the drum, still reverberating in his hand, is a reproach to himself as well as to Jack.

"Wilson followed me after lunch," Jack says.

Distressed at his own condition, Gonpo sorts through the Tibetan pantheon for a guide through this discussion. He begins to visualize the yidam Yamantaka, but the image is cloudy, imprecise.

"He is proposing a trip to Dolpo and wants me to go," Jack says.

The ferocious bull-headed figure of Yamantaka grows in Gonpo's mind.

"He knows I've been to Inner Dolpo; he knows I've seen Dorje."

The bull head clears and individual skulls appear; flames flicker as the visualization begins to vibrate with life. Gonpo opens his eyes. "Tell me about Dorje."

Jack hesitates. "That's difficult. I no longer know what is real and what is hallucination."

"Please."

Gonpo watches the ferocious devouring bull dissolve into a lotus as Jack begins a detailed account of his visit to Dolpo. At the heart of the lotus blossom the syllables of the mantra are glowing. There is no ripple on the water. The light is intense. The way is clear. But Jack is shredded with self-doubt. Instead of flowing like water around stone, he is trying to push through it with his head. Gonpo surrounds Jack's words gently, like water around pebbles, trying to better understand his meaning.

Jack is talking about his visions in the cave. Clearly, Dorje has given him a glimpse over the crest of enlightenment. But why send him back into this world where his presence in Kathmandu causes rumors to circulate in so many quarters? Why should a recluse notify the world of his presence in this way?

Jack stops speaking. The lotus glows serenely.

"And the sound comes to you here in Kathmandu, and is accompanied by pain?"

"Yes. I'm afraid I'm losing my mind."

Gonpo rings the bell once. "There is nothing to lose, my friend. All is mind."

Jack is a strange stone for Dorje to throw into a still pond. But disturbances now ripple in all directions. What lama could hope to control the consequences of such irresponsible action?

"Tsering has been reporting my activities to Lama Z. And he's been in contact with my embassy and the Nepalese."

The network of lamas reached everywhere and soon this odd contact with a physicist would be known, and Dorje's activities would reach the Dalai Lama in India and the lamas in England, Europe, the United States. And what about Wilson, the man from Denver, without psychic capacity or true interest in the Vajrayana? Why should he be drawn to Dorje? Of course the Americans had armed the Tibetan guerrillas, but both the CIA and the Dalai Lama had abandoned them in order to appease the Chinese. So why would Wilson want to go back there now, even if he were CIA? Whatever the reason for his arrival in Nepal, Wilson has bored a hole through Jack's hard surface, exposing his heart.

"And why did you refuse Wilson?" Gonpo asks.

"Would you take a man like that to see Dorje?"

"Not precisely the point, my friend. Why did *you* refuse?"

"Because I want to go on my own and stay indefinitely. I have no interest in *studying* Dorje. Wilson wants to take cameras, tape recorders, what else . . . encephalograms, rectal thermometers? The whole idea is repugnant."

"And yet Dorje warns you against refusing Wilson."

Jack blushes. "Yes. I don't like Wilson, yet I go to lunch with him."

"I hear much concern for *your* wishes. Have you considered the nature of your quest?"

"Of course. I've found a man who can liberate me."

"Liberate *you*."

"Yes."

"Why should *you* be liberated?"

Jack pauses. "So that eventually all sentient beings can be released."

"Precisely. And what do you think Dorje wishes?"

"How would I know? I can't even speak the language."

"You have had a series of communications from this naljorpa and still profess not to know what he wishes?

"How can I ask? Send a telegram?"

The hole in Jack's chest gapes wide, the lungs and heart show blue and vibrant. This man is lost without a guide, and Gonpo begins to wonder whether the guide may not also be lost without this man.

"*Why* did you go into Dolpo? *Why* did you strike the Khampa with a stick? *Why* did Dorje send for you, and then release you into the world? Do you think you have control over such events? Has it not occurred to you to ask Dorje what he wishes?"

Jack is silent. He's not stupid, but he's thinking stupidly now.

Whenever the superficialities of mind are disturbed, this man of science is as lost as a child. What good is such a physicist to a Tantric adept like Dorje?

"Ask him," Gonpo said.

"Ask him?"

"Yes."

"How?"

At least Malloy has been reduced to single-syllable responses. This is progress. "He gave you dreams. He gave you visions. He gives you his voice. Now use them."

Jack is silent a long while. "Speak to Dorje?"

"Yes."

"But how . . . ?" and then he stops, as if the meaning of the past days has finally snapped clear in his mind. His face clears, his breathing deepens. Good. Very good. Gonpo waits.

"Show me!" Jack speaks from the heart, but his voice is weak with doubt.

A chill rises in Gonpo's bowels, seizing his stomach and chest, constricting his heart and clogging his throat. This simple request, so dear to the teacher's heart, has created panic in the teacher.

"Come here," Gonpo says. "Take my hand."

Jack reaches out, but Gonpo's hand is trembling. His mind is muddy with alcohol and rich food, his chakras are clotted with impurity. This man, open to the way, cannot be failed, yet the teacher has lost the way.

"Let us practice your visualization," Gonpo says, stalling for time. "Visualize Yamantaka. Let him speak to you through symbols."

While Jack closes his eyes, Gonpo fights the constriction in his chest, trying to open his own chakras. But he's weak and helpless.

Jack's eyes flick open. "I'm blocked. Help me focus."

Jack's hands burn with psychic energy, his channels are open and receptive. In desperation, Gonpo picks up the dorje and vajra bell, the means and the voice. Let the bell speak for him. Jack is sweating now, his shirt wet at the armpits, his hair limp and damp, and Gonpo yearns to occupy this mind before him, as Dorje has done in Dolpo. He wants to speak without words, as a true master, and staring at the sweat beaded on Jack's face, at his shallow breathing, Gonpo tries to enter this desperate being before him. But it's hopeless. The master totters on the razor's edge.

Suddenly Jack's eyes open. "I see you."

Gonpo's stomach lurches with the judgment.

"Your love pushed me down a hole until I was looking up through darkness at a ring of light. The syllables of my mantra were glowing about the ring." Jack's face is radiant.

Gonpo's own heart is pounding and his palms sweating. He waits.

"The ring became a face. Dorje spoke."

Gonpo is ashamed because he has to ask, "What did he say?"

"I must do something. I must *do* something." And Jack's eyes flicker wildly. "I don't know. Translate for me, Gonpo, what must I do?"

Stinking sweat pours from Gonpo's body. He smells himself—the fear and the loss. Dorje has spoken. The web shakes. Gonpo must be a channel for the pure diamond light. There can be no mistake now.

"I think," he begins slowly, "that Dorje is risking direct intervention. But to intervene in the texture of cause and effect is very dangerous. Only a few yogi in a thousand years can do such a thing. And there is a very fine line between the Dharma and the black arts."

Gonpo gropes for a comparison. "It is like your man Einstein, a good man releases an idea into the world but even his great mind is not wise enough to control the way the idea spreads. A very wise yogi, however, can guide his intervention so that the Dharma is furthered."

"And there are such men?"

"There have been."

"But what can *I* do?"

Gonpo sits quietly a moment, sweat running down his own face. "You were given the answer today."

"What do you mean?"

"Accept Mr. Wilson's proposition."

As if the floor has vanished beneath him and he is falling, Jack's mouth opens in surprise. "Ah," he says.

But Gonpo has slipped on the razor and cannot catch himself. He watches the awful words emerging from the hole in Jack's face:

"Then you must come with me."

Terror grips Gonpo. No more Bordeaux, no more fine meals, no more tourist women. Those who would assist this quest were trapped like flies. A very powerful naljorpa indeed! Gonpo's vocal cords are paralyzed, his hands are trembling, when the outer door slams open. At the sound, his body splits open like a melon.

Oh, she sees them all right, the drunk and the serpent, hunkered in Gonpo's chamber face to face like a couple of lovers. She smells incense as she slams the outer door and kicks the walking staff skidding across the stone floor. In her own house she has to put up with this. Seeing Jack pass the institute in Wilson's blue Mercedes had done it. He could leave the house immediately. Gonpo, too. He'd lived on the streets before and could go back to the streets again. Lama Z was right—her life would change. Perhaps she would leave for India.

Upstairs she throws down the briefcase full of foreign newspapers, kicks off her high-heeled shoes, and sits looking out over the river toward the gleaming temple of Swayambhunath and the hills beyond. The monsoons have passed into a hot, humid September. But ten thousand feet up on the plateau, fall will have arrived—the willows changing color along the river, the grasses dry and brittle with wind, and a dusting of snow along the shallow lakes already crusting with ice.

When the figure appears in the doorway, she does not turn her head. Let him stand. When hands touch her neck, she doesn't move.

"It is time to leave," the voice says.

Hands brush through her hair, down her shoulders, but she doesn't move. Hands, ending in familiar tapered fingers, grasp her arms. The temple gong sounds. Evening fires have been lit; parrots and mynahs fly from roof to roof; crows circle squawking over the city. And she tastes salt before she feels tears on her face.

Somewhere, very high up, a bitter wind whines through stony passes, a wind that bites off your toes. You do not look back at the black robed figures struggling through the snow; you do not look back at the horse with the broken leg; you only look ahead at the Khampa warriors breaking the snow toward the pass; the wind flicks needles into your face. A blizzard now means death for all of them. But the man beside her, his mustache frozen, is smiling and pointing up. A blue-black sky breaks overhead, closes, opens again. She tries to smile. Her feet are without feeling. Behind them, the horse screams and thrashes in the snow. And soon enough they are falling forward, the weight of their bodies pulling them down into Nepal and a new life.

And now looking toward the great temple and mountains beyond, she feels a face slide alongside hers, feels its beard soft against her neck, its breath dry in her ear.

"Come with us."

Like a wild animal in a snare, she whirls, jerking her head to one side and pulling at the enslaving arms. She looks up. The scientist's face has vanished behind the mask of a stranger. She shakes tears from her burning eyes. Words spit from her lips, driven by more than anger.

"So you're returning home?"

"Yes."

"So you've played out your game and can abandon the natives to their quaint country?"

"No."

"I saw you drive by with that American." She looks into his face, but someone else is watching through his eyes.

"Come with us," the voice says. "You must."

"Where?"

"To the country which is nowhere."

It takes her a moment to recognize the Tibetan phrase. The country which is nowhere is beyond the crest of enlightenment. An unexpected force grips her body. She trembles, trying to resist the loneliness sweeping over her. At this time of year she almost died on the crest. The passes will close in less than three months. She shakes her head.

From the room below comes a shattering sound, the trumpet blown once, twice, followed by a flurry of pellets on the damaru. And then the chant. Coming nearer, the drum rattles again. Nearer. It is Gonpo ascending the stairs. He appears at the door. He enters the room as if emerging from a monastery into the bright fall sunlight of Tibet. She waits with Jack's hands on her shoulders. Another wild flurry on the drum, pellets beating on her own skull. And then in Gonpo's radiant face, she sees herself. Once she, too, had dwelt in a country which is nowhere—the country of youth and hope. She raises her arms, enclosing the angular figure before her. The lama watches them embrace with a curious expression: as if they were two figures on a temple frieze, a Tantric couple intertwining sensuous limbs. But the man in her arms is sinewy and bony—not carved on any temple.

"So," Gonpo says. "It has begun."

These rigid Western arms can never manage the sinuous postures of a yogi; these limbs tend to push away when they pull close. Yet neither can she manage the sensuous dances of Durga. And she, too, pushes away what she wants to enfold. She laughs bitterly, but the sound emerging from her lips is not bitter. Jack begins to laugh, an absurd honking sound that redoubles her own laughter. Pellets rattle on the skull drum. Then either she is dragging him down or he is dragging her down, because they are both slumping to the floor in each other's arms, their laughter an insane hiccuping, out of control.

Gonpo in his frayed robes stands over them, the drum dangling from his fingers. He, too, is braying and cackling.

"This is a very great power," he says. "This is a man I must meet."

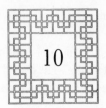

10

Wilson was taking breakfast in bed—fresh orange juice, ham, two eggs over easy, and American coffee. Translated into rupees, it was a breakfast that would feed a Nepali family for several weeks. But he wasn't about to make that comparison again. The hundred rupees to the bullock driver had galled him all night, and he was just remembering Malloy's smug expression when the phone rang. It was Malloy, sounding very contrite, and Wilson smiled. He hadn't expected him to capitulate so quickly. Very gratifying.

During the opening pleasantries, Wilson refilled his cup and leisurely stirred in cream and sugar. Of course, he said, he was glad that Jack was reconsidering his offer. Yes, the permit would be difficult, but some avenues of influence were open to him, and he was reasonably certain that a purely scientific expedition, as opposed to a tourist trek, would be allowed into the area.

Wilson sipped his coffee, pleased with himself. He had the high ground now. "What!" Wilson sat upright in his blue silk robe, a birthday present from his mother. "It's out of the question."

Taking a drunken monk on the expedition was ludicrous, especially since the vice-consul had revealed that Gonpo was something of a joke around town. Wilson was embarrassed at having taken him so seriously yesterday.

Now Jack was explaining his proposition. "Yes," Wilson said, "he *is* fluent in English, that's true." His eyes flicked rapidly as he tried to think ahead of Jack. "Yes, a lama in Dolpo might be an advantage." But this one?

Something besides Malloy's proposition began to trouble him, as if this phone call had stabbed him in the stomach, and his expression turned inward, looking for signs of his pre-ulcerous condition. Under the attention, his stomach rumbled and gurgled appreciatively, and Wilson grew troubled.

They'd have to carry that tub of lama lard in a litter. Of course Malloy was right, these people were so fanatically religious that a holy man traveling with the expedition could do no harm. But a discredited and dissolute lama, for Christ's sake, wasn't quite the thing. Before Wilson could even begin to digest the idea, Malloy introduced another preposterous one, and Wilson's stomach lurched again, a hot, familiar pain shooting through his intestines.

"Out of the question, Malloy. Absolutely out of the question. I'll think about the lama, but not her. If you can't get by without your woman for a few months, we'd best forget your participation."

His belly writhed and gurgled, a dramatic increase in activity.

"It's a harebrained idea, Malloy! What possible use can she serve? A woman is nothing but trouble on an expedition. So she's Tibetan. So she was born up there. She's still a Communist . . ."

That was a mistake. He'd offended Malloy and had to backpedal. "Well, actually, no," he replied, trying to modulate his voice. "I kind of assumed from what Lama Z said that she was a Marxist. Yes, it is irrelevant on a scientific expedition, I grant you that, but the border is sensitive, especially now they're mopping up the Khampa. If there were any sort of trouble, I'd hate to think what might happen, and how on earth can I possibly explain her presence?"

In his agitation he gulped more coffee, which hit his stomach like acid. His bowels constricted wildly, and the distant warning down there became a loud Klaxon of alarm. His goddamned body had gone into revolt, and his forehead was damp with fever.

"I thought we were taking the lama as translator. Why didn't you mention her first?"

He gulped more coffee, and sweat burst out on his face. Jesus, he slammed the cup down on the nightstand and reached for his cigarettes. Malloy was getting the upper hand here, because Wilson was sick. What the hell had he eaten that would cause the shits like this? The expedition hung in the balance, and all he could think about was his bowels. If he *had* to take two Tibetans, it was possible to do so. But why should he *have* to? *He* was bankrolling it. None of them could go without him. He had all the aces in his hand. All he had to do was call Malloy's bluff and make the bastard kowtow.

"Malloy . . . ," he began, but pain skewered him between the hips and he whimpered into the phone, "It's simply a shitty idea."

But Malloy didn't waver or pull back, as if there were simply no question about the woman and lama going. Normally, he could have handled Malloy except for this goddamned rebellion of his body. But even to his own ears, his objections sounded ineffectual, and the situation down below was becoming critical.

He jerked on the phone, but the cord wouldn't reach to the bathroom. He was going to have to hang up, but Malloy's voice had him hypnotized. Malloy was already arranging porters and Sherpas and food.

"But," Wilson objected desperately, "with this woman and lama we'll need more porters. It'll slow us down. Do you want that?"

"Slow is fine," the voice said.

A new jolt of acid flushed into Wilson's bowels. "But if winter catches us back there . . ." Wilson was whispering into the phone, clenching his sphincter.

"Better skiing than Aspen," the voice replied.

Naturally, Malloy had no fear of being stuck in Dolpo because he *wanted* to be isolated back there. Perfect! Isolated with his woman and his sidekick Gonpo who were used to those winters. They could sur-

87

vive. But could he? Something slipped inside his body—a shocking deterioration of the situation.

Six months living on ground barley and rancid tea in a filthy cave. It was impossible. He had to return to Denver by December at the latest. Malloy was saying they could lighten the expedition and speed things up, if Wilson wished, by carrying their own gear.

"What?" Wilson said, acid flushing into his bowels. "Carry our own?"

"Sure, toughen up by carrying weight at the lower altitudes. Acclimate. You need to get in shape," the voice said cheerfully. "It's rough country. Rockslides, chasms, no bridges . . ."

Wilson was puffing wildly on his cigarette and trying to keep a grip on his intestines. "Let's discuss the matter later, Malloy," he said, jabbing his cigarette into an ashtray, but Malloy was going full bore now, arranging details. He wanted Wilson's approval to get started immediately.

"Goddamn it, what difference can a few hours make?" Wilson's voice was plaintive.

"What's the problem?" Jack said. "Let's get the show on the road."

"All right, all right," Wilson cried, sliding his legs over the edge of the bed. They were white and trembling as the legs of an old man. "I'll take your woman as translator and the lama as Buddhist adviser. Are you happy now?"

Malloy said he was very happy and would come to the hotel that afternoon.

Wilson didn't bother hanging up. He simply stood up and let the phone fall to the floor. It was already too late to make the bathroom. The bathrobe was ruined. He could smell himself. Grimacing and hunched over, he waddled forward trying to control himself. Finally, he gave up, and gathering the robe between his legs like one of the natives in the street, he let the burning fluid drain from his body as he hobbled into the bathroom. The tile was cool, clean and white under his feet. He let the robe slide down into a stinking heap and hunkered up gratefully on the cold porcelain toilet.

Jesus H. Christ, he thought, they didn't pay him enough for this sort of thing. This goddamned hotel had guaranteed boiled water. What about the ice cubes? He'd had drinks all over town. Or the salad at that Russian restaurant with the lama and Malloy? Or that filthy, leech-filled water around the Mercedes? You couldn't get the shits through your skin, but had some splashed into his mouth?

His intestines writhed like snakes. Jesus H. Christ. Where they were going, there were no toilet seats or tile floors or running water. His stomach did a complete loop. Running water. He could practically see the microbes wiggling out of the tap. Jesus H. Christ.

11

Of course," Lama Z said over his tea, "I am delighted that you are accompanying this expedition." Tsering watched his face—supremely benign this morning. "However, I have made some discreet inquiries. Since Wang Dai was killed, groups of Khampa have refused to turn in their weapons. The Dalai Lama has sent a second emissary. There are reports that some villages are still terrorized by these countrymen of ours who have become so . . . misguided."

The same men the Dalai Lama had encouraged and the Americans had armed against the Chinese were now being abandoned, because the Tibetan resistance was now incompatible with the long-term goals of both. The American imperialists had shifted the balance of power by appeasing China, and since the decline of the Red Guards, the lamas hoped to return to Tibet by appeasing China. Politicians like Lama Z had once ruled Tibet, and they were capable of endless duplicity and corruption, she knew. These were only preparatory remarks, and she waited for him to come to the point.

"The application for your expedition is currently under review," he said. "There has been considerable pressure to expedite the process."

She waited.

"Since you, Malloy and Gonpo are involved, the institute itself has become involved. It is a curious thing to the government *why* we should be."

She waited.

"I believe, correct me, that you are employed as an interpreter."

Tsering sipped her tea.

"And Gonpo goes as an adviser on the practice of the Vajrayana."

Tsering set down her teacup, smiling as sweetly as she could manage.

"This displeases certain lamas, as you're well aware. Gonpo is not our chosen representative of the Dharma. Also, your friend Malloy is under close scrutiny by the government of Nepal for his previous activities in this region."

Jack was no longer *our* American but *her* friend. It was clear enough where they were headed, but she was oddly relaxed. After fifteen years in Beijing, Lhasa, Kathmandu, the patient endurance of a nomad had returned to her. She was going home.

"Mr. Wilson proposes to take cameras and recording equipment to a sensitive border." He waited, but she made no response. "The expedition is not propitious. Permission will be denied."

"Unless . . . ," she said.

"Unless I know what representatives of this institute are doing. I must have accurate information about what happens in Dolpo."

"Is there more tea?" she asked.

"Cold," he replied. "Let me summon some warm." A monk with a fresh pot of tea answered his bell. The lama filled her cup, sipped from his own and then folded his hands in his lap. "A disaster on the frontier would jeopardize our position here."

She breathed the fragrant green tea. There was that to be said for the Chinese opening the new road from Tibet: such things as this tea were in greater supply.

"On the other hand, we are naturally interested in this naljorpa who has excited such interest, and we have no reason to oppose a scientific expedition. If I could assure the authorities about the precise nature of our participation."

Normally, she couldn't have tolerated this long preamble to the obvious, but her state of mind was so relaxed that she waited patiently, enjoying the dance. It would be very beautiful, sharp and clean, in the high mountains this fall, walking day to day toward the plateau, higher and higher, until, at some point, she could see north.

"If I may speak frankly?" the lama said.

They both understood these preliminaries. There was no need for any response from her.

"I do not believe the stated purpose of Mr. Wilson. Nor do I believe Mr. Malloy fully, although his earnestness is beyond reproach. I think we have here the tentacles of a foreign power. The CIA has run the Tibetan resistance for years. I think Mr. Malloy was sent here to establish connections, and now Mr. Wilson has appeared. I have no control over Gonpo or Malloy. However, you and I have an understanding."

"*Had* an understanding."

"As you wish. But the expedition will not receive a permit unless I can assure the authorities of our intentions. I must pass on any information about the Khampa. If this naljorpa is a Khampa leader, that information must come to me. I must have a full report on the activities of our two foreign friends. If there is any connection between them, I wish to know that, too."

He was probably overestimating his own importance in this matter, she thought, since there was little respect for the Tibetans among the Nepalese, while the Americans, on the other hand, were a powerful presence in Nepal. She was inclined to think that Wilson's American connections must be far stronger than anything the lama could muster.

"I made myself clear several days ago—I am no longer your eyes and ears in the outer world. I offered my resignation, you may recall."

The benign smile did not slip, nor did the glistening eyes lose their luster, but there was a slight sagging of the skin. The lama was, after all, nearing seventy, and there were certain times when the secular affairs of the institute weighed upon him.

"Ah," he replied. "You understand the repercussions of such a decision?"

"You've made it very clear."

She stood. "The tea has been delicious, your company also, as always. But now I must arrange the transport of manuscripts to Dharmsala."

"Of course your work here may continue," the lama said. "I shouldn't be surprised if both Americans return home in a few days."

"Nor should I," she said, not believing it for a moment.

Exhilarated to have the fate of so many in her hands, she dropped to her knees and performed a grand prostration before the lama, for the first time in their relationship, and the irony was not lost on him. His smile vanished. So he was bluffing. Wilson would prevail, and she would owe nothing further to this man.

Ravaged by dysentery, Wilson allowed Jack to organize the expedition, and Jack, in turn, used the efficient Tsering to help him bargain in the bazaar and with Sherpas and porters. She paid more of Wilson's money than necessary, but, out of deference to Jack, not too much more. He insisted on heavy underwear for her, a down vest and down parka. More precautions than were required for her own country, she told him, since she had lived on the high plateau most of her life without long underwear. After all, she had crossed these mountains in a blizzard wearing tennis shoes.

"Yes," he replied, "and lost your toes."

Burlap bags of grain, flour, jars of ghee were prepared for transport to Pokhara by bus. Wilson packed his cameras and film and tape recorder in waterproof aluminum canisters. Sherpa Pasang, employed for this return to Dolpo, supervised the retention of porters under Tsering's watchful eye.

Gonpo prepared himself by alternating drinking bouts with repentant meditation sessions. He said he would travel as lamas had always traveled in these mountains, with no possessions. One morning, Tsering looked into his bloodshot eyes and put her hand on his knee.

"Do you know why we are doing this?" she asked.

"Because we have no choice."

"Of course we have a choice," she replied.

He managed a pathetic smile through his ferocious hangover. "Really? To live in this house without him? Knowing where he has gone?"

"Yes," she said defiantly. But it was hard to keep her eyes on his face as she said it.

Gonpo's sickly smile remained. "Please, my head hurts sufficiently. You can no longer deny your love for him."

"Don't use that word. He fascinates me. And now he provides an opportunity to leave the institute."

"This is your true reason?"

She lowered her eyes. "Also I wish to see my country."

He patted her hand gently. "I understand. It is humbling to do the bidding of others. To admit one's true feelings."

It *was* humbling. As Gonpo had said, desire blinds. Despite her distaste for Wilson and his boundless money, she was in the position of hoping that he would prevail with the Nepalese authorities in order to free her from the lama's tentacles. And despite her contempt for the Dolpo shaman, she had submitted to this course of events that he had set in motion.

"And you?" she asked suddenly. "What about you?"

Gonpo's expression became instantly intense and inward. "I *must* go."

"And would you call that *love*?" She spit the word out disdainfully.

"Yes. Love of the Dharma. And because . . ."

She waited a long while, but it seemed he would not complete his thought. "And?"

"And because there is something much larger here. I cannot see it clearly. My mind is clouded."

But she saw in his drink-blurred face a sure knowledge—that he was seeing the end of his own life. And more. More that he did not wish to tell her. Her heart constricted with fear.

"What do you mean?"

He patted her hand. "I am going to the country which is nowhere. There is no greater purpose for a Buddhist. And since Jack needs guidance, I must guide."

She was terrified by this acceptance of his own fate. Her shallow breathing and tight heart hurt her breast. She was afraid. Because Gonpo was also reading her fate.

"And me? Tell me truly. Am I following this man for love, like a movie from Hollywood? Is that what I am doing?"

He looked at her a long time in silence, and her heart shrank to pebble size. She had asked, and he would tell her, and she did not wish to hear the answer. "In your own way, you are giving yourself to the Dharma. You, too, are going to the country which is nowhere."

And it took all her strength not to ask precisely where that country was. Because Gonpo might tell her, and she could not bear to hear the answer. She lowered her face, and Gonpo placed his hand on top of her head.

"Now you know."

She nodded dumbly.

When Jack saw Lama Z, for what turned out to be the last time before their departure, he was feeling triumphant. The expedition was prepared to leave, and he was taking Tsering away from the lama's influence. But the lama looked as enigmatic as ever.

"Your interest in Buddhist practice is commendable," he said, "although I fail to see that a return to the mountains will facilitate your calling. The area is backward, the tradition is in decline. It is not a place for a novice. Your progress here at the institute would be more useful. But my advice in these matters is of small interest, I understand."

"Not at all," Jack said. "But the opportunity to return to these mountains is very important to me."

"Ah, yes. To return. On such a border, matters are very sensitive just now. It is probable that your expedition will not be allowed."

"Mr. Wilson has been assured that we will receive permission."

95

"Should you be denied, however, you are of course welcome to continue at the institute. As is Mr. Wilson, if his interest in Buddhism is as genuine as your own."

Jack, accustomed to this roundabout manner of speech, understood that Lama Z resented his loss of control. Jack was returning to Dolpo, and with any luck would winter there, locked away from this world of political intrigue among lamas who had once ruled Tibet and still believed they would return to power.

"We shall extend your blessings in the region," Jack said.

"Of course," the lama said. "And if you succeed in going, would you place this atop the highest pass?" He handed over a small, smooth stone inscribed with a mantra. In the most remote places, such mani stones were left by pilgrims, sometimes stacked to make walls at propitious points along the way. Jack accepted the stone.

"May it bring you good fortune."

"We'll likely need it at this time of year."

"In this part of the world, protection is always necessary."

"Then we have your protection?"

The lama did not speak for some time. At last he said, "It is always my wish to spread the teaching. If this expedition does so, it has my blessing."

"Is there any reason to doubt?"

"In this part of the world there is never certainty. We are trying to release sentient beings from desire and hence from suffering. It is possible that, how shall I put this, that you are *too* desirous in this expedition."

At the lama's words, Jack's stomach clenched. Was he deceiving himself and leading them all into danger rather than transcendence? Was Dorje's power a creation of his own ego, and were the omens he saw—Tsering's new docility and Gonpo's strength—likewise deceptions of a blind ego? The lama's warning chilled him.

"Tashi shok," the lama said.

Jack prostrated himself before the lama-politician who, in an effort to spread the teaching to the West, had compromised his spiritual authority. Nonetheless, he had shaken Jack. Was this return to a her-

96

metic figure on the high Tibetan Plateau anything more than self-deception?

The lama had closed his eyes in meditation. Jack was dismissed.

"You're feeling better," Jack said. Wilson was drinking bottled soda water at the hotel bar and had lost the inward-dwelling expression of the diarrhetic. His face had regained color.

"I'm fine," Wilson said. "However, the permit situation is worrisome. Since the government killed one of the Khampa leaders and is mopping up the remaining Tibetans, obstructions have been raised. A month ago, my connections would have cleared the way. Now . . . it is suggested that all three of you being connected to the institute poses a problem."

"Problem?"

"A guarantee is required . . . that you are actually traveling on behalf of the institute."

Jack's heart constricted. So, Lama Z had carried out his threat. "On *behalf* of the institute? At Lama Z's request?"

"It looks that way. I'm not sure how to go about it. He has no love for me. Gonpo is a renegade. I thought you might have some ideas."

Just when it seemed they were free, Dorje's web jiggled and these new complexities arose. Would the entanglements never end? By way of answer, a faint tingling between his eyes reminded him that Dorje did not appreciate doubt. There was one person who could sway Lama Z on their behalf.

"I suppose Tsering could speak to Lama Z," Jack said.

Wilson looked pained.

"The insides bothering you?" Jack asked solicitously.

"Just a bit, if you'll excuse me."

While Wilson was gone, Jack tried to appraise the situation. Wilson, Gonpo, Tsering had all been admitted to Dolpo. Now Lama Z was necessary. So word of his defection from physics was spreading in all directions, from Berkeley and the network of exiled lamas to the CIA. And there seemed nothing he could do about it.

When Wilson reappeared, his pallor had returned. "Would you talk with . . . her?" It hurt him to pronounce her name.

"If your connections have failed. But it was your assurance—"

"Do you think I like this? How could I know the Nepalis would begin cleaning up the Khampa after tolerating them for twelve years? Try, will you?"

They were sitting in the living room when Jack broke the news to Tsering. "The permit is denied unless Lama Z sponsors the expedition. I just talked to Wilson."

Lama Z's complacent face appeared before her; his satisfied smile was more than she could bear. "Why?"

"Because you and Gonpo and I are going, and the authorities think that involves the institute. But the institute has nothing to do with the expedition."

"Why would Lama Z help us?"

"I don't know. He's curious about Dorje, too. Perhaps he would do it as a favor."

But Tsering knew only too well the conditions of Lama Z's approval, and staring at Jack's face, made gaunt with dedication these past weeks, she was shocked at his begging. But when it came to Dorje, he had no pride.

"As a favor to whom?"

"You."

"But if anything should go wrong—"

"What could go wrong?"

"Who can trust Wilson? If anything happens, the institute can be expelled from Nepal."

"I've been to Dolpo, Tsering. What could go wrong? I know the monks and Dorje."

"And Wilson?"

"I'll make it clear to him what is at stake."

"You're willing to accept Lama Z's control?"

"Not really. Once we've left the last police outpost, there is no control."

"I would have to assure him otherwise."

"I've told you, there will be no trouble."

"You *want* me to do this?"

Looking straight into his eyes, she tried to make clear precisely what he was asking of her: that she sell herself to Lama Z as a spy. But Jack's eyes remained hopeful and pleading. She had worked with the Chinese invaders, with the Tibetan lamas in exile and with the Nepalis, but she had never had to beg as he was doing now. His long arms hung down sadly, palms out in supplication for the sake of a primitive shaman. She did not want to feel sorry for him.

"I'll talk to him," she said.

Jack's smile was ingratiating, like a guilty boy's. "You no longer believe in Buddhism, Tsering; I know you have nothing but contempt for Westerners who turn this way. So I appreciate your—"

"Enough!" She put her hand over his mouth to stop his apology. "Lama Z may refuse. Who knows."

When she removed her hand, Jack's laughter was delighted and boyish. But her own laughter, when she managed it, was far older and more knowing. In trying to free herself from Lama Z, she had sold herself to him. If Jack had been listening more closely, he would have heard the bitter undertone. But he didn't care, because she'd agreed to buy Lama Z's intervention. And now, instead of accompanying Jack and Gonpo as a free agent to see her home, she was being used. As she had been ever since the Chinese took her to Beijing.

12

From those blades of stone and ice, Annapurna and Machupachare, plumes of snow and cloud streamed in a high wind, telling another story. Down here banyan and banana trees, muddy villages where children played naked in the streets, water buffalo and thatched roofs, tea shops, saris and caste marks told of lowland Asia in high fall.

The procession straggled toward that epic gash in the earth's surface, the Kali Gandaki gorge. Jack ranged restlessly ahead, or dropped back trying to cheer the others during the first hard days in the heat. Wilson had enough energy to take some photographic interest in the countryside and to do a minimum of complaining. Tsering struggled gamely with her unaccustomed pack and blistered feet, walking in silence and managing to keep ahead of the twelve heavily burdened porters. Gonpo, in lama's robes, trailed far behind, shuffling forward in tennis shoes at the edge of exhaustion, sweating out rich food and drink and soft living. Whenever the porters stopped to rest, Gonpo caught up and stumbled past counting his beads. An hour later they would catch up with him slumped in the shade of a tree, fingers still moving the beads, eyes closed, tennis shoes standing beside his swollen bare feet.

"Are you all right?" Jack asked him.

"The way is difficult," he said.

"Yes." Jack knew too well the way ahead.

"So difficult." His fingers closed on the beads and began to count: *om mani padme hum*.

Jack propped his walking stick against the banyan and knelt. "Gonpo," he said. The eyes did not open and Jack looked down pityingly on this ex–holy man laden with flesh. "Gonpo!" This time the eyes opened. "Why don't you stay in Thakhal among the Bhotia. You would be welcome there."

Although the body could not move, the eyes flashed at him. "You think all you need is a strong body."

"I was not intending a philosophical statement."

The eyes closed. Above Gonpo's head, Annapurna smiled down in the fine September clarity, baring her fangs.

Gonpo struggled to sit upright. "You are unworthy of this quest without . . ."

"What?" Jack asked.

"Humility."

With painful dignity, Gonpo stood, and carrying his tennis shoes began to shuffle forward barefoot. Humility. Wilson weak with the shits; Tsering weak from carrying the pack and hardship; Gonpo weak with flesh. Yes, he was impatient with them all.

Chiseled into rock buttresses, the trail climbed north through the Kali Gandaki toward Tibet. Still swollen with monsoon, the river tore across the flanks of Annapurna and Dhaulagiri, cutting her way through the still rising range. An obstinate river.

Now that she was back among Tibetan-speaking Bhotia of this ancient trade route, Tsering felt clearer. With a pack on her back, in boots, dirty trousers and sweat-wet shirt, she walked again among people who spoke her language. But the once-prosperous villages were poor, some houses abandoned, since the Chinese had closed the border. It was like following a trail of debris, traveling this old caravan route.

101

Sherpa Pasang dropped back, the porters shuffling ahead of them like burdened animals. "They are refusing to carry past the next village," he said to her.

"Do they want more money?"

"Of course."

"How much will they ask?"

"This American has a great deal of money?" he asked.

She considered her answer only a moment. "Yes, a great deal."

"Then perhaps five rupees."

"But the people are very poor in this valley," she said. "What if he takes local porters?"

"That would mean delay."

She smiled. So Wilson's obsession with time had even reached the porters. "But it will be impossible to replace them after we leave the valley. Isn't it wiser to wait?"

"They will ask for more then."

They walked together in silence before Pasang spoke again. "Your friend Malloy has changed since our trek in May."

"Oh?"

"He was very strong then. Now he is like a hungry ghost. The porters think he makes unhappiness. He makes you unhappy."

"No," she said. "It's the other American who makes unhappiness. Jack is only preoccupied with what he is doing here."

"But he doesn't help the lama. Gonpo cannot reach Dolpo alive."

"Gonpo won't *allow* anyone to help him. He was a very strong lama in his youth. It is better to leave him alone."

Gonpo had invested everything in this return, she knew. He would live or die according to circumstance, and there was no need to pity him.

The river tore angrily at the black rock below, exposing fossil shells, and she felt the water cutting down through her thirty-five years, exposing her memories of the nomads on the trail, their animals, the sound of bells. It was harsh, grinding away the years in Lhasa and Beijing and Kathmandu. But when she emerged from this gorge into the world of hard light and wind, she would be ready.

Suddenly her pack frame struck a stone overhang, and she stumbled. The trail was cut for squat Tibetans and laden yak, not for tall Westerners or their tall pack frames. She caught herself on the edge, staring down at the river—which was stronger than stone.

Wind whipped past the stone wall where they sheltered. The ample fields of the lower valley had given way to dust of the upper valley where monsoon did not reach. Here, meager plots of grain were irrigated, and the dominant colors were shades of brown. Somber-robed people worked the fields, tended flocks of goats and sheep and hid from the perpetual wind. Dust swirls raced over the open stony ground, and village houses hulked in sheltered groups, their interiors low-ceilinged, smoky and unventilated. Jack's heart lifted: this was the edge of the habitable world.

"The bastards," Wilson was complaining. "It's highway robbery."

The porters had refused to carry farther unless they were given an additional five rupees per day. Of course, Pasang said, new porters could be arranged. But that would take several days. Wilson had capitulated, but he hadn't stopped complaining.

"It's their living," Jack said. "It means little to you or your purveyors."

"Your translator had assured me we had a firm agreement."

"She has no control over these things. Relax and save your energy. You gave them the extra money, let it rest."

Wilson looked sour. "Jesus," he said, staring at the bleakness ahead of them and listening to the wind wuthering on the stone wall at their backs. "Can you imagine living in a place like this?"

A lammergeier coasted against the wind; a prayer wall stretched up the stony path out of the village; the walls of a monastery hung from the cliffs. In this landscape, bare as if blasted by radiation, faith endured, but the battle was constant and harsh, the lines clear. Jack stood and looked over the wall at a distant red spot—Gonpo laboring up the trail. "Yes, I can imagine living here."

He turned west toward Sangdak, the first of the passes guarding Inner Dolpo, and left Wilson squatting behind the stone wall.

≈

From that night's camp, they had fine views north toward Tibet and east toward Annapurna. For the first time Gonpo did not collapse inside his tent as if shot, but wandered off alone. Jack found him sitting on a ridge facing Tibet. Without turning his head, Gonpo said, "I knew you would come."

"You're feeling better."

"Perhaps I am the chela. I begin to see my origins again. These nomads we pass, they move all their lives up and down with the season. They have no home." Those wild men and women and children in rags, always on the move with their flocks and tents.

"They're like the spirit of this place," Jack said.

"But their world is going away. Everywhere boundaries, prohibitions. If they try to cross over there, the Chinese may shoot them." Gonpo was looking toward the invisible border. "I think this is coming to all of us soon—exile of the spirit. I too have lost the way."

"No, Gonpo, you are returning to the way."

"As are you, my friend. The path is open but you must see with clear eyes. There is strange news."

Jack looked at him. "News?"

"Tsering talked with the caravan we passed this morning. They encountered a foreigner traveling our direction. They call him by his smell, the Onion. He travels with a single Sherpa and two porters."

Foreigners often attempted Dhaulagiri, Jack knew, but Gonpo was trying to tell him something else. "Why do you mention this?"

"Because in the coming days you will need more strength than you currently possess. There is only one source of such strength—you must seek the white light."

"I am."

"Perhaps you are." Gonpo was silent a long moment, his face drawn, eyes sunken. "Has Dorje spoken to you?"

Jack blinked in surprise. The expedition had been launched by a vision of Dorje summoned in meditation. But Jack was still unable to take this mode of communication seriously. "I have had dreams recently, but they are not important."

"Please."

"Landscapes a little like this, very bare, as though human beings have vanished. Blasted by radiation, I believe. That is the feeling."

"And you feel these are unimportant."

"I've had apocalyptic nightmares for years. I share them with my guilty physicist friends at home."

"And you think this has nothing to do with Dorje?"

"Indirectly, I suppose. Ever since I killed that man in Dolpo, I've had doomsday on my mind. The coincidence of the Indian test haunts me."

"There are no coincidences. There is only ignorance. All events have meaning if we dispel ignorance. And it is imperative that you keep your mind clear. Now meditate with me."

But Jack found it difficult to focus; he kept drifting back to California where his friends were confronting the mysteries of the universe and meditating on koans of their own: the sound of a quark, the shape of a resonance, the nature of strangeness. When the sun set behind Dhaulagiri, the cold descended instantly, and Gonpo began to chant. It was the familiar universal Tibetan mantra, and Jack joined him, the two of them linked by sounds that had no meaning other than the act of saying. In Berkeley his friends were chanting their own mantras.

There is no coincidence, Gonpo said. Only ignorance prevents us from understanding chance events. And physics might yet agree with him that consciousness, rather than chance, rules the universe. Even now, experiments on Bell's theorem in Berkeley were showing that when either of two correlated particles was observed, no matter how far separated in space, the other was instantly affected by the observation—as if the two particles were embedded in the observing consciousness itself.

Delicate, sharp as ringing ice—a bell on the wind. Annapurna stood alone in the last sunlight. Banked clouds to the east and south surrounded the mountain, and within moments obscured it. Like the ringing bell, a momentary vision. Of the isolated mountain, nothing remained but recollection.

Gonpo rang the bell again. "Good," he said.

He stood and Jack followed, legs cramped by cold. A sudden movement at the base of the ridge caught his eyes—delicate and quick as the bell—a flash of blue. Their abrupt standing had surprised a watcher. Both Wilson and Tsering wore blue parkas.

"What is the importance of this foreigner?" Jack asked as they descended.

"Dorje is more reckless than I thought."

"Reckless?"

"To involve so many observers."

The flash of blue told him it was true. They were all observing one another. And thus creating one another.

He rolled over in his sleeping bag and put his hand on her shoulder. "Awake?"

"Yes."

The tent fly flapped like a big wing over their heads in a cold night wind. Night came early on this north side of Dhaulagiri massif, and they were high enough to know the pure sting of altitude.

"I understand there's a foreigner ahead of us."

Her body stiffened. "Who told you?"

"Who do you think?"

"What did he tell you?"

"That you had spoken with the caravan."

"I did."

"And what did they tell you?"

"That a man was traveling our direction with a small group of porters and a single Sherpa."

It was difficult to understand her reticence, as if he had to pry every word from her. "A foreigner?"

"Yes . . . *Urusso*. But their idea of a Russian may be a long way from the truth."

106

"Russian?" Had Gonpo not passed on this information, or had she not told him?

"It is almost impossible for a Russian to receive permission to come onto this border right now. He may not be Russian. He may not even be a foreigner. It is difficult to tell out here, people travel without permission, in disguise. He could be almost anyone."

"Except for Gonpo, you wouldn't have told me."

"Perhaps not."

"Why?"

"It was not important."

"A Russian in these mountains?"

In the darkness, her voice was flat, impersonal. "Of what importance is his nationality?"

She was right, of course.

"It is your silence which I find odd."

"Do you? You think silence conceals information?"

That was precisely what he thought.

"If that makes you suspicious, you are surrounded by silence. Your silent friend Mr. Wilson, for example. Did you know he is armed?"

His body tensed.

"I saw him cleaning a pistol inside his tent. Does that interest you?"

It interested him. The wind rose and the tent fly flapped overhead as she explained what would happen if police discovered the gun at one of the checkpoints: their expedition would be terminated. A huge web of silence surrounded him, and two new particles had stuck in the web: a Russian and Wilson's gun. What else did he not know, which, once known, would jiggle the web of silence, as each observation of particle physics jiggled the quantum web of the universe? Of course, he and his colleagues never knew whether the universe itself was jiggling, or only their observing minds.

Frantically, he tried to quiet his mind—counting breaths and listening to the wind and to Tsering's breathing as she fell asleep. He simply had to purge these nightmare thoughts, because the paradoxes of quantum physics could drive him crazy. Jack was no longer certain

107

who controlled this expedition. He had thought he was doing so as Dorje's agent. But Wilson was also an agent; so was Tsering for Lama Z, who was himself an agent of the Dharma. And now the Russian.

When he finally did slip below consciousness and drift into the desolate region of his dreams, a gun replaced the familiar walking staff in his hand. Huge as one of the three-headed demons of the Bardo carrying a battle-ax, whose teeth protruded and who made strange whistling sounds and sang *a-la-la*, Jack strode through a greenish radioactive glow across an ash-covered landscape.

He entered the hermit's cave.

A-la-la, he sang. *Ha-ha*. He raised the gun in one of his six hands. A battle-ax, a skull cup of blood, a sword rose in his other hands, and the skulls hanging around his neck thudded dully against one another. He fired point-blank at the man responsible for destroying his familiar world. The muzzle of the gun flashed blue and green flame.

13

"Do you suppose it's drugs?" Browny asked. "They're rife in Nepal."

Drinks had appeared after their September meeting, and Browny was on his second cognac.

"Worse," Mukerjee said. "A midlife crisis of faith and hormones. Do you believe it? Falling in love with a Tibetan woman and crawling into some shaman's cave."

Lia sipped her second glass of chardonnay. She allowed herself one glass alone, two in company, but in recent weeks had begun to see little reason for any prohibition. The summer months had been a bleak confrontation with her solitary life. It was banal. Work at the lab was monotonous; Mukerjee had turned querulous, and Browny's sudden decision to retire from teaching had made her consider the end of her own career. In some obscure way, it was Jack's fault, but she couldn't bring herself to blame him.

"Why are you always so cynical about him?" she asked Mukerjee.

"You know bloody well why. Some mystic tells him about a nuclear test that Western intelligence knows nothing about. And he does it without any language? And controls Jack hundreds of miles away by mental influence? Really. This last letter is too much and you know it."

Jack's letter, discussing his return to Dolpo with a Tibetan woman, a lama and some American psychic, *was* bizarre. In trying to explain a large pattern of events that was being orchestrated from a Himalayan cave, involving the government of Nepal, the local Buddhist community and even the CIA and the Pentagon, he was nearly incoherent. Somehow this entire web of events depended on him, who was both instrumental and helpless at the same time, but it was such a classic example of paranoid thinking that even Browny was shaken.

"It does seem crazy. A mysterious quantum web reaching from a remote Himalayan cave all the way to the Pentagon. Consciousness as waves and particles, probability patterns, quantum numbers—"

"Not very mysterious," Mukerjee said. "Thanks to Jack's craziness I've had security people at my house twice since I returned from Bombay, asking about him and the conference. My phone has got odd sounds these days. Somebody in a beige car parks across the street day and night. They've probably got this place bugged."

The quibbling seemed so petty to Lia because they all loved Jack; yet because he'd abandoned their careful little world, they were turning on him. "As if *we're* the ones in danger," she said, addressing the empty end of the couch where her mother had always sat. "Because of Bell's theorem, we're willing to admit superluminal communication and even throw local realism out the window, but when Jack says the same things, we dismiss him."

"One thing Jack is not," Mukerjee said, "is a quantum event. We're talking people, not quanta, and psychic mush is not quantum theory. Jack's crazy. I agree with Browny."

But Browny, as usual, had wandered ahead of their bickering. "Quantum theory is metaphysics at its most esoteric and bizarre, but so long as we can keep the physics discrete from the rest of our lives, like a chess game we can fold up and put away, fine, we break out drinks and become normal people—or what passes for normal, although what we're saying is crazier than his letter. We keep ourselves safely partitioned. Jack's crossed the fence. I think Lia's right. Maybe we should listen to him."

"Listen to him!" Mukerjee said. "Listen to what? Some hermit's mind controlling events hundreds, thousands of miles away?"

"Remember what Jeans said?"

"What?"

"The universe is more like a great thought than a machine."

"So?" Mukerjee sulked.

"So physics is a study of consciousness. Heisenberg, Bohr, Jeans, Planck, Schrödinger were mystics in one way or another. Einstein. Oppenheimer. What's our fear of Jack?"

Browny had worked at Los Alamos, had known Heisenberg, Bohr, Einstein, Schrödinger, and was a direct link to those giants who had demolished the cozy Newtonian universe and built a crazy world of relativity and quantum theory. The litany of their names silenced Mukerjee.

"So why don't we see what thoughts are circulating in the universal mind and what quantum theory can tell us about ourselves? Perhaps our thoughts are just jiggles in the big pudding of consciousness."

"Brahman," Mukerjee said sourly. "That's what the Hindus call your universal pudding."

"And the jiggles?" Browny asked.

"Maya. The world of appearance."

"Doesn't that sound familiar?" Browny asked. "The universal mind, represented by Schrödinger's wave equation and collapsed by our individual observation into appearance. Each time a jiggle."

"You had better stick to physics," Mukerjee said. "There, you are brilliant."

Lia drained her wine decisively and poured a third glass. "Very well, then," she said. "I'll tell you something I did last week down at Stanford. I've not been able to sleep ever since, thinking about Jack and this mystic."

Lia had been invited by Stanford Research Institute to participate in some psychic experiments called remote viewing. A psychic viewer at Stanford sat with an interviewer while another member of the experimental team, known as the beacon, drew a target location from a list unknown to any of the participants, using a random number generator. The beacon went to the target location while the interviewer recorded the psychic viewer's impression of what the beacon experienced there. Written results of the interview were matched against photographs of the entire list of target locations. People who knew nothing about the experiment, or were even hostile to it, were used to judge the results. Lia had been asked to judge.

"It's uncanny," she said. "But some of the reports are so accurate. It's as though the viewer is actually present at the site describing what the beacon sees, hears, smells, feels. They can even draw pictures of the target location."

Mukerjee was doing little to conceal his skepticism, but Browny listened intently.

"Distance doesn't seem to be a factor either," she said. "They've actually done experiments across the country or between countries. Even time seems irrelevant. The beacon and viewer are instantaneously connected." She looked pointedly at Mukerjee: "A Bell's theorem of the mind."

"We aren't particles and you know it," he said. "This is rubbish."

"Then why are you so hostile?" Browny asked him. "Can't we at least hear what she has to say? Is that dangerous?"

"I simply can't listen to this," Mukerjee said.

"Aren't you even interested how they got started at Stanford?" Lia asked him. But he wouldn't give her the satisfaction of a reply.

"How?" Browny asked.

"On the quark detector. Sorry, Krishna, but this psychic, Ingo Swann, altered the magnetic field right through the superconducting shield."

Silence.

"And you know what else? They gave him coordinates anywhere on earth, and he could describe the place. That's how they started the remote viewing experiments."

Mukerjee sighed. "I can't believe I've come all the way from India to escape magic and superstition, only to run into it now in the name of science."

Browny looked at him sternly. "What's quantum theory but magic and superstition?"

"You're joking."

"Not really," Browny said. "We're the modern alchemists and priests."

"I'm not quite done," Lia said. "The Pentagon is interested because the Russians have been doing these experiments for years. They're even engaging in psychic espionage."

Mukerjee jumped to his feet and headed for the bathroom.

Lia's face was flushed from the third glass of wine, and also because the empty space at the end of the couch seemed to be occupied by some presence other than her mother.

"So what are you proposing?" Browny asked her.

"Why don't we try to see what Jack's doing for ourselves? Let's try the Stanford experiments."

"You really believe this, Lia?"

"I've seen the records. I served as judge. They've invited me to participate as a viewer. Now I lie in bed and can't sleep because things come to me like dreams. I see my mother, I see Jack, I see far-off places I've never been. It's as if my mind is a lattice and there's a wind blowing toward me. Only a few particles of reality get caught in the lattice, the rest blow through. I'll never feel them, never know them. It's such a loss."

She didn't care that she was sounding like Jack or had exposed herself to Browny, who was looking at her with the strangest expression, leaning forward with his canny old man's eyes gleaming.

"You're really shaken, Lia, aren't you?"

She nodded.

"Then why not?" he said. "What do we have to lose?"

Mukerjee emerged from the bathroom to find them discussing a protocol for viewing Jack seven thousand miles away. Lia had poured a fourth glass of wine, Browny a third cognac, and they were sitting side by side in the September twilight, like children plotting some grand adventure. Mukerjee poured himself another gin and tonic and sat down in the big chair. Lia was explaining about the mental noise—how they must not make any assumptions about Jack's location or try to reason in any way about his probable whereabouts. The viewer's mind must be a blank screen, and the interviewer's questions must remain neutral. Mukerjee supposed no serious harm could come from such a game, unless someone at the university or lab heard about it and thought they were serious. The lights of San Francisco were soft in the distance, the air was lilac-colored. Gradually he let himself be drawn into the conversation.

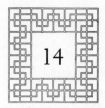

14

Four dark figures mounted on yaks in a snowstorm; the yaks walk
head-down, tails to the wind. But the trustworthy yak, surefooted
guide across treacherous snowfields, has now stopped in the snow and
mist, sensing danger—a crevice, a rotten cornice? To one side, three
blue sheep watch the yak's indecision. Slowly, mist rises, revealing a
deep tropical valley, green against the snow, but the yaks turn their
bulky shapes sideways to the wind, refusing to go forward. The sheep
leap away as if frightened. A figure clad in dark wool and wearing a
hood has crossed the trail. An assassin descends toward the valley.

Jack hears Tsering's deep breathing and listens to the tent flap in
the wind. He has been turned away from Shambala, the hidden kingdom, by a dark, sinister figure. Wilson. He opens the tent flap on an
overcast, windy dawn. Tsering watches him dress but says nothing as
he slips out of the tent. The porters, huddled against a huge boulder,
are boiling tea over a small fire of sticks brought to this altitude. They
watch Jack walk toward Wilson's tent, shouting "Wilson!" into the
wind. The tent flap opens and Wilson's myopic face emerges. He is
dressed, sitting with a notebook in his lap.

"What is it?"

"I want to talk to you."

"Those goddamned porters again?"

"No. Your gun."

A faint flicker of hostility on Wilson's face. "Gun?"

"Tsering saw you cleaning a pistol. It's a very serious matter."

"One that doesn't concern you."

"We go no farther without an explanation."

Wilson studied him warily. "*We* go no farther?"

Jack ignored the challenge. "Why jeopardize everything?"

"Isn't it obvious? Any sane man needs protection up here."

"May I see it?"

"It's no concern of yours."

"It's a concern to all of us. The one thing we don't need is to be caught with a gun near the border, you goddamn idiot. Now show it to me."

Wilson looked him over and then drew a long-barreled pistol from his pack.

"What is it?"

"A Browning nine-millimeter automatic."

"How much ammunition are you carrying?"

"About fifty rounds."

"It's loaded?"

Wilson managed a thin smile at the absurdity of the question. "Of course."

Knives, staves, vicious dogs were common fare; the Khampa were heavily armed. But a scientific pilgrimage led by a professional gunman left Malloy at a loss.

"Dorje can spot that thing miles away," Jack said, surprised at what he was saying. "It gives off emanations like a beating drum."

Wilson's smile broadened. "Who is Dorje?"

"You know damned well who he is, but that thing will kill any chance for your alleged psychic research."

"Will it now?" Wilson looked faintly astonished. "And what about your innocent walking stick? *That* doesn't seem to have harmed relations with the shaman."

Of course Wilson would know about the incident on the pass, if

Lama Z had known, and once again, Jack shrank from the knowledge.

"There's never an excuse for taking life," he responded lamely, "yet it happens. All things die, and there are always agents."

Yes, ignorance, desire or the intellectual pride of Los Alamos. Or the blind instinct that cracks a man's skull. Again he felt the bone give. Last night, like one of the monsters in the Bardo, he'd held a gun on Dorje. Now Wilson was holding the gun, teeth exposed in a grin, eyes magnified. But he had only two hands and feet.

"Well, in that case," Wilson said, "there should be no objection to this weapon. It's best to have all our cards on the table, isn't it? We ought to discuss your last trip to Dolpo in more detail."

Jack had used this despicable person to enter Dolpo, and now he had to listen to his smug blackmail. A familiar pain between his eyes reminded him of the reason for his own presence, and he turned away, frightened at the inability to control his thoughts. Lama Z had said Dorje practiced the black arts, and right now, Wilson was good evidence. Once again, he felt the urge to strike out blindly with his staff.

She watches him return with the same long angry strides, and when he reaches the tent, she is standing outside and ready.

"He has a gun."

"I told you."

"He knows I killed the Khampa. No one knew except you and Lama Z."

"And Gonpo."

His bearded face is wrenched by anger and he seizes the front of her parka. "Gonpo would tell no one." His hand tightens the cloth tight around her throat. "You would, it's your way of life."

The Sherpas and porters watch; Wilson peers from his tent. But they will do nothing. And neither will she.

"There are many ways your activities may be known," she says. "Word travels in this country. Do you think your actions are invisible?"

"You are spying on Gonpo and me, aren't you?" He shakes her.

117

"Aren't you? Is this Russian part of your doing? Have you arranged for him, too?"

He has staked everything on a quest for which he is not prepared, she sees, so now he must blame others. Seeing paranoia overwhelm a man of science horrifies her.

"Lies and dishonesty everywhere I turn. I can't stand it any longer."

"A week ago you were swimming happily in a river of inevitability, but now you balk. Why? Your lama is dying, you said, and you must return. You use Wilson. You use Lama Z. You use me. And now you feign innocence, as if none of this is your responsibility."

His grip loosens. "I can't stand these doubts . . . that I'm putting Dorje in danger."

"You cannot *will* yourself to believe, Jack. If you lived all your life in Asia, you would still not believe. I have told you this repeatedly. You simply have no capacity for faith. You must return to your science."

But his mood has shifted abruptly. He's so volatile these past days, and now he's crying. "I *must* believe. I must believe that there is a way out."

"No magical way," she says gently. "Only what we can do with our own intelligence." She takes his hands in hers. "It is what you are good for."

But he is shaking his head, rubbing at his eyes. "Are you spying for Lama Z? Tell me."

"He asked me to do so. In order to obtain the permit."

"Did you agree?"

"Did we receive a permit?"

His look is full of fear, anger, distaste. She is so heartbroken at his innocence that she even risks putting her arms tentatively around him. He does not refuse her. "But that is not why I came," she adds.

He stands rigid in her arms—the only answer he is capable of.

"I came with *you*. And to see my own country once again."

The poor man does not believe her, she can feel it in his body. But he is so desperate to believe that he tries awkwardly to kiss her. And she lets him, responding with as much passion as she can muster.

"I think our friend is capable of great mischief," Lama Z had told her. "I do not yet understand what he's up to, but I will risk his return to Dolpo to find out."

"Our friend" was capable of very little mischief, she now realized, because he was helpless in his own innocence. Watching him storm toward Wilson's tent had made it clear that they were not conspiring together. A man able to penetrate the mysteries of the universe had been thrown into turmoil by this minor affair of the gun. Poor Jack, caught up in a conspiracy of his own making and frustrated that nothing was what it seemed. His blindness was almost endearing. Lama Z would be pleased.

Suddenly, the wind roared overhead, blasting their camp, and sparks flew from the fire. A huge mass blocked the rising sun.

"No go," the Sherpa told Wilson. "Bad weather." But Wilson refused to accept the verdict and persisted in asking for a better reason. They were only a few hours from crossing the pass, and he did not wish to lose a day. They were stalling only in order to demand more money. First, the goddamned porters demanded more money, then more provisions, and now every passing cloud threw the expedition into confusion, which could only lead to more money.

Sheltered from the wind under a rock overhang, Tsering and Malloy watched Wilson rant at the Sherpas, who simply reiterated, "No go." When one of them was unwise enough to mention the true reason—"Bad spirits here"—Wilson began to sputter and jump about, demanding assistance from Jack and Tsering: this kind of blockade simply must be prevented or the expedition would never reach Dorje.

Gonpo began to chant, and the rebellious porters joined him, a plaintive sound in the growing wind and thin air of sixteen thousand feet. Gonpo brought out the damaru—the joined skull cups covered with leather and attached to a handle—and began to rotate the handle. The pellets beat upon the skulls: *"Om mani padme hum."* The universal mantra/prayer/propitiation of Tibet. He rang the vajra bell in his other hand, a clear sharp sound in the rising wind. The chant grew and Jack joined in. Tsering, wrapped in a yak-hair blanket, stood silent beside him; Wilson withdrew to his tent in disgust.

Cupped by the *om* of all creation and the *hum* of all annihilation lay the jewel in the lotus: the Vajrayana. Six simple syllables about which volumes had been written, but not by these illiterate porters, who were chanting as if their lives depended upon it. *"Om, mani, padme, hum."* They had entered the region of demons, spirits, hungry ghosts who controlled the weather, and he wondered how Tsering would acknowledge this ancient propitiation. She looked on coldly. This part of her heritage had left her forever.

Sitting erect against a stone wall in these mountains, Gonpo was no longer a Tibetan debauched by the West, but a lama come home. He radiated the ferocity of belief. His spiritual strength had grown geometrically as his body wasted, and now in the cold he seemed to give off heat like the sun. Moving slightly with the chant, holding the damaru ready in one hand and the vajra bell in the other, he had become a lama. Jack could feel him root down into the stone and rise up into the storm. He had become one of the impersonal forces of the universe.

Suddenly came the damaru, a wild swirl of pellets against the drum head, like hail on a roof. Again a flurry of pellets broken by the clear bell. And then the hail itself. Huge stones fell out of the sky. These storms could destroy crops in minutes and were considered the work of local demons. For travelers they could be a warning, for pilgrims a test. It was the lama's job to sort out the causes, to ward off evil storms and to assist true spirits in their pilgrimage.

Now, standing beside Tsering under the stone overhang, Jack felt the force field closing around them like deep violent water. The few pitiful smoldering sticks on the porter's fire had been extinguished by the hail. Above tree line in the most formidable mountains of the world, they had entered a world utterly indifferent to human wishes. Jack and the porters and Sherpas chanted the six-syllable mantra as if their lives depended on it. The hail was dangerous in its ferocity, but no one moved. So, this is what it means to be stripped of everything

120

that gives identity, he thought. To be stripped bare as a hermit, to wander these mountains exposed to the unimaginable universe that the Buddhists believed was our own creation. He created this hailstorm. If only he could believe that.

And why not? In the quantum world such acts of creation were commonplace. Using an accelerator and detection chamber, the physicist created particles, or at least verifiable attributes of particles, from quantum chaos. Yet for his own sanity, he could not believe in quantum chaos. Einstein had even hoped that the quantum theory he helped devise was flawed, because he could not accept the quantum randomness of the universe. There *had* to be a hidden variable that would establish order. The greatest mind of the century had defied its own reason in a ferocious act of faith. But now the physicist Bell had forced them to confront quantum reality. If there was no hidden variable, as tests at Berkeley suggested, then there was no boundary to the quantum lake in which they swam. The shores fell away to an infinite distance, and the ripples appeared infinitely far from the swimmer. In this realization, Gonpo and the lamas had advanced beyond Jack and the particle physicists. Gonpo believed that mind-created distortions of the lake's surface were the cause of human suffering, so he devoted his life to clearing the lake. It was really very simple, he insisted, since the lake of consciousness had no shores or ripples. But without shores and ripples a particle physicist was lost.

Outside the laboratory, Jack was terrified and vulnerable. He was deep in the quantum lake chanting six meaningless syllables in a blind act of faith. Hail swept into windrows, cascaded off the cliffs and boulders, bounced over the stone pavements. Three days' walk from here, Jack had killed a man and dog. His stomach clenched as the syllables blew away on the wind. Five months ago, he had made a psychic ripple in the region, just as the Indians had blown a dome into the desert, sending P waves to the far side of the earth. He had created a disturbance that now, through interference with other waves, had been amplified into this storm. This sudden violence, he thought, came inevitably from his own violence.

"*Ommmmm* . . ." It came deep in his bowels. *Mani*, the jewel, *padme*, the lotus, *hum*, the great unification of void and creation. Together, a compassion for all life caught in the illusionary forms of samsara—Tsering was wrong, he could believe.

As suddenly as it began, the hail stopped. The wind picked up, whipped across the crests above and swirled clouds down into camp. Hailstones rolled wildly over the rock, the tents flapped, and then the wind stopped. There was only the sound of the mantra, triumphant, inscribed all over the Himalaya on prayer wheels and flags and stones. Silence fell. Total silence, as if all of them had known the precise moment to stop.

Wilson opened his tent flap and lay propped on his elbows like a rifleman. His face looked as though he were watching poisonous snakes writhing in a pit instead of the very psychic phenomena he had come to study. Tsering stood shrouded in her heavy blanket, her flat Mongolian face no longer that of the secretary to the Institute of Tibetan Culture, but that of a nomad's daughter encamped in central Asia. Whether she had been chanting or not, she had given herself over to the power of place and returned home. Around her, hail hung in lees and pockets, revealing the rough topography of stone.

The porters and Sherpas began to laugh and chatter. Even Wilson looked cheerful—they could leave now—and began to drag gear out of his tent. Jack walked over to Gonpo.

"What happened?" he asked.

Gonpo looked at him, not understanding.

"I've never seen a storm so sudden."

"What storm?"

Gonpo's face was calm and inward-looking. He was not joking. Perhaps he was still holding his visualizations and had not understood the question. Jack pointed at the hail piled around Gonpo's legs. He picked up some hailstones and let them fall like pebbles.

"What storm?"

The white lines of hail bled up crevices toward the high fields of ice and snow and disappeared into mist and cloud. Either the hail climbed toward the cloud, or the cloud leaked hail. Jack began to giggle. "What storm?"

And for the first time since he had known him, Gonpo laughed from deep inside, an alarming series of hiccuping gurgles, belches, long choking trills that drove Jack's own laughter into hysteria, into that unstoppable, suffocating laughter from which people have died. The porters and Sherpas looked curiously at them, smiling and giggling themselves.

When Gonpo recovered at last, he said, "Let us see what else Dorje has to teach us."

"What storm?" Jack said, and his diaphragm convulsed again at the edge of vomiting. They were being admitted to Dolpo. Even Wilson, the assassin, was being admitted. They had passed the gate. How propitious. And how amusing, Dorje's gentle reminder of the forces at work here: a hailstorm, a dead man and dog. Clasping the metal spider in his pocket, the dorje, Jack was surprised at the tingling sensation, as if his fingers caressed the sharp edge of a knife.

Wilson stared in rigid disapproval at the idiotic laughter, but the camp was breaking up in good humor. Gonpo had accomplished that much by intervening with the gods of the place, and even Wilson knew how much good humor meant to the progress of their expedition. It was worth half an hour's delay and this relatively harmless horseplay.

When Jack returned to their tent, he found Tsering's pack gone and finally saw her blue parka on the trail above. She had set off alone for the eighteen-thousand-foot Dolpo pass, beyond which they would never drop below fourteen thousand feet. They were entering the highest inhabited region on earth. Perhaps it was only lack of oxygen that accounted for his hysterical laughter, which continued like the aftershocks of a major earthquake. Above ten thousand feet, it was said, one begins to suffocate.

Up they went toward the ancient Tethys sea that was Tibet, the rupture in the intestines of the earth. If a seabed could be transformed into the highest mountains, what was not possible? The region taught a hard lesson, but they were being admitted. On their own recognizance. "In Tibet," Gonpo had said into Wilson's tape recorder, "the mind is different." So it was. They ascended into a mystical aura flickering like the blue flames of marsh gas or Saint Elmo's fire.

Wilson worked at being cheery, walking for a while with Jack. "I hope there's no trouble between us about the pistol." He was trying to look eager and ingenuous, as he had three weeks before when they first met.

"What pistol?" Jack said, and began laughing again.

"I don't feel so hot myself. This goddamned altitude. I'll be glad to get over the pass."

That Wilson wanted to cross the crest of enlightenment struck Jack as amusing, too. But this was too much for Wilson, all this good cheer, and he bolted up the trail. No woman was going to beat him to the pass.

For the first time, Jack was quite happy to lag behind. He followed Gonpo, who rang the vajra bell every so often, keeping company with some inner mantra. Suddenly Gonpo turned back, face radiant, and pointed above. Jack stared at the end of his finger. The top of Dhaulagiri had appeared, brilliant in October sunlight. They were nearing the crest. For how many hundreds of miles beyond the Himalayas was Dhaulagiri visible? he wondered. From the top of Dhaulagiri, how far could he see into Tibet? How far into holy India?

He leaned on his walking staff, contemplating these miraculous vistas. When he remembered where he was, Gonpo was far ahead, tinkling his bell in the waning sunlight.

15

From the stony wasteland on the banks of Barbung Khola rose the filthy, dank houses of Tsharka, stacked one on top of the other up the hillside. The inhabitants had no potatoes or barley to sell, and they were not inclined to replace the truculent porters who refused to carry farther into Dolpo. However, it was possible that some yaks and drivers could be arranged. It was a miserable and sullen village. The Tibetans of this region, Gonpo had said, were notoriously unclean, and the evidence was everywhere among the dense-packed stone houses that looked like a medieval fortification: human excrement, sores on lice-ridden children, filthy rags on the people. In one of these houses lay a foreigner who was ill and whose porters and Sherpa had deserted him. He did not speak anything faintly resembling Tibetan or Nepali and was known by his smell—the Onion.

"All right, what's going on this time?" Wilson asked Tsering. Since their own porters had rebelled again, he was in a vexed state.

"It may be possible to arrange yaks to carry for us."

"Yaks? They're slow."

"But obdurate," Jack said. "The yak will prevail."

In fact, these shaggy beasts they had met on the trail never ceased to amaze him. Although domesticated, they suggested a primordial time when both men and animals were hairy. In addition to acting as tractors and trucks, they provided a virtually limitless supply of useful materials: blankets and tents, fuel, rope, meat, fly whisks, milk, cheese, yogurt, and the omnipresent butter that was drunk in tea, burned in temple and home lamps, and smeared on bodies as a universal unguent. The yak was even smart, at least smarter than the water buffalo whose fur he had borrowed for a trip to Tibet and then never returned. To this day the buffalo hides in the water awaiting the return of his hair. The idea of traveling with yaks pleased Jack, but not Wilson, who was almost pathologically worried about the onset of winter. Tsering had derived a good deal of pleasure in passing on local weather lore to him: the marmots were thick-coated this season; nomads were already driving their animals out of the uplands; an early and hard winter would close the passes by the first of November. Perhaps sooner.

"So we leave today," he said.

"Without porters?" she asked.

"*With* the goddamned yaks if necessary."

"Then we may get more cooperation by assisting this sick foreigner."

"Anybody would be sick in this place. Who is he?"

"I don't know yet, but yaks seem to be dependent on our helping him."

"Is this their idea?" Wilson asked. "Or yours?"

Wilson accompanied her and Jack through the raw sewage of the stinking streets, where people wore black rags tied around their bodies and seemed particularly wary, unlike the curious folk of other villages. She explained that a major enclave of Khampa had occupied the area and that the people still expected some reprisals from the Nepalis. "It was here," she said, "that the Dalai Lama's representative played a tape recording of the Dalai Lama asking the Khampa to turn in their arms. That the Dalai Lama could occupy such a small box is considered a miracle."

Weaver Yondon's house had two stories, the lower occupied by sheep and goat pens, the upper by a crude circle of firestones, coarse yak-hair blankets, a primitive low table. A rich smell of human and animal confinement, contained by fire-black walls and a low ceiling, filled the house. The blankets seemed the likely abode of lice. Since windows were a luxury in an area so hard to heat, there was little light, and the smoldering dung fire dimmed what little there was. Chimneys were also a luxury. Human occupants hunkered on the floor, eyes red and watery, faces streaked with soot.

In one corner of the room, bundled in a fur coat and a wild tumult of black hair and beard, was the Onion. Through the smoke, it was difficult to make out anything about him except that he looked squat and muscular. Weaver Yondon spoke rapidly to Tsering.

"*Urusso?*" she asked. He explained something further to her, and then she spoke directly to the man in a language none of them recognized at first. His face opened in a grin, and he sat up, grimacing at some internal pain, as words tumbled from his mouth.

"What's he saying?" Wilson demanded. "Who is he?"

"Shut up," she told him. "I'll let you know."

Sitting up and smiling, the man looked like a large and friendly dog. He was a Russian named Boris who had arranged this solo expedition for himself because he had been on several expeditions in Soviet Central Asia as a young man and wanted this opportunity to see part of Tibet.

"Bullshit," Wilson said. "We had enough trouble getting a permit; the last thing they'll let up here is a Russian. Russians aren't floating around taking trips. Ask him what he's doing in Nepal. How did he get out of Russia?"

"You ask him," she said.

"I just did." Then realizing the need for tact, he added, "Find out what he's doing in Nepal. Please."

After further discussion, she reported, "He's a Russian engineer from Leningrad working on a dam in India."

"Sure he is. And he just happens to be in the same area we are."

Wilson's assumption that he owned this part of the Himalayas and that anyone else in the area had designs on his expedition annoyed Jack. Unfortunately, Jack's own paranoia overlapped with Wilson's,

127

and he too wondered about the Russian's presence. What was Dorje arranging for them now? "Look," he said to Wilson, "let's just help the man out and then get on our way."

"He has a bad case of dysentery," Tsering said to Wilson. "Very debilitating, as you know. Did you bring medication?"

Wilson nodded.

"Why don't you give him some?"

If Wilson wanted his expedition loaded on yaks in the near future, there wasn't much choice but to oblige. Grudgingly, he went outside for the medicine. While he was gone, the Russian became increasingly good-natured and outgoing. In his sheepskin and fur hat, he appeared distantly related to one of the yaks: a pair of red eyes staring out of a lot of fur.

Wilson returned wearing his orange Denver Bronco cap and carrying his day pack. He extracted a vial of pills and handed them to Tsering, who passed them over to the Russian. "Now explain the dosage," she said, and Wilson did so while Jack wondered why he had brought the day pack, and why he had donned the absurd orange cap. Was it an assertion of Americanness against the evil Russian?

Cheered by the sudden recovery of his sick foreigner, Weaver Yondon brought out a wooden bowl full of chang, the weak barley beer. Jack sipped and passed the bowl to Wilson, who sniffed the liquid skeptically and passed it on to Tsering, who drank and handed it to the Russian on his blanket. He took a large swill of the the moldy liquid, said something to Tsering, drank vigorously again and gave it back to her, leaving his hand on her knee. On the next round, Wilson ventured a delicate catlike sip, trying to keep his lips from actual contact with the wood. Weaver Yondon looked very pleased with his own hospitality, and the prospect of getting a sick foreigner off his hands.

After long abstinence, Jack felt the effects immediately and found himself speculating on the hairy presence of the Onion. Tsering had managed to discourage his hand on her knee, but it was clear she liked the man as immediately as she had disliked Wilson. After years living down her collaboration with the Chinese, and recently her collaboration with the lamas, she was now compromising herself with a Russian, in language that protected her from scrutiny. Once again her facility with language allowed her to move freely in a strange setting. Now Boris was speaking rapidly and pointing at Wilson.

"He likes your hat," she said. "He's offering a trade."

The Denver Bronco cap for a genuine Russian fur—not bad, Jack thought, but Wilson's delicate sips of chang had not yet warmed his taciturn nature. "If he gives his real reason for being here, I'll trade him."

"He told you," she said.

"Horseshit!"

"Yak shit," Jack said. The chang was stronger than it tasted.

The Russian spoke briefly.

"What did he say?"

"He's offering to travel with us."

"What!" Wilson said. "No way he travels with us!" He stood up indignantly, banging his head on a low beam.

"Do you want the yaks?" she asked.

"Not on his terms." He rubbed his head. "I want out of this sewer. And give me back that medicine."

"Come on," Jack said, "you wouldn't refuse a sick man medicine."

Wilson continued rubbing his head but said nothing further. It was difficult to know who was teasing him—Boris, or Tsering with her translation. But now Wilson, eyes streaming from yak-dung smoke, had been isolated by his own petulance.

He squatted, coughing below the smoke. "All right, you say he comes from Leningrad."

"He says he comes from Leningrad."

The Russian spoke again, and Wilson waited. "Well?"

"Leningrad very beautiful city. Many famous buildings."

"He said that?"

"He's proud of his country. Why don't you tell him about the Grand Canyon and Wall Street."

"Ease up," Jack told her.

"Eeezup," Yondon echoed, practicing his English.

"Did he study engineering at Leningrad?"

129

She spoke to the Russian, who seemed to have a little difficulty explaining. "Biology and physics," she translated.

"Biophysics? At the Lenin Institute?"

Boris stopped looking jolly. Weaver Yondon, a contented smile on his sooty face, echoed, "Biopiss, biopiss," and poked the smoldering yak dung. He poured another round of chang, and, feeling quite expansive, gave Wilson a friendly whack on the shoulder. Wilson tensed and grabbed his knapsack, before realizing that he had misinterpreted the blow and thus revealed the contents of his pack—the pistol or tape recorder, or both. Yondon, impervious to this drama, passed the chang bowl, and this time Wilson drank deeply. The Russian's eyes glittered as he watched.

When the bowl had made its round, Wilson went on the attack, speaking directly to the Russian. "Do you know Nina Kulagina?"

Boris's face retreated into fur, leaving only a pair of watchful eyes shining out at Wilson. He had been caught off guard. *"Nyet,"* he said to Tsering, as though she had asked the question. And she was sufficiently startled by his behavior to ask Wilson the first sincere question of the afternoon. *"Who is Kulagina?"*

Scowling silence from Boris at hearing the name again, and a gratified look from Wilson. "A key figure in Russian psychic research. However, such people are not compatible with Marxist doctrine, as you would be only too aware—"

"Stop it!" Jack warned Wilson.

Surprisingly, he did. "I've seen films of her work," he continued, "quite astonishing and difficult for the Soviets because she's attracted so much international interest. And she has a large cult following in the country. So, you bastard," Wilson said to the Russian, "you're checking out the Tibetans, aren't you?" He glared at him and spat out a series of names that Jack later discovered were Russian psychics: "Vasiliev, Romen, Ivanova."

Boris grabbed Tsering's arm and began shouting at her. She tore loose, shouting first at him and then at Wilson, while Weaver Yondon waved his hands in despair. All his chang wasted. Jack was appalled at the new complications—Dorje's net drawing tighter in such unex-pected ways. Now a Russian counterpart to Wilson.

Tsering stood angrily and left the room. Without a translator, the interview was terminated. Taken by surprise and confused by Tsering's translation, the antagonists had revealed more than they intended. Any future chats, he was certain, would be much more wary. But the Russian extended his fur hat. Wilson examined it with his usual lack of enthusiasm. The Russian held up the bottle of pills and smiled. Wilson managed a grimace. And when the Russian looked expectant, Wilson reluctantly took off his Denver Bronco cap and held it out. Yondon smiled and poured more chang, which had taken over as interpreter.

When Jack left, descending the notched log in clear September light, he watched a bearded lammergeier, half-eagle, half-vulture, coasting the bare hills. Hunting what, the living or the dead? The bird dived out of sight behind a crude stone building on the ridge above the village—the ghompa where Gonpo had gone to visit the local lama. And without thinking, Jack followed the bird up the slope. Up there, he could wait quietly for the shape of things to come.

Coming into the interior and taking off his hiking boots, he took some time to adjust to the dimness. Gonpo sat with an old lama in rags. The man's poverty reflected the life below. Two butter lamps gave a dim light. Gonpo indicated that Jack should sit beside him. "This man is deaf," he said, "and nearly blind. Have our friends arranged porters yet?"

"Yaks," Jack replied, "and a new member of the party."

"Ah, the Onion."

"He and Wilson didn't hit it off too well. Two dogs working the same territory."

Gonpo looked amused. "And what is their territory? Have you ever understood it?"

"Psychic research, of course."

131

"Ah, yes, psychic research. They come here"—he looked toward the old lama, emaciated and watching them dimly; one eye was white, the other infected and swollen—"the two most powerful nations in the world come here where the light has gone out. The monasteries are in disrepair, ignorance and squalor abound, only the most degraded Buddhism remains, and yet two psychic researchers come *here*. Don't you find this amusing?"

"Not especially. Nor do I find the behavior of our friend, the former Chinese collaborator, amusing. She is keeping an eye on all of us."

"Stop," Gonpo commanded. "Do not enter the net of suspicion by questioning. All is a creation of our own mind, and all reasons exist within. You have saved my life. I will never leave Dolpo." There was an expression on Gonpo's face that made this prediction simple fact. "I've come home."

"To the country which is nowhere."

"Yes. Nowhere and everywhere."

"Perhaps I will join you and remain in Dolpo."

Gonpo looked at him closely. "Perhaps."

"Don't you wish it?"

"It's not for me to wish. Your karma is your own. I think it must be very difficult for Westerners who are accustomed to imposing their will. But it is a very narrow thing, human intention."

"So I've discovered. Still, it is difficult to return to Dolpo and feel that others have taken over my purpose."

Now Gonpo's face became more severe. "Please, there is no longer time for such thinking. You insist on these doubts. It is fatal. Do you still think this is some sort of game you are playing, in which you can move pieces at will? We have entered a . . . it is hard to find a word. You understand *ālaya vijnāna* . . . ?"

Jack had read the esoteric concept of store consciousness, a place where the seed causes of all things are stored but which is also active, like an ocean or river from which individual seeds of possibility flash in and out of being. It sounded very like the world represented by the quantum wave function, from which discrete energy packets, quanta, emerged from the ocean of possibility into human observation. He nodded his head.

"Your gomchen can focus seed causes; it is possible with sufficient training, but I have never heard of such things in modern times. There is a great risk here as well as great possibility. This man has created a whirlpool in the river of causes, a vortex drawing people from other countries, a circle widening outward. We can be certain that our friend Lama Z is broadcasting news through the network of lamas. Now the existence of the institute itself may depend upon this expedition."

"But," Jack interrupted, "I began the circle of causes with my desire to return to Dolpo. I brought the others." Even to his own ears, his voice sounded plaintive.

"Please," Gonpo said with a distasteful expression, "you became aware of seed causes. But dimly. Mistaking your own intention for universal possibility is a grave danger."

Jack was silent under this rebuke.

"You are nearly as blind as this lama, who at least knows that outward sight means nothing. If Dorje is able to draw from America and Russia people uninterested in the Great Liberation, possibly even hostile to it, then he is doing something that the great Siddhi of the past tried. But no one these days has such powers."

"And if he did have such powers?"

"Then your country and others might well be interested in him. They are always attracted to power. But a true Siddha would block their mundane interest rather than invite it. This I don't understand. It makes me suspicious. Have you told me everything about the Indian nuclear device and Dorje?"

"Yes. He knew I was a physicist, and he knew about the Indian test, even though Western intelligence was surprised by it. He was warning me of imminent catastrophe. I don't understand how my return can prevent the catastrophe. And these others have no function that I can see."

"Never rule out possibility. They, too, have the human privilege of the Great Liberation. But it is your karma as physicist that is crucial here. It has brought these others to Dolpo."

"Hardly."

"Didn't Dorje speak to you as a physicist? Did not the Indian scientists come to you? Was not Tsering attracted by your profession? Did not Wilson seek you out as a scientist? Perhaps even the Russian—"

"That's absurd."

"Can you never learn that such a judgment itself is absurd? You tell me the universe is without reason, yet you constantly cast out that which does not fit your reason. If you are intended to prevent catastrophe, perhaps these people are here to help you. You and I have these conversations; Tsering translates for everyone but herself; Wilson pays for the expedition; and now this Russian appears who, as you have said, is like Wilson." Gonpo paused, thinking. "It is very complex. Can you do what is necessary?"

Since the expedition had taken on its own life, Jack was no longer certain. "With your guidance," he replied.

"I lack the power of this naljorpa who may be dealing in the black arts."

"You really believe that's possible?"

"It's possible, yes. Wilson, the Russian, even Tsering are no friends of the Great Liberation. Yet they are here, and you think they are spies."

"It's very difficult for me to accept their presence."

Gonpo was silent a long while. "We must guard against the black arts, but I believe that our only hope is to accept what is happening. A greater wisdom than our own is working here."

So Jack must give up his control of the expedition. Although his own desire to return had created the vortex of particles circling Dorje, he had no more significance than any other particle. Just as no particle in an accelerator beam had significance before it struck the target in a detection chamber. And even then, it was only a chance encounter with another particle that produced meaning.

"Ommmmm . . ." Gonpo had begun to chant. The deaf and blind lama reflected the sound, *"Ommmmm . . . ,"* and Jack felt his limbs relax. He would sit and prepare his spirit. As Gonpo asked, he would accept, wait for impact on the target, and see what new particles were created by the energy of collision. Like his quantum colleagues in Berkeley, he would observe the world created by his own observation. But now he was both observed and observer, creating others and himself created.

"Ommm . . ." He had never in his life felt like an accelerated particle. It was not without its charm.

16

Boris sat in the sun against the wall of Weaver Yondon's house, looking resentful and suspicious in his Denver Bronco hat, the bill drawn down against the sun.

"It seems to me," Jack said, "that we'd be better off knowing where he is by taking him along."

"I already know where he is, and I don't like it. He stays."

"Very well," Tsering shot back, "then I stay."

Wilson thought about that a moment. "Really?"

Impossible, Jack thought, that they were engaged in these endless squabbles while on the other side of the Himalayas the man they came to see was dying in a cave. He looked up into the blue sky, where a puff of cloud rode a lowland updraft from India. Was it a sudden wisp of cloud forming in the sky? Or a wave function collapsed by his presence? An emptiness transformed by his observation? The cursed uncertainty of modern physics, which he had left behind, now poisoned his every thought.

The cloud grew rapidly, a towering plume of energy made manifest, roiling into the stratosphere. He blinked. The angry voices had subsided.

"You'll *what*?" Wilson said to him.

Tsering watched him, her chapped and burned face opening with surprise. "Do you mean that, Jack?"

Had he said something? Jack searched back through his mind and found only the roiling cloud.

"I can equally well go alone," Wilson said.

"Oh?" Tsering said. "Alone, with an early winter coming? No translator? No support if anything goes wrong?"

What had Jack said to cause such a commotion?

"You'll give up your guru for *him*?" Wilson meant the Russian.

Now Jack knew what he had said. "Not just for him. For all of us."

Wilson's face changed, as if realizing for the first time that Jack was terminally ill. "Are you all right?"

"Perfectly," Jack said, looking up into the sky. "Perfectly fine." The cloud had vanished as quickly as it appeared.

"Then I want my hat."

"You'd better keep his," Jack said. "Where you're going, it will serve you better."

"Goddamn you," Wilson said.

"Goddamn you," he replied.

"If he goes, we need a protocol for traveling with an enemy agent."

"Enemy? Up here?" Jack pointed down the river canyon toward India, and then swept his hand over the bare hills toward the crest. "Up here?"

If nothing else in the past two weeks, Wilson had learned when to capitulate quietly. He put on the fur cap. The Russian said something.

"What's that?" Wilson asked.

"He thinks you're cute," Tsering said.

"Goddamn you both."

"Goddamn you," she said. "Shall I negotiate with the owner of the yaks?"

Weaver Yondon, sitting cheerfully in the sun and smoking a pipe, began to practice this most recent addition to his vocabulary: "Godom," he said. "Godom." And then rehearsed the rest of his English. "Eeezup, biopiss. Eeezup, biopiss."

When Tsering left, Wilson spoke confidentially to Jack. "Can't you see they're thick as thieves?"

It was true. Boris sought her company as the only person he could talk to, and she enjoyed practicing her primitive Russian. She alone moved freely among them all—the porters and Sherpas, the villagers, the Americans and Russian. The woman of silk blouses and high heels from Kathmandu had vanished into this person with her hair tied back in a ponytail, a sun- and wind-chapped face, wearing boots and a wool shirt. At a distance, it was no longer possible to tell her from one of the Sherpas, except for the blue parka. The higher they moved, the more she merged with the landscape, and the less possible such petty emotions as jealousy seemed. She no longer belonged to any of them.

"What difference does their friendship make?" he asked.

"They're both Communists, for God's sake. Who knows what they're talking about? Can we believe anything she says? We have only her word."

"Can we believe anything *you* say?" Jack shot back.

"You're crazy," Wilson said.

"None of us speaks the same language. Only one person knows why we are here, and he's not speaking."

"Who?"

"Wooo," echoed Yondon.

"The man we're going to see."

"You believe that?"

"Don't you? You're the psychic researcher."

"Do you want to explain yourself further?"

"If Boris is here, he is intended to be here."

"Intended?"

"I would call it that."

"You *believe* all this?"

"I'm beginning to. Try it. Accept the Russian as necessary in a grand scheme none of us understands."

"Suppose there is nothing the least bit mystical about his presence? Suppose *she* arranged this meeting? He's recovered from dysentery pretty fast."

"Your drugs, of course."

"More likely that woman of yours. They've known one another in the past."

"We all may have known one another in the past. It's a karmic bond."

"A Commie bond."

"Can't you forget ideology up here?"

"Are you kidding, on an American expedition? Who pays for the yaks? Who gives him drugs?"

"A financial arrangement can be worked out, if that really bothers you. Perhaps he'll do you a good turn one day."

Wilson looked disdainfully at the Russian under his orange cap. "I don't want any goddamned mooching Commies trailing along. I want a clear financial accounting. He pays his share."

"Who's paying *your* share? You sound as though this were coming out of your own pocket."

"I need to keep strict accounts. We have a limited budget."

"Limited to a Mercedes and the Oberoi Hotel."

"All right," Wilson said. "Let's assume he goes. Let's assume I give in, so you and the woman don't have to follow up on your threats. Then could we get the goddamn yaks loaded?"

"Good," Jack said. "You're learning. Like the rest of us."

Wilson stomped off toward Tsering, who was talking with the yak man. Tanned by constant exposure to the sun, dirty from the trail, growing a beard, and now transformed by the fur cap, Wilson had begun to look faintly human.

Shadows flickered—fire against stone—and the figures of the three porters from Tsharka, the Sherpas, the yak drivers and Tsering were cast like shadow puppets. Voices rose and fell as he watched through the tent flap, drifting in and out of sleep. One of the porters was a woman, Angmo, powerfully built, and he recognized her voice and Tsering's, but couldn't distinguish the others. Ringed about the fire were the tents of Wilson and the Onion, who were probably also watching, wondering what the Tibetan speakers were saying. It was their last night south of the Himalayas. Tomorrow they would cross the last pass and enter the highest desert in the world—the Transhimalayan region. Then it would become clear whether this was a grand design, or only the deception of his own ego.

He was dreaming of a dakini, a hideous old woman with pendulous breasts, when he awoke to a presence in the tent. Tsering had returned, was lying in her bag next to him, looking at him with the bright, mischievous eyes of the old woman of the dream.

"You are awake," she said.

He blinked. "I was trying to imagine what you were saying out there. I envied the group of you talking in the firelight, while the rest of us here in the tents were cut off."

"It would please you," she said. "These people are locked in ignorance thousands of years old. They believe the land is occupied by spirits; they go to the lamas for propitiatory rites; they believe in dreams. The land lives for them. Do you think you can make yourself ignorant enough to reenter their world?"

"Perhaps. Superstition and science may be closer than we suspect." He looked through the tent flap at the bodies huddled against the stone. "But I'll never know what happens in their minds, nor will they know mine."

"But you yearn for their simple life, don't you?"

"No. I'm beginning to think this moment of common consciousness . . . it's sufficient."

"Ah, the good Buddhist Gonpo has been brainwashing you again."

"Not really. I've been thinking of my friends at home and our work. They're not so different from those folk out there. We all want to live in a world of meaning."

The few precious sticks of wood on the fire had died to coals, and the Tibetans lay in dark bundles.

"They are good people," she said. "I am reminded of being a girl in the nomad camps when for hundreds of miles there were no lights, no roads, no towns or houses. Just a few tents, our families and animals. When the season moved, we moved. Stories of demons and magic rise up in me on nights like this, when I see spirits and fear dance in the eyes of these people. They make me a girl again. But they are ignorant. Because of their ignorance, the hills are stripped, the terraces abandoned. There is no living thing to hold the land. Their ignorance destroys. I always remember these things."

"So you would never go back?"

She looked at him. "On nights like this, I could go back. But there is no back. The Chinese have built their airfields and roads and communes. The nomads must register. I would return to a reeducation center and close supervision by the Chinese. They would never trust me again. I would be a minor bureaucrat at best. There is no back." She paused. "I suppose we must go a long way to return to what is lost."

"I didn't think Marx or Lenin allowed such sentiments."

"There are times I doubt. You know that the porter, Angmo, is married to two brothers? They sleep together in the same bed, naked."

"Apropos of Marx?"

"The brothers are not jealous; they could not afford a wife otherwise. Through ignorance, they transcend bourgeois notions of love. We must do it through education."

"You think this is possible?"

"Of course. These people transcend property. They leave their houses to the highland nomads in winter and go south to India and become nomads themselves, while the nomads become domestic and take care of their livestock and old people. These are things I miss." She moved toward him until he felt her breath on his face. "The mood is strange tonight," she said. "Even Boris is unsettled. Even he is susceptible to a place like this. It is the altitude. Or for them . . . a spirit."

Jack moved closer to her, feeling her warmth and remembering the story of Angmo and the two brothers.

"He is a good man," she said. "He has a wife and two children in Leningrad. He will return to them in a few months."

"Why is he here?"

"To see these mountains."

"You believe that?"

"It is sufficient."

"You're the only person who can know what is going on here."

"Yes."

"And yet you won't tell me."

"Haven't we just spoken?"

"Indirectly. I can't get out of my mind that you are *gonyipa*—even now collaborating."

There was no pause in her breathing, and she did not move away. "Perhaps we are all *gonyipa*. We all seem to be collaborating with this guru of yours." Suddenly she took his fingers in her mouth and closed her teeth: a sharp, unexpected pain.

Instantly, he was unzipping his bag, thrashing to get free of encumbering clothes. The nylon tent thrashed with him, as she unzipped and pulled at her long underwear. When he placed his face over hers and closed her lips, he heard the Russian stop snoring. Writhing beneath him, nails clawing at his back, was the hag woman of his dreams. They rolled wildly against one another, his breath came shallow and his heart flickered. The bright starfields seemed to cast shadows down through the tent. The Russian began to snore once again. Wilson coughed. And the yaks shuffled their feet on stone, restless. There was a soft, woman's cry from among the porters. Once only.

The two-headed one beside him slept. Until tonight, he had never thought of her girlhood in mountains such as these, on the limitless grasslands and deserts of Tibet. But in the firelight, he had seen another face. The translator and collaborator with no homeland, driven by hard Marxist rationalism, had seen shadows flickering in the eyes of the porters. She had understood the loss. Perhaps she was right—they were all two-headed.

~~~

Four yaks, two drivers, two Sherpas, three porters, the stocky Russian in long leather boots and Denver Bronco cap, Wilson lean and tidy under the bulky fur cap, Jack carrying the walking staff and looking gaunt, Tsering grown squatter and more powerful moving as strongly as the men, and Gonpo in his robes, walking steadily in the thin air and moving the beads in his hands. They had entered a valley of low-lying fog. The rising sun behind cast long shadows ahead into the mist, like holograms.

Struggling up onto the pass where five months earlier he had decided to enter Dolpo, Jack paused beside the familiar prayer flags and looked over the ocher hills of Dorje's kingdom. He had returned, not in spiritual simplicity but in complexity and doubt, just as he had left Bombay, blind to understanding.

In one pocket of his parka, he felt the smooth stone given him by Lama Z, the spiritual politician. In the other pocket was the dorje provided by a spiritual master. He took out the stone, studying the familiar symbols of the universal Tibetan mantra, and placed it beneath the tattered prayer flags. Lama Z's blessing had been delivered. Then he took out the dorje and held it like a compass in his hand, the long axis pointed toward Twilight Mountain. Since Gonpo had spoken to the yak driver, Dorje's hermitage had a name now: Twilight Mountain, for its location in the shadow of the Himalayas. In two days they would discover why the lama of Twilight Mountain had summoned this odd group.

17

Wilson panned his Nikon from left to right, zooming in on the yak driver, on Sherpa Pasang, on the new female porter with rotten teeth and chunky thighs, on her two sullen male colleagues, and on Malloy. Wilson paused. Malloy looked worried—they were only two days from his mysterious friend Dorje. He shifted the camera to Gonpo, much less flabby these days, who looked almost noble, standing on the summit of the Himalayas in his tattered robes, chanting mantras and staring toward Tibet. Wilson moved to Tsering. A striking woman in Kathmandu, he had to admit it, but in twelve days turned into a harridan who looked more like the grubby female porter, Angmo. Tsering's teeth were better, but she wasn't displaying those for the camera, since she didn't think much of Wilson or his avid photography and was delivering her familiar scowl. He shifted the camera again and discovered nothing but a pile of stones. Devout believers built the pile by adding a stone with their passage, in homage to the Buddha. To his surprise, Malloy himself had placed a small black stone on the pile. It was covered with Tibetan and had come from Lama Z, the wily politician's contribution to their expedition. Now where was the goddamned Russian? He looked up from the camera.

"Where's Boris?"

"He went ahead," Gonpo said.

Wilson walked quickly to the edge and looked over. The Russian trudged down the slope toward Inner Dolpo. No cameras for Boris. Wilson smiled as he zoomed in on the retreating figure and snapped the shutter.

"He shouldn't go down there alone." It was Malloy behind him.

"What difference does it make?" Wilson kept his camera trained on the Russian. "We're all starting down in a few minutes."

In answer, Malloy's pack abruptly blocked his view through the camera lens, and he looked up. Malloy was running down the pass after the Russian. Running! Wilson refocused his zoom lens, snapped a shot, and then looked up again. A few hundred yards down the pass, the Russian was kneeling and steadying his right hand on his pack held in front of him. Toward him were riding half a dozen horsemen. Wilson zoomed the two-hundred-millimeter lens on the Russian. He was pointing a pistol at the horsemen, for Christ's sake! Malloy was jogging up behind him with his stick raised over his head, like something out of a samurai film. Foreshortened through the lens, Malloy seemed to be charging the armed horsemen. Wilson triggered the Nikon as fast as he could advance film, the lens blinking like an eye. But Malloy wasn't after the horsemen. He brought his stick down on the Russian and a shot echoed up the pass. Both men were down in a tangle on the frozen stones. The horsemen were dismounting. Angry voices drifted upslope. Tsering entered the scene and Wilson cranked the Nikon for all it was worth.

An explosion of angry voices behind his back snapped his head around as if he'd been shot. The two male porters were running down the other side of the pass toward home, their baskets bouncing, and Angmo was shouting at the yak driver. Wilson rushed to his pack and pulled the Browning Hi-Power from his long underwear; then, heart beating frantically and camera slapping against his chest, he rushed back to the edge of the pass.

Jack, the Russian and Tsering stood surrounded by the Khampa, with M-16s trained on them. The rifles had been flown here from Taiwan, Wilson knew, but he'd never expected to encounter these few

145

remaining Khampa guerrillas—men in dark robes, bright leggings and wool caps. They were ludicrous yet inspiring in a way—horsemen fighting modern warfare. Something he'd never see again. He stuck the Browning in his pants and reloaded the camera.

Boris almost fired before the horsemen split to either side. He sensed movement behind him, but too late, as the breath left his body and the pistol exploded in his ear. He fell, scissoring his legs and tripping the man behind him, throwing an elbow hard to one side. He heard the man gasp. It was the American down on his knees, gagging. The elbow had caught him in the belly and his walking staff lay on the stones.

Boris moved his left arm gingerly. Nothing broken, but it was numb. The horsemen ringed them. His pistol lay on the stones, but he didn't move. There was no hope for escape.

Tsering spoke rapidly with the horsemen.

"What is this?" Boris asked her. "Why have these bandits attacked us?"

"Not bandits," she said. "Warriors."

"Bandits," he said.

"No," she said. "They have fought the Chinese for years and come to meet us. Leave your gun."

The men's faces had lost hope. They had fought all right. And lost. So, the psychic lama had his own army, a pathetic rabble armed by the Americans and defeated by the Chinese. For the moment, it was necessary to put the best face on what had happened, and Boris attempted a smile and held out his good hand. The left arm was definitely numb.

Gonpo descended the steep and rocky path, leaving Wilson and the yaks and Sherpa on the pass. "*Om, mani, padme, hum,*" he chanted to his steps, beads in one hand, bell in the other. His body felt light. Coming home.

Ahead, Tsering and Jack and the Russian stood in a circle of horsemen—stately, delicate, a mandala the naljorpa had imposed on the entire region. Armed men in a ring. The sky stood high and autumnal, like a great glass bell overhead. The animals, the people rested lightly on the hard earth. Yes, they waited for him. It was time to speak.

The horsemen clasped their hands together as the lama approached. The warrior on foot spoke: "Welcome, we have waited for you."

"There was a delay," Gonpo replied. "Certain obstacles had to be overcome. But we are all here at last."

"No," the warrior replied. "One has not come."

Even now Gonpo felt the incompleteness. He should have known, but had not yet learned to trust this land where messages came so freely on the wind, as though this great teacher breathed over the landscape.

"There was nearly a tragedy," Tsering said. "Jack stopped him just in time."

Gonpo looked at the two men, still angry with one another. "This is where you killed a man five months ago?" Gonpo asked Jack. Of course it was. The mandala had perfect symmetry.

Jack nodded. "That's Aten, the other man." He meant the warrior who had dismounted and approached them. "We are ready," Aten said. "Bring the rest of your party."

Tsering glanced up at the Dolpo pass, where the yaks and porters and Wilson waited. "They're afraid of you and won't come down," she said.

"Then I will speak with them," Aten replied.

Now the Russian was speaking rapidly.

"What is it?" Jack asked Tsering. "What now?"

"He wants to know if we are prisoners or are free to leave."

Still breathless from the blow to his stomach, Jack whispered, "A meaningless question. He wouldn't leave if we begged him."

Pleased with Jack's response, Gonpo looked at the Onion. A curious thing, this smelly man with his pistol. Why had he and Wilson, in every way antithetical to the teaching, been allowed to come so far? But such questions belonged in Kathmandu. He must remain open to

147

the moment and to the forces at work in this place. A shadow crossed the landscape and he looked up. The gigantic lammergeier, bearded carrion eater, carried his bulk over the land. A remarkable man, this Dorje. If he *were* engaged in the black arts, it would be a very unequal battle for them.

"Go with Aten back to the crest," Gonpo told Tsering. "The others will come down with you."

Aten spoke to one of his men, who dismounted and offered Tsering his horse. She swung into the saddle easily, as if the intervening years were only minutes. It was a fine sight—the two Tibetans riding side by side toward the crest.

Gonpo turned his back on them. "*Om,*" he chanted, and swinging the bell in rhythm with his steps, he began a slow and dignified movement forward, the respectful steps of a pilgrim who carries only his humility.

"*Hum . . .*" Annihilation that must precede creation. "*Om . . .*" The stones ground together under his feet, the sharp wind tore at his face and his lips stretched in a smile.

"Where are you going?" Jack shouted after him.

Casting his mind forward over the landscape, he found emanations—not so far off—a steady beacon of welcome. Each step rang with certitude. In order to return nowhere, it was necessary to have left the country which is nowhere. *Ting, ting, ting.* The bell gave out a sharp clear sound in the void of this landscape, where water and wind exposed the bones of an ancient sea.

They formed a caravan, the laden yaks, Angmo the remaining porter, Sherpa Pasang and the six horsemen riding to either side. Tsering insisted they were honored guests, but the M-16s did nothing to reassure Wilson. They came and went, these disaffected national groups, and you used them as best you could. But he didn't like the feel of this at all. On the other hand, Malloy's fight with the Russian was gratifying. Jealousy would keep Malloy off balance, although he seemed harmless enough—a maverick physicist plunging into mystical Asia.

Stranger things happened in California. But how could a physicist believe this shit? A lama with his beads and bells, chanting, spirits in a hailstorm, throwing holy stones on top of the pass—you put this stuff in a laboratory and it evaporated like dew. But that Berkeley crowd was flaky enough for anything to be possible. Why shouldn't one of them hunker up in a Himalayan cave the rest of his life? Give up one priesthood for another? But without the pay and benefits. It was always possible Malloy was just what he seemed. But he was Lama Z's agent, and who could trust Lama Z? No, something was up, all right. He'd figure it out in time.

In the long run, having the Russian along was all for the best. They were the ones investing in this psychic business wholesale, the KGB was in up to their ears. They'd even imported lamas to Moscow. It'd be interesting to see what this Dorje could do. Even more interesting to have the KGB watch him filming and taping it.

This damned woman—look at her now—a peasant, all muscle and bone, and filth. She was an enigma and a pain in the ass, and he hated the control she had through her languages. Impossible to believe she spoke Russian by coincidence when this bastard showed up. She was a Commie and probably figured, like a lot of Tibetans, that the Soviets were the great white hope and would treat minorities better than the Chinese. The poor bastards believed Radio Peace and Progress.

No point in worrying it further. If he got out of here in one piece, he'd take his vacation in the Aspen cabin. That girl Mudra could leave her kid and stay a while. A few days of good whiskey, good dope and good sex . . . but that was a long way off now. A long way. Lucky to be skiing by January. And if Malloy had his way, they'd get stuck back here. Then what? No Mudra, no pussy, no Scotch, nothing but roasted barley in stinking salt tea and a few rotten potatoes.

Tsering looked at the warrior Aten riding beside her. Such men had fought the Chinese well. But without ideology, they were pawns for the Americans who had abandoned Tibet for China. The only hope for Tibet was Russia. She glanced at Boris walking beside her. He

149

might have been descended from Cossacks riding across central Asia. There was something primitive and unruly in his soul, unlike Malloy, who was all mind.

She felt certain of herself here. She understood the Khampa, yaks, the country itself, the peasant Angmo. Only the naljorpa was unknown, and why these foreigners were showing such an interest in him. Jack was a special case, of course. But why Wilson and Boris? What could these agents, with their money and weapons and lies, wish from this physicist and his guru? All of them trekking to this remote border as if for a great secret—a little naked shaman in a cave.

She laughed out loud.

Wilson shot her a look, but she continued to laugh, opening her mouth wide. The air was wonderful.

"We have an excellent satellite shot, sir. Just to locate you on the map, here's the Russian border, here are the Chinese test sites at Lop Nor, these are the Kunlun mountains, you see the road they have completed here, and along the Himalayas, here. They have an airfield here and here and some sort of construction near the Nepal border here. We think they may be moving nuclear facilities to the Himalayas, as more difficult targets for the Russians."

"That's fine," Colonel Yanker said. "Now where are our friends?"

"Well, curiously enough, sir, not that far from the Chinese construction. Right about here in the part of Nepal called Dolpo."

"I see. Can you take it down?"

"This is the equivalent of about a thousand feet," the sergeant said. "Below that we lose resolution."

"Who's that?"

"We think it's the physicist. See the stick?"

The figures did not have much distinction, and it was not really possible for Colonel Yanker to see the stick. He took the sergeant's word. It was a man. There were others. "Which one is Wilson?" he asked.

"There. See the baseball cap?"

150

Yanker followed the pointer.

"Who's that?"

"Don't know, sir."

"And that?"

"Don't know, sir."

"Who are the horsemen?"

"Carrying supplies, I expect, sir."

"Take it down to five hundred feet."

As the focus changed, the figures began to blend with the background, become grainy, and then dissolve into unrecognizable patches of shadow and light. They began to vanish.

"Is that the best we can do?"

"Yes, sir. But it's very clear at this time of year. We should be able to shoot regularly if you wish."

"If this is the best you can do, I don't see much point. Keep track of their course and pinpoint this guru's location on the map. After that, we can simply wait."

"Yes, sir."

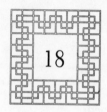

18

The shallow lakes lie like mirrors scattered in the grasslands of the Chang Tang; the ice-clad mountains rise bare and sterile, already locked in winter; the Tsangpo flows quietly toward Lhasa and the forests of eastern Tibet; and the great wall of the Himalayas drops to the hot, dusty plains of India. The autumn sun casts long topographical shadows and the plateau stands in stark relief, like the surface of a planet seen for the first time.

Among the glowing peaks and rock walls, individual chunks of torn stone appear; in a valley below one of the ocher peaks of the Transhimalaya, a small group of horses can be seen. A nomad's black tent stands nearby. The light is failing. At the north end of the valley, a woman emerges from a cave and looks up the stone cliffs of Twilight Mountain at another higher cave; a heavily bearded man emerges and stands beside her. He puts his hand on her shoulder and they remain in twilight.

The six-armed black figure holds a drinking cup of brains, a flaming dagger, rosary of skulls, leash, trident and drum. It is Mahakala, who stands watch over all that will prevent enlightenment and who will protect the seeker from selfishness and self-absorption. But the seeker is weary after hours of sitting, and while Gonpo and the two monks sit erect as cobras, he is stiff and restless. He cannot carry the weight of expectation.

Light appears in the cave entrance, a moon rising out of India. Twilight has passed. Perhaps he has slept. Gonpo and the two monks remain deep in their sadhana.

"Why have you come?"

A familiar voice in his head, but for a moment he can't remember the answer. "To see you."

"Why have you come?"

His answer was dangerously incorrect. "I wish to cross the crest."

"So, now you stink of Buddha. This odor we were spared on your last appearance."

He is silent.

"You wish to see the other side?" the voice says.

He nods his head ambiguously.

"Then where is the mountain?" the voice asks.

A Zen roshi once asked him such questions, to which all rational answers are wrong. And the inability of a theoretical physicist to satisfactorily answer such koans finally frustrated his Zen studies. Now he's abandoned his life in science for a cave stinking of incense and rancid butter. No wonder Tsering finds him ludicrous. But this time, as he never did in his Zen studies, he voices his frustration:

"There is no mountain," he shouts. "There is no crest, so there is no climber." He pauses. "And besides, I'm a fucking idiot."

Silence.

"And you're a fucking—"

"Yes?" the voice asks.

He would not continue this dialogue with his own voice from the past: *If we ask whether the electron is at rest, we must say no; if we ask whether it is in motion, we must say no.* Oppenheimer's conundrum of twenty-five years ago had followed him to this cave.

"This is pointless," Jack says. "I may as well leave."

"By all means, go home," the voice replies.

153

Home. Berkeley and physics. An ex-wife. An estranged daughter. Home had exploded in Bombay, and the alternative, this brittle parchment figure, this pile of dust that a slight breeze could destroy, only frustrated him. Jack's hands were full of weapons—sword, skull cup of blood, intestine noose—and the brass knuckles he had brought back to Dolpo. He pulled the dorje from his pocket—a handful of razor blades to cut through illusion—and flung it at the old man. The scepter struck him full in the face, and the curving prongs gouged his eye from the socket. The eye dangled, watching him.

A hand touched his arm. "You have been sleeping," Gonpo said.

He turned toward a cowled emptiness.

"Even this does not exist," a voice said.

Jack clutched Gonpo's hand.

"No," Gonpo said, pulling his hand away. "I cannot help. You are alone in the Bardo, moving between two worlds."

"I must see Dorje." Jack's voice was drawn and frightened. "I'm going crazy."

"There are worse things."

Gonpo rang the bell; Gyatsu blew once on the kangling, a mournful sound, and then Sonam crashed the cymbals together. "Now go below," Gonpo said, "and explain to the others."

"Explain what?"

"What you already know."

Jack found himself standing obediently, as if he were once again a graduate student at Princeton leaving Oppenheimer's classroom. He descended the stone wall in moonlight, as Gonpo watched from above, and as the trumpet and drums roared behind him. His feet crunched across the gravel valley floor, walking toward the lower cave where Wilson, Tsering and the Russian waited with alarmed faces. Sleeping bags, pots, pans were strewn around the floor.

"Good evening," he said.

"What was that awful squalling?" Wilson asked.

"Bad dreams," Jack replied.

Tsering examined him closely. "Are you all right?"

"So far as I know."

"So when do we get to see him?" Wilson asked.

He saw Tsering's concerned face, Wilson's cameras ready to record psychic activities, the Russian with his notebook and pipe, and heard his own voice screaming in the cave above, cursing Dorje, cursing Buddhism, throwing back what he had come to seek. His meditations were fragmented and unsatisfactory, and he was lost. He no longer had any idea why they were here, or what was expected from him. The hostile Khampa camped at the mouth of the valley prevented them from leaving.

"This is what you came for," he said bitterly.

"No way," Wilson said. "Two weeks' trek and how many thousands of dollars and dragging along the Onion . . . to sit in this cave under guard? You're crazy."

"Precisely."

"There's nothing going on here. If there's a lama up in that cave, I want to see him. We have another two weeks to get out of here. If you won't help, I'll find him myself."

Jack turned from Wilson to the smoldering coals at the center of the cave and poured a cup of the strong tea the Russian had prepared. Beyond the fire, against the cave wall, were the frightened faces of Angmo and Sherpa Pasang.

Behind him, Wilson was saying, "Gonpo will help set up a meeting if you won't."

Jack sipped the tea, blisteringly bitter. "Perhaps."

Disconcerted by the lack of opposition, Wilson said, "Is that all right with you?"

Jack turned back toward this officious American who, with his magnified eyes and scruffy beard, looked like some minor Tibetan ogre. He expected Jack's resistance; he was waiting for it; he wanted it. And suddenly the answer was blazingly obvious. The way opens when least expected. Wilson was the way!

"Is what all right?" Jack asked.

"If I set up a meeting with the lama?" Wilson said.

"What lama?"

"Goddamn you!" Wilson went flying over the precipice of

Dorje's intention, and Jack couldn't suppress a knowing grin, which infuriated Wilson further. He stormed past the Russian, who was puffing generous clouds of smoke at the cave entrance, and who watched his exit with interest, but no amusement. That should have been some consolation to poor Wilson, whose anger had just tethered him to Dorje.

Tsering's concern deepened to a frown.

"I just learned something," Jack said.

"And what's that?"

"I was the problem."

"Indeed!" she said bitterly. "These Khampa have not forgotten the man you killed, and they don't like Wilson."

"And what about your friend Boris?"

The Russian stood bulky and solid in the cave entrance, and his smoke rose in twisting drafts of air, the smell rich and alien in this place. He glanced up at his name.

"They trust him," she replied. "He's done nothing to deserve your hostility or Wilson's. His arm is still stiff where you struck him."

"Then why is he here, Tsering?"

She paused, and he saw conflicting emotions in her, as if Boris's arrival had been no coincidence. "Sometimes ..." She paused. "Sometimes I feel powerless here."

He took her hand solicitously. The Russian watched them, hearing their words but understanding only their touch. And oddly, Jack felt as if he were touching the Russian, too, through his translator. She pulled away, and while Jack sipped the Russian's bitter tea, he watched her talk to Boris and heard the concern in her voice. She must be explaining Wilson's sudden disappearance.

A half hour later, Wilson returned in triumph. "Gonpo says we can all go to the middle cave. Even *him*." He pointed to Boris.

It was so simple, Jack thought, to allow these people to lead the way.

The female porter and Sherpa Pasang sat at the back of the cave watching and listening as Tsering translated between foreigners.

156

Wilson, cocky and self-assured, led the way up to the middle cave. The Russian and Tsering followed, and Jack brought up the rear. Inside the cave Gonpo and Sonam sat meditating. The monk Gyatsu spoke at some length with Tsering, who glanced at the three foreign men seating themselves awkwardly. Wilson and Boris were alert, looking inquisitively at the musical instruments and wall hangings. Jack simply waited for the pattern of events to unfold.

"What do you wish here?" Tsering asked Wilson for Gyatsu.

"What I wish," Wilson said, "is to see his holiness, to talk with him."

"Who are you?" came the reply.

Wilson looked a little puzzled at the question. "I am an American," he said.

"Why?"

Wilson looked at Tsering. "Is this getting through?"

"Yes," she said.

"This doesn't make any sense, why am I an American?"

"Your presence here makes no sense either," she replied.

"Goddamn you! Is she translating accurately?" he asked Gonpo. But the lama did not open his eyes or respond, and in frustration, Wilson turned back to Tsering.

"I don't understand his question," he said testily. "Does he mean why am I here?"

Gyatsu made no reply to her translation, and Wilson's frustration at being dependent on her boiled into a small tantrum.

"One can't help where one is born," he shouted. "I'm an American who came to study psychic phenomena. I don't know what word you would use for this."

The smoke of incense and butter lamps rose like a screen between the two monks and the four intruders. Tsering had trouble explaining *psychic* to Gyatsu.

Finally Gonpo opened his eyes: "Messages on the wind," he said. "Mr. Wilson would like to hear messages on the wind. But for that it is necessary to gain complete control of the mind."

"I know my mind pretty well," Wilson replied.

"But are you sincere?" Gonpo asked.

"Yes. Of course."

"Is *he* sincere?" Gonpo indicated the Onion.

"Ask him yourself," Wilson shot back. "I know nothing about the man."

Tsering spoke to the Russian at some length, and the Russian's degree of sincerity was sent directly from his language to the two Tibetans.

"Then sit with us," Gonpo said.

"Sit?"

"Yes."

"Can I get my cameras?" Wilson asked.

Jack had to squelch his objection to this obscene request. *The way opens when least expected.*

After considerable discussion between the monk and Gonpo, Tsering delivered the response: "If you wish."

Wilson looked smug. "Now we're making progress," he said. "We'll be out of here in a week."

"But," she added, "he says that you would be better concentrating your mind on a single point."

The two monks and Gonpo closed their eyes and began to rock slightly from side to side. Listening to Tsering's instructions, the Russian looked bewildered. Wilson glanced at Jack for direction, and Jack grinned. Wilson clenched his jaw. It seemed so absurdly easy, allowing the moment to unfold without any attempt at control and without even the means to calculate what would happen here. *We cannot say that the electron moves; we cannot say that it does not move.* We cannot say anything about the moment itself.

The Russian and Wilson had closed their eyes. He glanced at Tsering. Her face was dark with sun, her hair tied back in a crude pigtail, and her trousers and parka splotched with soot. The high heels and silks and gold bangles had been left in Kathmandu. Behind her eyes, he again saw the familiar shifting shadows, the images of Tibet that had entered his own mind in sleep. Her eyes flickered, half seeing him, half looking through the granite of Twilight Mountain at the land beyond. Tibet. She was drifting away and he was frightened for a moment, wanting her to see him fully, to know him, to recognize his presence in the cave. But her eyes were blurred. He let go and closed his own eyes.

When he opened them again, Wilson was on his feet stretching and the others were watching him.

"Go and rest," Gonpo said. "All of you. Tomorrow will be a long day."

"I'll bring my cameras," Wilson said.

Gonpo was silent.

Wilson went to the cave entrance. The Russian followed. Then Tsering stood up, waiting for Jack.

"Go ahead," he said. "I'm comfortable here. I'll be down later."

Her eyes focused, saw him. The Russian said something and she turned. Jack was silent. It was difficult, but he remained silent.

Long after they left, when his mind was clear again and he had forgotten the expression on Tsering's face, Jack lay down and slept under a rug. Gonpo and the two monks chanted, their words forming a canopy over his dreams. Near dawn he woke and looked at their dim shapes, still seated and breathing quietly. His own mind was focused now, as if during the night he had become a true disciple of Lama Dorje. A mute.

He descended to the lower cave where dim bundles lay strewn on the cave floor. Wilson sat up with a start, groping for his knapsack. "What time is it, my god it's still dark."

"The moon is setting," Jack said.

He could tell in the dark that the Russian and Tsering were also awake in their sleeping bags. So was the woman porter Angmo and Sherpa Pasang.

"It's time," he said, and then stepped outside to wait for them.

A near full moon was setting to the west over Ladakh and Kashmir. It would be throwing long shadows in the canyons of the Hindu Kush and Karakorams and Pamirs, and shining brilliantly in the Persian deserts. In Greece, the last of the season's tourists would be drinking beneath a brilliant Mediterranean moon; and in Berkeley, where this moon was only a promise, his colleagues would be wrapping up another day at the lab. *The world thus appears as a complicated tissue of events, in which connections of different kinds alternate or overlap or combine and thereby determine the texture of the whole.* Heisenberg might have been describing this moon rather than the mysterious world that lay behind quantum physics.

The Russian emerged from the cave, wrapped in furs and smoking his pipe. He looked at the same moon. Was he considering the angle of moonlight in Leningrad, or the angle seen by his wife and children watching it rise out of the Russian heartland? Jack did not have the language to ask, but it made little difference, since the precise angle of light inside Boris's head would always remain a mystery. From down the valley, a figure emerged from the big tent of the Khampa and stood looking up. This moon had already set over his homeland in eastern Tibet and dawn had broken. He would never see that particular angle of moonlight again.

But then neither would any of them. *The present is the only thing that has no end*, Schrödinger said. And so this moment slices through time and is eternal. And so this lumpy moon is forever setting over Dolpo. And so, from inside a remote Himalayan cave, there is always a commotion. Angmo is dragging Wilson's camera bags to the cave entrance, and he is shouting at her, "Get away!"

Tsering watches, amused, and does nothing to help.

Wilson tugs on his cameras, but Angmo won't let go.

"She wants to carry them for you," Tsering says. "She knows nothing but service."

To Jack it looks like a bit more than service. "Am I mistaken," he says, "or is our sole remaining porter smitten with our psychic researcher?"

Wilson turns an angry face. "That's pathetic, Malloy. Tell Tsering to stop her. The equipment is delicate, and she's clumsy as an ox."

Tsering speaks to Angmo, who listens with an enormous, snaggletoothed grin. "She insists you need help," Tsering tells Wilson. "She finds you charming."

"Damn it!" Wilson replies.

But now the energetic Angmo is loading his camera gear into her carrying basket.

"Easy, for Christ's sake," he snaps.

Squatting on her powerful thighs, she looks up at him with an adoring grin. "Eeeez," she hisses.

"Very valuable," he says to her. "Very expensive. Much money." He rubs his fingers together, and her gap-toothed smile in the moonlight is dazzling.

Gathered outside in the last of the moonlight, they let Angmo ascend the stone face first, while Wilson watches anxiously from below. Her bare feet, callused as shoe leather, grip the stone surface, and she climbs with the certainty of a mountaineer. Wilson follows with a bag slung over his back. Then the Russian.

Tsering doesn't move. Her face is molded in complex shadow from the moon's final light and the coming of the first oblique light of dawn. She is touching Jack's arm. "Go with them."

"And you?"

"I want to see the other side."

It takes a moment to be certain what she is saying. "You're going *over* the mountains?"

"Yes."

"It's dangerous up there."

"No more dangerous than your cave."

A distant peak cuts into the moon, and the light dims around them. "It's possible the Chinese have troops on these borders."

"Unlikely," she replies. "They have nothing to fear from Dolpo. Certainly not from this pathetic band of Khampa."

He puts his hands on her shoulders. Looking into her eyes, he sees the precise angle of moonlight inside her head.

"How far will you go?" he asks.

"How far will you go?" she replies.

Slowly they untangle from one another. She starts down the valley

161

toward the Khampa, and he watches, both hoping and fearing that she will look back. The crest can be crossed only in the absence of human attachment. Even love for another human must be transcended. Love. It's a word she considers a bourgeois obscenity. She does not look back, and he turns to the rock face. As she disappears into shadow, he climbs into the last moonlight.

Gonpo instructed them to observe each breath and consider where it begins and where it ends. When that became impossible, they should consider where the mind that observes the breathing resides. Then they might consider at what point their breathing became past, present and future. But always come back to breathing.

It was amazing what Wilson would endure since taking charge of the expedition. The Russian also sat, trying to follow whatever instruction Tsering had provided him. He was breathing steadily, his large chest emptying and filling regularly. Jack joined them. He heard Wilson shift uncomfortably from time to time; daylight came and the voices of the Khampa and yak herder could be heard down the valley. Occasionally, Gyatsu rang a bell, but for long periods there was that peculiar silence that comes with communal meditation.

It was late afternoon when he felt a vibration in his solar plexus, a tightening and ringing, and then a tremendous explosion that for a moment blinded him as sound became light. When he looked up, he was surprised to see Wilson and the Russian on their feet, hobbling on stiff legs toward the cave entrance, as if they had heard something outside. The monks and Gonpo had not moved, however.

Again came the explosive sensation in his belly, and this time he too rose on stiff legs and went to the cave entrance—just as three jet fighters swept over their valley, rising rapidly as if delivering bombs. The shock wave from the planes struck the cave like an explosion. Below, the Khampa had scattered for cover with their weapons pointed up.

"MIGs," Wilson said. "Chinese."

And Jack thought of Tsering, climbing toward the invisible division between Nepal and Tibet, exposed on the bare hills above.

"What do you suppose they're up to?" Wilson asked.

"Perhaps routine border patrol," Jack replied, not believing his own spoken words. A *complicated tissue of events*—according to Heisenberg. Even three jets flying over a Himalayan ascetic's cave, as observed by an American physicist, were connected in meaning.

"Odd they came over twice," Wilson said.

"At that speed they won't see much."

After such a violation, it was difficult for Jack to concentrate again. In minutes those jets could appear over Kathmandu, a distance it had taken them ten days to traverse. Perhaps, in the world beyond these mountains, the long-awaited holocaust had begun and the Chinese were attacking the Indian nuclear installations. He tried to calm himself, allowing his breathing to still, but the jets had struck as suddenly as the Zen master's stick. Could the minds inside those cockpits possibly be related to the minds inside this cave—as ripples were related by the lake? *There is only one mind. The stuff of the world is mind stuff.* Now, in Heisenberg's complex tissue, three Chinese pilots had appeared. Like ripples on the quantum lake of one mind.

When he descended to the lower cave, Tsering had not returned, and the Khampa band had vanished with their horses.

Sherpa Pasang was highly agitated. "Very bad. We go now," he said.

"No, we stay," Jack told him.

It was a familiar argument between them, and as always, Pasang was difficult to convince. Five months ago, Jack's entrance into Dolpo had made him nervous. Now the surly Khampa made him nervous. The Russian made him nervous. Tsering's disappearance made him nervous. And the jets made him very, very nervous. But finally, given the alternative of leaving alone and Wilson's refusal to pay if he did, Pasang agreed to stay.

Jack was worried, too. Something had happened beyond the crest—he could sense the violence. Tsering was in danger. And despite his resolve to accept what happened, that evening he climbed out of the valley looking for some vantage point. It was too dark to see much, although he did make out a shadowy figure on the far side of the valley. Bulky and powerful, it was not one of the Khampa. It was Boris scrambling over the broken granite, looking for his translator.

A series of stone faces blocked Jack, and he realized that she could not have come this way and that he must return and wait for daylight. But when he turned back, he discovered a vast presence behind him. The moon. The great mirror was rising beyond the mountains, reflecting sunlight into Dolpo, and as he walked to camp with his feet and lower body in shadow, his eyes were dazzled by light. Tsering, if she were still alive, would be seeing this same reflected light.

Angmo was waiting anxiously in the valley and began speaking rapidly as soon as he appeared. But he understood nothing until he asked Pasang to translate into fragments of English: "Khampa bad. Tsering hurt."

Then his own fear exploded in a series of questions to Pasang and Angmo. "Hurt?" he asked repeatedly. But slowly he realized that they knew no more than he did. Pantomime and a few hundred words of English had magnified their concern, and he nodded wearily. While they all stood in shadow, the rock above glowed in moonlight.

"We'll find her tomorrow," he said. "Don't worry."

But even Wilson, waiting in the cave, was worried. "Do you suppose the Chinese have got her?" he asked.

"I doubt it."

But that was precisely what Jack thought. While he had committed himself to acceptance and patience, lives were threatened. Either Dorje was in control of events and meant well, or he was malevolent. Or else these events in Dolpo lacked any mystical connection or significance. In which case, immediate, decisive action was required to save their lives. In which case, Jack's passivity was criminal.

Late that evening, a somber Boris returned and slipped into his sleeping bag, where he began to sing a mournful song that must have come from the steppes of central Asia. It mingled with the sound of the monks chanting in the cave above and the occasional wail of the bone trumpet.

From his sleeping bag Wilson said meditatively, as if responding to the mood of the Russian's song, "I wonder if anyone is *up* there?"

"He's there," Jack replied.

"But you say he's dying. Maybe . . ."

"He's there."

It was below freezing, but porters slept out in such weather and a native Tibetan like Tsering could survive a night in her parka. At dawn they would launch a search for her. Angmo and Pasang sat near the smoldering fire talking, no doubt brooding on the events of the day. Jack remembered the night on the pass when Tsering and the porters had talked in the firelight, and he had been envious of their closeness in the high mountain night. Tsering had returned to the tent full of nostalgia for a lost Tibet. Now she had gone to the lost country, and there was nothing for him to do but wait for sleep, listening to another of the Russian's mournful songs. If Lama Dorje had intervened in the complicated tissue of events, then Tsering's absence was necessary, no matter how painful. If not, then Jack had killed another person through his own egoistic self-delusion.

When a hand touched his shoulder, he rose on one elbow certain she had returned, but it was the silent monk, Sonam, squatting at the head of his sleeping bag. And then Jack knew that she was dead and the messenger had come. Since he slept fully clothed, he slipped quickly into his boots and followed Sonam outside. The Russian, breathing heavily, turned on his side; Wilson whimpered in his sleep; Angmo lay huddled in a blanket close by. Even restless Pasang did not wake, as if Sonam had cast a hypnotic spell over the sleeping cave.

Jack followed the monk out of the cave into the waning moonlight, where the loss of Tsering exploded in his mind, along with her last words, "How far will you go?"

Sonam climbed and Jack followed. They passed the middle cave—

empty—and kept climbing toward the upper cave. So the test had truly begun, and now he must put Tsering out of his mind. He saw her frozen corpse lodged in the rock of the Tibetan border range, but he must put her from mind. For if one is caught in human desire, it is impossible to leave the wheel of karma.

Once again, he climbed from darkness into moonlight. But now, near dawn, the light was pallid.

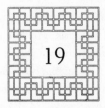

19

Jack followed the monk up familiar hand- and footholds to the upper meditation cave where Gonpo and Gyatsu sat—erect shadows. He prostrated himself, cold stone against his forehead, smelling the ancient seabed in which fossil shells were embedded like sacred ornaments.

Sonam left him alone in front of Dorje. The change in five months was shocking: the man wore a death mask—rigid and brittle. The eyes were open but lifeless; loose hair hung around his face like dry grass; his ribs were individually exposed beneath parchment skin. And there was a strong odor that Jack could not identify, but which was not that of human habitation. One summer in Montana his father had opened a rattlesnake den with a bulldozer, and the smell of many reptile surfaces intertwined had boiled from the earth. Stunned, Jack turned toward Gonpo for help, but he sat in deep meditation.

He sat down before the wooden meditation crib from which the shadow of what might have been a man rose like a cobra in the dim light. In Kathmandu, he had seen this figure beyond the quantum door, and it had drawn him beyond the equations of sanity. Now, in this frightful smell, in this frightful presence, the harsh face of the universe was exposed. He knew that the short path of Tantric Buddhism,

167

seeking enlightenment and release from the world of illusion, plunged straight into the abyss of demons. He knew that benevolence only delays the ultimate confrontation. But this knowledge did not prevent him from being terrified. And he had no means of protecting himself, no way of telling good from evil. He sat, helpless, before this man whom he had sought and tried to kill in dreams.

"Have you arrived?" Gonpo said.

Jack turned, grateful for a human voice. "What?"

But it was not Gonpo speaking. "Have you arrived?" Gonpo's mouth opened and closed, as if he were hypnotized. Had he been taken over by the dark forces he had warned about? Was he, too, helpless in the grip of the black arts? To whom was Jack speaking?

"Yes," he said.

"Do you accept?"

Of course he accepted. But his insane screaming of the night before had not been acceptance. Those were the screams of a threatened ego. If only he had had time to prepare himself with Gonpo, but this summons had caught him asleep, unprepared. Still he must answer. He knew none of the parameters; he knew none of the mathematics. Each response was a test, each question a whipstroke on his back.

"Yes," he said.

"The path is narrow. It vanishes over a cliff. No one has ever walked it before. There are many fierce beasts. There is a river that cannot be passed. There are tremendous storms of fire. No human being can survive. Will you go on?"

The familiar metaphors of the dangerous short path did not strike him as quaint or rhetorical in this cave. It *was* impossible to walk such a path; no human could hope to do so alive. In the terror of ignorance, he strained not to cry out for succor or explanation from Gonpo. There were no answers now. He was blind. Just as he had been blind all his life in physics, because he had never challenged the paradoxes. He had lived a kind of controlled ignorance all these years. Yes, particles moved backward in time. Yes, they were waves. And, of course, they were not waves. We cannot say that they move, Oppenheimer

168

said, we cannot say that they do not move. It was necessary to accept these conundrums, and he had done so. Now his own life depended on a deeper understanding as it never had in physics. Now the answers *must* come, and he was panicked because they could not come from reason. Either there was a part of himself he had never seen, and it would speak, or he was lost. They were all lost.

"Yes," he said.

"There is no way. You understand?"

There is no way, but you must go forward. There is no far shore, but you must cross the water. There is no crest, but you must climb. He recognized the familiar Zen paradoxes that he had tried to resolve and failed, and which in physics he simply took for granted. But this time he must plunge into the water and climb the mountain.

"No one can help. You are alone."

"I have always been alone," Jack replied.

"You have never known the meaning of this word *alone*, but you will."

"And the others?" he asked.

Silence.

"I accept responsibility for myself. But the others?"

"You accept responsibility for yourself?" Gonpo's mouth opened and closed like the mouth of a fish, slow and soundless.

"Yes."

The face before him melted, became flesh, teeth, bone, eyeballs. The cave walls pulsed in on him like living tissue. He wallowed in viscera. Fragments of arms, torsos nudged his face. Blood poured over his head like a waterfall. He had the suffocating sensation of being drawn under the tremendous pressure of some fluid.

"I am astonished by your profound ignorance," the voice said.

He was crawling on his face through slime. Ignorance. Under crushing pressure he had become a fossil. He was the stone that held the fossil. He was the void that held the stone.

"Responsibility. A wingbeat in the emptiness. This is beneath contempt. I spit on responsibility. You think you understand what it means to be alone? To be responsible?"

Jack reached for the edge of Dorje's crib, whimpering, trying to pull himself erect.

"You alone know what to do. And you must act. The forces are immense and all my strength goes into holding them. I do not have patience with your ignorance. One misstep, and everything collapses. Do you understand? One misstep and the world ends. One misstep and you will be responsible for all that has happened, for all that will happen. One moment of paralysis, one moment of doubt . . . *this* is responsibility. I am beyond my strength. I can spare nothing for your personal guidance. You must go now. And you must act."

Jack was up on his knees, moving away from the awful voice, from the naked man who wore a death mask over his tremendous concentration, who held the world together in his mind while Jack had the presumption to speak of his own responsibility. His being alone. Backing from the cave, he felt light on his feet, legs.

"When another comes from beyond the mountains, you will begin. Remember, you alone know the way."

And then there came the sound that he had heard months before, as if a single vocal cord were isolated and scratched by a fingernail. As if the rock itself were vibrating. The sound carried him backward into some other death than what lay ahead of him. It drew him back down into that nightmare vision of slime on the bottom of a sea. The lama's face stretched around a huge, circular hole. His mouth gaped in the death mask.

At last he understood. Dorje was delaying his own death, waiting for Jack to act. That single vibrating cord, like rough twine stretched to the breaking point, was all that stood between them and oblivion.

He looked down the cliff. It was daylight. Wilson and the Onion stood side by side staring up at him. Behind him, he heard chanting, the wild frenzy of the damaru and vajra bell and kangling. Now they were all in free-fall, launched into the void. They were all alone and all together. They were all home and all in exile. They were all alive and all dead.

And if Bell's theorem were proven, as Lia had suggested in one of her letters to Jack, then every particle was instantaneously connected to every other particle in space and time; quantum events could not be dammed into a comfortable puddle of local reality to be studied by science; instead they flooded out of control into a sea beyond imagining. And without a shore on which to stand, the physicist was nothing more than an agent of creation, making more waves in his struggle to understand, jiggling the entire web of the universe with each observation. But that was madness. Dorje had nailed him into the box of his own intellectual paradoxes. And now, unless he acted, the box would become his coffin.

Wilson and Boris stared up at him. He stared down at the two men, but saw instead two women. Tsering was alive. And she was not alone. Jack descended from the upper cave to the valley.

"You've seen him?" Wilson said eagerly.

Jack nodded.

"Did you ask when I could interview him? Will he allow himself to be photographed?"

"You never entered the conversation."

"What did he say?"

"We're waiting for somebody."

"*Another* person?" Wilson said with annoyance. "Up here?"

Jack nodded.

The Russian, lost without his translator, was watching their conversation with frustration.

"Like hell we are. We've got enough of a circus here. I'm going up there myself."

And then Wilson suddenly stopped talking and pivoted down-valley. Boris turned in the same direction—toward the sound of hooves on stone and creaking saddles. Jack did not need to look. She was coming back with the Khampa warriors—faces wrapped against the cold—four horsemen trailing two horses. On one of the horses rode a slumped figure, on the other rode two people. When Jack turned to look, he saw Boris racing toward the horses waving his Denver Bronco cap.

"Looks like somebody's hurt," Wilson said.

The injured man was one of the Khampa. On the other horse,

Tsering rode behind someone and Boris strode beside her, chattering eagerly, but her face was grim and she was silent. The Khampa dismounted and carried the injured man into the tent. They looked exhausted and murderous. Tsering dismounted, helping the other person down. Together, they came toward the cave—it was a woman dressed in the unisex uniform of the Chinese. She was limping and sullen, her face puffy and bruised.

Jack moved to greet them. "Are you all right?" he asked Tsering.

She looked at him from far off. "I don't know."

There was no way to touch her now. She was back, alive, and he was relieved, but whatever had happened beyond the mountains had dropped between them like a steel shutter. She and the woman entered the cave, the Russian at their heels. Tsering spoke to Sherpa Pasang. He stirred the fire and put on a kettle of water. She said something sharp to Boris, who shut up and retreated to a wall. While Pasang prepared tea, the Chinese woman slumped down against the far wall, and Tsering turned to Jack and Wilson.

"If you don't mind," she said to Wilson, and drew Jack outside.

"Who sent the Khampa?" she asked.

"I have no idea. They disappeared the day you left."

"This is very serious," she said.

There was no questioning the expression on her face as anything but serious, but he must wait for the answers.

"I found a way down into Tibet."

"You went *down* the other side? You mean . . ."

"I went down the other side. It was evening. I think I intended to come back, but I can't be sure. I saw a single figure below and kept descending. We approached one another. I can't say what I intended because I was descending into Tibet as a kind of challenge, to see how far I could go. Perhaps to test myself. I don't know. I was in a strange state of mind."

She spoke as if reciting a script; he had never seen her so austere and remote.

"Her Tibetan was no better than yours, so I responded in Chinese,

172

which made her very cautious at first. I said nothing about our expedition or the Khampa, only that I had come from Dolpo. She wanted to know how I spoke Chinese. I did not tell her that I had learned in Beijing. She was equally evasive to my questions. She was an engineer attached to a large military installation a few miles away. She had walked into the mountains for relaxation. Then, I risked the truth. I told her I was a Tibetan exile. She asked if I was returning. I said I wasn't certain. She said that Tibetans were better treated. Red Guard excesses were being remedied. I must come with her. Perhaps I would have done so. Perhaps not. But two Chinese soldiers appeared, walking toward us. As they approached, I no longer had a choice. If I tried to flee they would follow, perhaps shoot. My fate had been determined for me. Or so I thought. I would never again see you or Nepal. Then these Khampa appeared, riding furiously toward us. The woman ran back toward the soldiers, I stood still, and a battle ensued. One of the soldiers was killed, the other escaped. One of the Khampa was killed. Lopsang was shot in the chest. We were taken prisoner and brought back here. They were very rough with Li, and with me. They abused her."

"Abused?"

"You know what I mean. They have fought the Chinese for so long it is natural to retaliate against a woman. They are vicious dogs."

"You were *both* prisoners?"

"Yes. They thought I was going to the Chinese. They trust none of us and are very dangerous now that the Chinese know of our presence. You saw the jets?"

"Yes."

"From what Li has said, there is a large airfield, a transportation depot, and some huge underground chambers being constructed."

Underground chambers. In his notebook were recorded the apocalyptic visions of his first visit to Dolpo. Those caverns and chambers he had taken for nuclear installations in Russia, China, India, perhaps the Sahara or Australia. But there had been rumors of the Chinese moving nuclear facilities to the Himalayas. Was the lama of Twilight

Mountain sitting right over the site? In that case, this incident was very serious and the Chinese would certainly cross the border in pursuit of the Khampa.

"The Khampa are disillusioned by your guru. They lost a man bringing you and now another man bringing this Chinese woman. They think you and Boris and Wilson are agents of foreign powers and that Dorje has lost control."

So, in the hour since descending from Dorje's cave, his search had been transformed into an international incident on a sensitive border where two Americans, a Russian, a Tibetan defector and a Chinese hostage were held by Tibetan guerrillas. Now who would believe they had come to see a mountain ascetic?

"I saw him," Jack said.

"Who?"

"Dorje. He is very near death."

"You spoke with him?"

"I think so. Gonpo translated. Sometimes I seemed to hear the voice in my head."

"And what did he say?" Her face showed no interest in the answer.

"Not to misstep."

"What?"

"We were waiting for this woman."

"You *expected* Li?"

"Dorje did, yes."

Her face changed from the distant expression of one in shock to a sharp focus on Jack. "You *still* believe in some mystical purpose here?"

"Yes."

"Which is what?" she asked bitterly. "To kill the rest of us?"

"I won't know until I've done it," he said. "It is not even possible for me to know."

"You are worse than these ignorant savages. They believe in demons. They drop stones on the house of the gods at every pass. They prostrate themselves before every lama and wear their amulets

174

and charms and chant their mantras. And they kill. What is your excuse?"

"I'm not the issue. We're Dorje's creation."

"No," Tsering said, "*your* idiocy created this madness, and now it is out of control. Now people are being killed because of your stupid quest. Li is badly hurt. Can't you understand that mystical games have consequences in the real world?"

"Which is *precisely* why we must continue. If he is willing to use his last hours alive on our behalf, we must help him."

"*We* must do nothing but leave immediately before the Chinese arrive. If I am taken prisoner here, I will be executed as a spy rather than reeducated. The Khampa will be killed. Boris will be imprisoned. Of course, you Americans may be spared since your criminal president has made accommodations."

"Nonetheless, I stay."

She laughed bitterly. "Why? Does this shaman have some secret worthy of the Russians and the Americans, and now the Chinese? Like what, a nuclear bomb? People are dying, can't you understand?"

"I understand. Dorje is also dying. And he is waiting for me to act. And I say that there is only one way out for us."

"Which is what?"

"To continue."

"Continue what?"

"Continue meditating. Continue our preparation."

"Continue *your* preparation."

"*Our* preparation."

"This is my only choice?"

"Unless you can think of another. You and Li must join us in meditation."

"Thank you, but I prefer to die with dignity. I will stay down here with her."

"Then I'd appreciate your telling Boris and Wilson as little as possible."

"I'll say whatever I wish." And she turned away from him.

Jack went back into the cave and said to Wilson: "There's been a little run-in with the Chinese. A Chinese soldier was killed, the Khampa lost a man, and they've brought this woman back with them."

Wilson seemed unperturbed. Of course, he had wanted action, and this was action. "So now what?"

"We continue to prepare ourselves. Dorje is willing to arrange a demonstration for you." The lie came easily to his lips.

"What kind of demonstration?"

"That will depend on the intensity of our preparation."

"I can photograph?"

"You can try."

Certain the Russian would follow Wilson, Jack turned away, and as he did so, the stone floor of the cave seemed to shift beneath him, like a raft. He glanced back, but none of the others showed any alarm; he stepped out of the cave gingerly, as if the mountain were alive and undulating beneath his feet. If Tsering's report of her conversation with Li was correct, the Chinese were blasting underground chambers in these very mountains. If it was a nuclear installation, then the cancer of the twentieth century had infected this sacred stone itself. These were the visions Dorje had planted in his mind and that had drawn him back to Dolpo along with the others.

Carefully, he fitted his hands and feet to the living stone, and trembling at the edge of understanding, he ascended toward the middle cave where Gonpo and the monks waited. By way of greeting, there was the forlorn sound of the thighbone trumpet and the rattle of stones on a skull drum. The Chinese woman had arrived. The final phase of this experiment had begun.

20

Wilson's flash dazzled the monks, and while Gonpo endeavored to explain these strange activities of the American in the fur hat, Jack brooded. The accursed cameras and tape recorder had disturbed the atmosphere beyond repair, and it was impossible for him to concentrate. When Wilson finally did settle down, he twitched on his blanket, waiting for the onset of psychic events. And whenever he jerked, the Russian looked alert. Both monks watched the cameras enthusiastically, waiting for another miracle. Only Gonpo, who had been through this sort of thing for years in Kathmandu, seemed able to concentrate.

In the cave above was the man who had brought them here with a strange chant. In a few hours or days that sound would cease. Then what? If he had achieved enlightenment, Dorje would return as a bodhisattva and help others off the wheel. Fine. But of what use was this motley crowd? Once again, his stomach was constricting into an explosive charge. *You* have the answer, Dorje said. But what was the question?

The screams from inside his belly dazzled him. When he recovered, he saw Wilson and Boris peering out of the cave entrance with drawn weapons. They'd brought their goddamned pistols into the

177

ghompa! He should have known, of course. Now the Russian was scrambling down the cliff, and Jack leaped to his feet. So the screams had come from *outside*. He bolted for the entrance, passing Wilson, who looked up from his pistol. "This is insane, Malloy. We've got to get out of here."

But Jack was descending and made no reply. At the base of the cliff two Khampa held the Russian at bay with automatic rifles. They watched Jack approach and did not try to prevent him from entering the lower cave. Inside, Aten and another warrior had backed the two women against the far wall, jabbing their fingers at them, the way children torment small animals. Tsering held Jack's walking staff raised over her head; the Chinese woman held a small knife in front of her.

"Stop it!" Jack yelled.

Aten turned toward his old antagonist with a wicked smile, but Jack looked beyond his grinning face at Tsering, just as she brought his walking staff down with a familiar, sickening sound. Aten groaned and dropped to his knees, stunned. As the other warrior turned toward her, something large and furry entered Jack's vision. It was the Russian, growling like an animal. Jack slammed into the man, driving him off his feet and landing hard on top of him. He delivered two short, chopping blows to the man's face with his pistol and sat up with the gun pointed at his head. Outside the cave the two remaining Khampa shouted and gesticulated with their weapons, uncertain where to aim because Jack stood squarely in the way. He stepped toward them, gesturing for them to put down their guns, when he heard a loud groan behind him. The Chinese woman was clinging to Aten's back, stabbing at his chest through the thick robes, and he was trying feebly to shake her off. Jack rushed back into the cave and seized her arm—she was trembling and panting like an animal. He pushed her back toward Tsering.

"Tell her to stop," he commanded, but Tsering's eyes had been transformed into opaque discs—she did not seem to hear.

"Tell Boris to release that man."

Still she refused to speak.

He took Aten by the shoulders and helped him stand. The knife had shredded his wool robe but drawn no blood. He steered him out-

178

side into the muzzles of the automatic rifles, where he felt a baleful presence in the cave above. He looked up—Wilson was sighting carefully along the barrel of his automatic pistol, but Jack's sudden emergence had blocked his line of fire.

"Put it away," Jack commanded. "It's over."

But Wilson did not move. Beneath the fur hat, his magnified eyes made him look like one of the local demons.

"Put it away!"

There was a long moment during which Wilson continued to stare down the barrel; a moment during which the Khampa became aware of Wilson's intent; a moment in which they might have used Jack for cover to fire up at him; a moment during which Boris might have fired from the cover of his hostage. But Jack stood in the way. He heard Tsering speaking to the Russian, and finally the other Tibetan emerged from the cave with one eye already swollen. And it was over.

Jack went back into the cave. "You must come above," he told Tsering, but the almost continual violence of the past hours had left her dazed.

"Explain to Li that her only hope is to go with you."

It was impossible to know whether she responded or not, but she did speak briefly to the Chinese woman, who still held the knife trembling in her hand. There was a sudden flicker of awareness in the woman's eyes.

"Now tell the Khampa to return to their tent. We mean them no harm."

"No," she said. "I do mean them harm."

"In which case your stubbornness will kill us. Tell them it's over. They have done a great service in bringing Li, at great cost to them. Now they must do Dorje's bidding."

Still she stood dumbly before him.

"Then send Boris and Li up to the cave, and you and I will go to the tent."

"I will send her up to the only safe place. But I will not talk with these men."

"You must. It is the only way."

"You," her voice was harsh, "you can't even speak this language, you know nothing of what is happening here. You have no right to command."

"But I have the obligation."

Taking Aten by the shoulders, he helped him toward the tent. Aten's eyes were cloudy, and he was not yet conscious of his actions, but he could walk. Reluctantly the other three Khampa followed them. Jack did not look back to see whether Wilson or the Russian had put up their weapons; he did not look back to see whether Tsering obeyed. He walked steadily toward the tent and pushed open the flap. Inside on a blanket lay the man wounded by the Chinese, obviously feverish. Jack helped Aten sit, and then bent over the dull eyes of the wounded man. He pulled away his robe and removed a filthy rag from his shoulder. The skin was puffy and inflamed around the wound. Infection was the principal danger now. Wilson could administer penicillin and wash and bind the wound. When he turned, four Khampa with automatic weapons sat watching him.

Aten's eyes flared with anger. His mind had cleared enough to know that he had been struck by this man's cursed walking staff. Once again, he had his M-16 leveled at Jack's chest. Except for the lama, he would have killed this foreigner long ago.

"Dorje," Jack said quickly, enunciating the magic syllables.

Aten slid his hand along the barrel, and spoke briefly with the other three men, who shifted their weapons and nodded.

From outside the tent came a voice: "Jack?"

Aten shifted his rifle muzzle toward the entrance.

"Enter slowly," Jack said.

The flap opened and Tsering peered myopically into the dimness. Aten spoke and she looked at him, her face savage as a Tantric goddess. She spat several words back at him.

"What do you want?" she said to Jack.

"I want to know what's happening here."

Her look penetrated him like a knife. "Ask your shaman."

"I need your help now."

The Tibetans were talking among themselves. Angered at their recent losses and by the long poison of exile, their faces were serious and tense. They glanced repeatedly at this Tibetan woman and her American friend who had caused so much grief.

"At the slightest provocation, they will kill us all," she said.

"Then help me."

She sat down. Aten said something to her, and she retorted so sharply that he swung the rifle toward her and frowned. His eyes were still not clear, but his anger and humiliation were evident.

"These bandits are defeated. Your CIA has cut off their weapons, the lamas have stopped supporting them, and now the Nepalis are hunting them down. They do not trust us. Yet you sit puffed with mystical nonsense."

"Perhaps. But why didn't he kill me last May? Why did he bring me here? Why did he bring you and Li back? Are these the actions of bandits?"

"Ignorant and superstitious men under the influence of this magician. They have an excuse. You have none."

"Why did they follow you across the border?"

"They won't tell the truth."

"Try."

She spoke. The exchange was short and angry-sounding, and Aten looked as though at any moment he would pull the trigger.

"The monk told them to go over the crest and bring back whoever they found."

"Why?"

"They obey Dorje without question. But they were not warned about the soldiers. They feel betrayed."

"And so they took it out on you and Li?"

She was silent.

"What will they do now?"

"They will leave."

"Why?"

"Because they believe you have made this an evil place. The Chinese will send soldiers."

"They *must* stay."

"Let the swine go. It's our only hope."

"Tell them to stay."

"You have no control over them."

"Listen to me. Now!"

She looked at him across thousands of miles of open grassland and desert; across frozen mountains; across the ruined monasteries; across the Chinese betrayals and her years of exile. Their eyes locked, and he felt the familiar pressure building in his belly. Twice it had exploded in the past days, once with the jets and again with the screams from the cave.

"Dorje will die within hours."

"Good."

"Tell them."

"Why?"

"Because these next hours are the only hope for us."

As she looked hostilely into his eyes, he felt his internal pressure join with her, a physical force that made her blink with surprise. The anger left her face as if she had been slapped.

"Do it," he said.

She spoke. The Tibetans looked at one another. "They ask how you know."

"I just know. Tomorrow they will see."

The words were coming to him as they had months earlier, as if by dictation. During the long exchange between Tsering and the men, Jack watched news of Dorje's imminent death throw them into disarray. Aten's eyes flickered with uncertainty.

Jack stood suddenly, and the conversation stopped. "Now let's help Dorje," he said, and stepped out into the clear mountain light. There was a flurry of Tibetan behind him. Who was this man? the voices were asking. What did he want in their country? What power did he have over Dorje? The questions were clear. The answers were not.

He looked around at the bare stone peaks blocking Dolpo from the world. The air was still, expectant. In this sky, dark as the edge of space, lay the answer. The answer lay in the stones, in the pure light drenching the mountains. The questions had been worn down to bare nubs of exposed rock; consciousness blew from the stones like dust.

She emerged, looking puzzled. "They will stay. But your presence puzzles them. They have not killed you because Dorje told them that you are a lama from another country."

"A lama?" Jack grinned at the absurdity. "Of course, a quantum lama."

She was not amused. "You suffer nothing."

"Only a knife twisted in my stomach."

"What knife?"

"Doubt. Finding no reason for my actions except belief in Dorje."

"Magic is no reason."

"No worse than science, which is also a knife in the belly."

"What do you know of knives? I might have returned to Tibet, except for them. I'm cut in two."

"You?" He looked closely, unable to believe that this woman, who so hated the Chinese, could possibly think of returning to her occupied country, or that such a shift could have occurred without his knowing. "You were going back?"

She nodded, as if embarrassed by the admission. "Do you understand being torn in half? Standing on the crest of these mountains, torn in half? Descending, torn in half? Torn in half by these men who treat me as a traitor? The pain is too much."

Her eyes blurred with anguish.

"Perhaps you are needed," he said gently.

"Why?"

"For Dorje's experiment. And because . . ." Because he did not want to lose her. They stood halfway between the black tent crouched at one end of the shallow valley and the cliffs and caves at the other. He tried to formulate his thoughts. "Last May Indian scientists forced together two masses of uranium isotope and achieved a critical mass. It was very crude and very simple. We did the same thing thirty years ago in New Mexico, and the cloud has been spreading ever since. Now India is contaminated. Li says the Chinese are building installations in these mountains. I think Dorje wants to stop the evil before it spreads farther. He needs us before he dies."

183

Tsering flashed her sardonic smile, familiar from their discussions in Kathmandu. "Ah, you and the shaman will save the world?"

"With your help."

They started walking.

"How can you be serious?"

"Will you help?"

"At the moment, there's little choice."

"Make it your choice."

"To act in your little drama? And what is their role?" She meant the Khampa.

"They're standing guard like the Tantric demons. They've driven us all into the cave of enlightenment."

"Like the hole in the Indian desert."

She was being ironic, but she was right—it was like being pushed into a hole. If Dorje had allowed him to remain in Dolpo five months ago, he would have remained in the hole alone. Now all of these hostile people were being shoved into the same hole. Like the uranium isotope, they would achieve critical mass.

"Will you and Li sit with us?"

Tsering actually smiled—thin and bitter, but the first smile in days. "How can we resist the honor?"

They had reached the cliffs and were standing under the watchful eyes of Wilson and the Russian, peering down from the middle cave. As Jack took her by the shoulders, Wilson shouted down, "Will you two cut the crap and get up here? We've got some serious talking to do."

"Okay?" he asked her.

She paused, her face roughened by exposure and burned a dark red-brown, her hair drawn back severely.

"I'll do what is possible," she said. "But don't ask me to believe it."

She followed him up to the middle cave, where Wilson and the Russian waited with the two monks. Li sat dazed against one wall, as far away from the rest as she could manage.

Wilson blurted out, "The goddamned Sherpa bolted, the yaks have left. We're stuck here, Malloy, with winter coming on."

184

"With a good roof over our heads, however."

"Cut the crap. What happened down there isn't funny. Those bastards are madder than hornets, and they'll never give me a target like that again. I could have popped them all off."

Jack grinned at his earnestness. "What's the problem? You can walk to Tsharka in two or three days. From there you can find help."

"What happens to all the gear?"

"You leave it here, of course."

"I'm not putting up with this shit anymore, Malloy. From now on, I run the show, and I want to get some things straight. I want to know what this Chinese woman is doing here. I want to know precisely when I get to see his holiness."

"First of all," Jack said. "You haven't been abandoned. The faithful Angmo waits for you below."

"Goddamn you, Malloy, this is no joke."

"And I have prevailed upon the Khampa to stay and keep us company."

"What!"

"They were going to leave."

For once, Wilson was actually shocked beyond complaint, and Jack continued quietly, "They were also pleased to know you would patch up the wound with your first-aid kit. He needs antibiotics."

Silence.

"Would you do that?"

"Are you kidding? One less of those bastards is one less for us to worry about."

"One less of them, and many less of us. Now will you go?"

"Not unless I know what's happening here."

"Ask."

"How can I trust her answers?"

"Try."

"What do you want?" Tsering asked him.

"I want the Onion to know who's running this show."

"Use his name," she said.

"See what I mean, Malloy?"

185

"Try doing what she says."

"Which is what?"

"Treat him with respect."

"He's a spy."

"Just ask what you want to know."

"Would you," he said at last to Tsering, "inform our Russian colleague that I am running the show from now on."

She spoke briefly to Boris, who tipped his Denver Bronco hat at Wilson.

"Well?"

"He thinks your anger is magnificent. Since you have grown a beard and wear his hat, you look Russian."

"You see, Malloy? This has got to stop. Now you make her translate accurately."

"She is. If you would quit the territorial squabble and settle down to business—"

"Sitting on our ass waiting to get snowed in is no business. I want to see your guru and I want to see him now."

"Attend to the wound first," Jack said, folding his legs beneath him and clasping his hands together.

"Malloy!"

Silence.

He heard Wilson depart, but his mind remained clear and steady. The test had begun in good order. He was relaxed and ready for whatever would happen. Boris talked at some length with Tsering before putting out his pipe and crossing his legs. Then she spoke with the Chinese woman, who had been watching them uneasily. Finally, Tsering herself sat, breathing steadily, waiting.

Jack let his mind drift. It would be full moon tonight. Where would any of them be on the next full moon? He smiled. We cannot say there is a moon. We cannot say there is not a moon. But this moment blazes through time and creates moonlight. And then he was no longer sitting in a Himalayan cave but in a lecture hall at Princeton, listening to Oppenheimer speak. Aha.

"Good," a voice responded. It was Gonpo. "Very good."

21

It was pretty clear that Malloy and the woman had cooked up a deal with the Khampa—because they never let Wilson out of sight. Getting the wound cleaned up hadn't helped—they followed him right back to the caves with the M-16s, and if he'd tried to enter Dorje's cave, they would have filled him with more holes than a colander. So, okay, he went back to the middle cave.

Tsering and the Onion were thick as thieves. It was hard to figure Malloy being so unconcerned unless he was in on it with them. Unlikely, but nothing was impossible. He couldn't trust Malloy, that was certain. And then what about this damned Chinese woman, cowering like an injured animal? The Khampa had lost a man bringing her, and for what? Since Gonpo had clammed up, there was no way to find out without Tsering. They'd probably rigged that too. He had no allies. The radio was either broken or not sending out of these mountains. It was just his wits and the Browning Hi-Power against the rest.

"Well, I'm back," he said.

No one looked up. Now what? Ignore Wilson and see what he does? With four automatic weapons down below, there wasn't a hell of a lot of choice but to stick with this crowd and wait for an opportunity. So he might as well get with the program and sit down on the hard stone. Another few days of this and his hemorrhoids would flare up. He crossed his legs gingerly and glanced at the rest. They looked tranquil. Even the Onion.

Okay, let's get caught up. Breathe. Give it a try. Follow your own breathing and . . . what was the rest? If the mind is an object where does it reside? That was easy. It weighed a couple of pounds and sat right inside his skull. What was the other question? Are past, present, future separate from one another, and if so where are the divisions? The second hand ticked off the division right before your eyes. Of course that was a pretty crude job, a stopwatch or some sort of atomic clock was better. At some point this moment became a past moment. And the future? Well, he had to admit that was a concept. You kind of thought there would be a future, but there were always surprises. What was Mudra doing now in Aspen? Still waiting tables? Still waiting for him? He wanted to get out of here and be skiing by January. Okay, so the future was fantasy, expectation. He could buy that. And in some sense the past was fantasy, too, if you looked at it that way. It happened, you knew it happened, but there were so many versions, and no way to reclaim it. Film helped. You could get a pretty good bead on the past if you had it all on film. That was indisputable. Still, this was intro to philosophy when you're nineteen with a head full of wine.

Breathing. Well, he could do that okay. The lungs just filled and emptied of their own accord. Nothing to it. Except when you thought about it too much. Then it seemed like you were opening and closing your lungs deliberately, taking deep breaths, like this, or shallow breaths, like this. And if you paused between them, there was a moment when it wasn't clear whether they would start up again. You sort of hung at the bottom or top. But so what?

His eyes closed. This was kind of peaceful, sitting here, letting the worries go. Thinking of Mudra.

The bell rang at greater and greater intervals. The monks and Gonpo began to chant; the voices of the Khampa died away. The light outside the cave shifted toward evening. The Russian spoke briefly to

188

Tsering, who replied. She spoke to the Chinese woman. Jack heard these voices at a great distance. From far off, he listened to the pellets rattle against the covered skulls of the damaru, to the rusty cry of the kangling. He heard cymbals crash together, a deafening sound inside the cave.

"Jesus Christ!" Wilson said. "What was that?"

Languidly, Jack answered, "The cymbals."

But in the absolute silence that followed, Wilson spoke again in a panicky voice. "There it is again."

Jack heard no sound.

"What?"

"The goddamned light. There!"

The cave was quite dim now and he could just make out Wilson's face, his eyes flicking back and forth in panic. The Russian was speaking rapidly to Tsering, and Li was moaning and holding her eyes.

"What is it?" Jack asked.

Tsering had difficulty understanding Boris. He wanted to know where the animals had come from. Li thought she was going blind.

"There was an earthquake just now and a flash of light," Tsering said. "Did you feel it?"

Jack had felt and seen nothing, and Wilson destroyed whatever chance there was to meditate on these events. He was on his feet flashing his camera, the brilliant light illuminating the faces of Gonpo and the monks.

"For God's sake," Jack said, "put that thing away."

But Wilson swept the camera from side to side, squinting intently through the lens. The monks, distracted, stared blinking at the camera. Only Gonpo continued to concentrate.

"What are you shooting?" Jack asked.

"Like fireflies," Wilson said. "There. And there."

"You're creating them," Jack said, "with that goddamned camera."

"There," Tsering said. "Feel it? A little aftershock."

But Jack felt nothing. He glanced at Li cowering against the wall. "What's the matter with her?"

"She sees only shadows."

Of course she had her hands over her eyes, and Wilson would have blinded anybody. Jack was half blind himself, and the cave was full of afterimages in the dusk. He watched Wilson frantically reloading his cameras. Tsering and Boris talked in querulous tones. Li sat up, looking with wonder as her eyes regained vision. The cave was growing brighter—a full moon had risen out of India, cresting the Himalayas.

Jack watched it rise through the cave entrance. It rose as he watched. Two moons forever different. This was the great frustration of nuclear physics—Heisenberg's shroud of indeterminacy cast over the actual, in which conditions could be known but never the thing itself, and the inquiring mind was forever trapped in its own consciousness. Of course, these lamas would admit no such limitation to consciousness, which, in their view, could find ultimate reality at any time—even after death in the Bardo. But he was no lama, and these photons striking his eyes and creating the illusion of a moon over India came from a reality that quantum mechanics could not penetrate. He was trapped in a Himalayan cave with people terrified by visions he had not seen, and for which there was no proof and never would be. And his physics would never explain what lay beyond their perception or his own. Neither alive nor dead in the quantum Bardo.

As the monks began to chant, Tibetan, Russian, Mandarin, English mingled in the air, and Jack added his own quantum murmurs from a lifetime of study—Schrödinger's wave mechanics, Dirac's quantum algebra, the von Neumann mathematical formulation of quantum theory—and gradually the mathematics emerging as dumb sounds from his throat took on the form of the mantra: *Om mani padme hum*. Peace settled over the gathering. The bell whispered intermittently; the damaru made the soft sound of rain on a lake. And at that moment, in the river of sound flowing from the cave into the brilliant night, Schrödinger's wave equation had no more meaning than any other mantra. It was an act of faith.

As the moon moved west, shadows shifted. The entrance of the cave cast a clear arc across the floor. From below, the Khampa joined the chanting: *Om mani padme hum*. He imagined the cold-faced moon swinging north, while the sun slipped south toward winter, the two balanced like dancers at arm's length. The waters would freeze, the monasteries fall silent. The few people left in the area would huddle with their animals in primitive stone and mud huts and wait. There would be no movement except for the prayer flags whipping on bare poles. And in the frozen silence, it would not be clear why human consciousness had ever dragged itself out of the great void in the first place.

Once again the bubble was forming in the region below his chest, in the chakra known to Tibetans as manipura. Twice it had exploded —with the MIGs and the scuffle among the Khampa—and he tensed against the pressure of what might happen. He slowed his breathing. The bubble expanded, as if the center of his body were about to rupture.

He heard the dry scratching of a single vocal cord, Dorje's sound; but the monks and Gonpo were deep in sadhana in the moonlight. The others sat as if hypnotized—the Russian, the American, the Tibetan, the Chinese—drawn so deeply into themselves that they might have been asleep. He longed to join them, but remembered the Bardo Thodol's warning that the hearer must not cling to the human world. It was illusory, and death was the great opportunity. The inhuman sound of Dorje's voice grated inside his mind; it was irritating, and his body tightened like a drawn bowstring.

His stomach and chest were forced apart and a passage burst open. He emerged like a thunderhead, like a nuclear plume over the Nevada desert, wanting to cry and laugh all at once. He was on his feet in the circle formed by the monks and Gonpo and the four reluctant disciples, and his arms and legs were making spontaneous, soft movements, trailing his body like shadows, as if his body had turned fluid and was draining out on the floor of the cave. As his body drained away, his mind remained like a crystal pillar at the center of his turning, and within the clear light of the pillar, mathematical symbols flickered. He saw the monks and Gonpo deep in sadhana. He saw the woman he loved deep within herself. The Chinese woman's face had

191

cleared of terror. Wilson had forgotten about his cameras. The Russian had closed his eyes in a beatific smile. They were human beings. It was such an honor to be human. And such a difficult burden for all of them. He turned slowly, radiating compassion while the symbols inside the crystal clicked together like hard-shelled insects. He turned like a beacon, and faces below him appeared and disappeared in the rotating light. But as each face flared up, he saw a grotesque mask, head thrown back, eyes and mouth wide but screamless, arms akimbo, body rigid in terror. His joy was reflected back to him as horror—as if he were the cause of their terror and suffering—and he shuffled forward in his strange Tantric dance, reaching out a benevolent hand.

The panic was instantaneous. The Russian drew his pistol and, baring his teeth, slid back toward the far wall. Wilson whipped out his own pistol and slithered along the floor on his belly. The Chinese woman remained paralyzed, her bruised face stretched beyond recognition. And Tsering . . . she looked up at him, mouth twisted horribly, clawing the air and trying to move as if her spine were severed.

He wanted to help, couldn't she understand? He spun toward her, but she dropped to the stone floor, twisting like a broken-backed snake. Li fell over, mouth working, face bulging. The Russian slashed his pistol back and forth. Tsering began to bang her head stupidly against the cave floor, and he yearned to take her in his arms, to draw her into his dance, but he dared move no closer.

Wilson opened fire behind his back, and Jack twirled, reaching for the sound, trying to stop the bullets, but Wilson was aiming toward the top of the cave where the ricocheting bullets flickered like fireflies in the shadows.

"Wilson!"

At the sound of his name, Wilson turned the pistol toward the floor, angling bullets out into the moonlight. A burst of automatic weapons fire answered from below. The Russian stopped slashing above his head and fired back, aiming straight out into the night.

Inside the crystal pillar the symbols scratched and rattled like stupid beetles in a bottle. The beacon light slowed its spinning, and the faces receded. He felt a human touch.

192

"Go to Dorje," Gonpo said.

Jack translated the simple command with difficulty, frowning with concentration.

"Your ego clouds this experience. Little time remains. Please, let us go."

How could he leave this carnage he had created: the cringing bodies, the corpses, the shattering explosion of guns and drums and bells? The gentle hand led him toward the cave entrance, and all the fluidity of the dance left him as Jack moved in awkward crablike jerks. Weapons flashed below and bullets struck the stone. He remembered the hailstorm on the pass when Gonpo had sat chanting, a still center in all that violence. Now they were on the rock face, exposed in the moonlight, climbing. Flames of light leaped from the cave below as if napalm had exploded. Lead hailstones cascaded off the stone, and a snake's spine of sound rattled through the valley, building in waves, shattering his ears. Screams tore from the middle cave, but Gonpo's gentle voice drew him on. "Don't look back. You can't help them."

He pulled himself clumsily from one handhold to the next, working his way up the twenty feet of sloping rock to the entrance to Dorje's cave. The dry smell of an ancient seabed met his nostrils. The gunfire died down and the patter of hail stopped. The unearthly light of the middle cave had been replaced by three butter lamps, and he crept into Dorje's cave, not on his hands and knees, but on his belly, like a snake. From outside in the moonlight came a single scream. And then silence. Without lifting his face from the stone, he heard the insect rasp of dry shell.

22

"Good of you to have me," Lama Z said in his precise English. An amiable-looking Tibetan in red-orange robes, the lama sat in a large overstuffed chair facing the window. "Your colleague has told me much about you and your work."

"He has written us of your work also," Lia said. "Would you care for tea? I have Darjeeling, oolong, and various herbs."

"English tea will be fine," the lama said, holding his beads in one hand. While Lia was in the kitchen, he admired the distant Golden Gate bridge.

"We were surprised to hear of your arrival in Berkeley," she said from the kitchen.

"I'm helping to prepare for the Dalai Lama's visit. Exiled lamas travel a good deal these days."

"Spreading the Dharma?" Lia asked, reemerging into the living room.

The lama seemed pleased at the question. "Your country has been very receptive to the Dharma."

She spread out the tea things. "The others should be here soon. We're all anxious for word of Jack."

"A splendid fellow," the lama said. "A remarkably clear mind and

194

very perceptive. It was gratifying to have him choose our institute for study."

She carefully set a tea strainer across the lama's cup. "It was a little surprising to us. There's been a good deal of consternation about his behavior."

"Ah, yes . . . ," the lama said. "Consternation? I expect from his family and such."

Lia was examining the lama critically. He did not look his age, which must be well over sixty. His hair was dark, the Buddha belly looked firm and inviting. He moved with an easy liquidity. All that yoga, she supposed. His face was warm and his lips had an engaging way of turning up quizzically, as they did now.

"Yes, but also among his employers and the government security apparatus. I won't trouble you with details, but we were hoping you might have some idea of his future intentions, whether he'll be returning soon. Or at all."

The lama poured a little tea, inspecting it for color, and then returned the tea to the pot. "As a matter of fact, his behavior has been enigmatic to us also."

Something about the lama's presence in the thin October light made her wary. One should be utterly frank with a lama, she supposed, but she felt reticent and hoped the others would be circumspect. "Enigmatic?" she asked.

"Where he has gone and why are not precisely clear. Perhaps you have some information."

"As a matter of fact," she said, settling down with her own pot of oolong, "we're not too certain ourselves. We assume that he is in the same region as his first trek." What was it about this lama that made her cautious? "There seems to be a dearth of accurate maps of the area. Although Dhaulagiri is easy enough to find."

"Yes," the lama said. "He's north of Dhaulagiri on the Tibetan border. But the circumstances of his return are a bit puzzling."

"Oh?" she asked.

"You know nothing about it?"

"Only that he hooked up with some character from Denver."

195

"A 'character from Denver.' " Lama Z mulled this description a moment. "I've met him."

"Really?" She sipped.

"Interesting fellow, a sort of researcher. Investigating psychic activities, telepathy, clairvoyance, and such. Rather a trivial business, actually, but he seemed very earnest."

"That's good to know," Lia said, "that you think Jack is in good company."

"However," the lama added, "their association is a matter of some concern. Mr. Malloy's interests are rather at odds with those of Mr. Wilson."

So far nothing the lama said was at variance with Jack's account of Wilson, but he was being too indirect for her taste.

"Jack's always been a bit of an oddball, it doesn't surprise me that he's hooked up with another one."

"But Mr. Wilson's expedition is rather awkward for us, you see."

Lia raised her eyebrows. "Oh?" she said.

"Yes, the Nepalese authorities are sensitive just now, political affairs being what they are."

"Political affairs?"

"This visit of your president to China . . ." The lama stopped before saying anything critical.

In Lia's opinion, the shift of China policy was long overdue. "What has Nixon's visit to China to do with your institute?"

"It has made the Dalai Lama's position rather tenuous. He can no longer count on American support for Tibetan independence. Tibetan independence fighters are no longer welcome in Nepal, which—how should we say in modern scientific terms—has become the interface between Chinese-occupied Tibet and the world."

What a peculiar, roundabout way of speaking. He had more on his mind than he was saying, and she was pleased at her discretion in dealing with him. "Are you suggesting Jack is involved in this political . . . interface?" The scientific cliché was not a term she used without irony, but in this case she managed.

196

The lama brooded a moment in the huge chair, his orange robes resplendent in fall light. "The Nepalese have asked the Dalai Lama's assistance in removing the Tibetan fighters. He agreed, and most of the guerrillas have put down their arms. However, the Tibetan community remains under suspicion, and Mr. Malloy and Mr. Wilson have now gone to a highly unstable area. Perhaps unwisely, our institute sponsored their expedition. The Nepalese are increasingly restive. I now endeavor to make certain there are no—how do you say in your language—no hidden parameters?"

Lia looked on with amusement. He was obviously a well-read man and more cosmopolitan than she expected. So the Tibet Institute had a *political* problem with the expedition, and Lama Z had come to make sure that Jack was only what he seemed—an oddball physicist— and that no "hidden parameters" were concealed in the American physics or military community. She smiled, pleased at having waited him out.

"The hidden variable notion," she said to him, "as you no doubt know, was proposed by Einstein to deal with certain paradoxes of physics that affronted his spiritual sensibility. He could not accept the cosmic disorder of quantum mechanics, so he postulated a hidden variable. However, recent experiments here in Berkeley confirming something called Bell's theorem suggest that there is no hidden variable."

"Mr. Einstein was wrong?"

"Not precisely. But perhaps, as one of our colleagues from Bombay speculates, the universe is more like the Hindu Brahman, and the hidden variable is simply our own mind. Maya, I believe."

"We call it samsara," Lama Z said, pouring himself more tea and adding sugar and milk like a good Englishman. "Mr. Malloy is aware of this experiment?"

"Oh, yes. It's no secret. What interests us are the implications for consciousness."

"There's nothing secret about your work then?"

She laughed. "Secrecy is quite unnecessary, since no one cares about us. There's no official interest since our speculations are unlikely to lead to any practical application. Besides, our opposition to military work has made us pariahs."

"So the expedition of a nuclear physicist to the remote Himalayas is of no significance in your view?"

"Doctors and dentists go trekking in the Himalayas, why not a physicist?"

"And in your view there is no special reason Mr. Wilson should accompany your colleague?"

"Since I know nothing of Mr. Wilson, I couldn't have an opinion. I gather he looked up Jack as a fellow scientist familiar with the region."

"So he said," the lama replied. "Among my colleagues in Denver, however, there is some question about the nature of Mr. Wilson's science. In particular there is skepticism about this Institute for Psychic Research."

"Skepticism?"

"That it is not, as it would seem, independent of the government. In fact, there is considerable evidence to suggest a connection to your defense establishment. Hence I am surprised to hear of Mr. Malloy's antimilitary attitudes. They would seem at some variance with Mr. Wilson."

"Perhaps Jack is unaware."

"Perhaps. But Mr. Malloy's work does not involve the military in *any* way?"

"The university is increasingly separated from military work."

"I see," Lama Z said. "So the connection of Mr. Malloy and Mr. Wilson is entirely coincidental in your view."

"I'm quite certain Jack has no interest whatsoever in military applications, and besides, what is the military application of a Himalayan cave? I find this suspicion of Mr. Wilson and Jack a bit farfetched."

"It is mysterious to us also. Although recently it has come to our attention that the Russians are highly interested in mental control. As you might expect, the KGB in particular has explored these areas for years. With some success, it is said."

The idea that an agent of the Pentagon, Mr. Wilson, was accompanying Jack to a lama's remote cave in order to perfect mind control struck her as droll, except that Jack had also mentioned the Pentagon and CIA, and Mukerjee continued to complain about surveillance.

"I'm sorry, but I can't take the Pentagon's interest in a remote ascetic very seriously. Surely we've not come to this."

"Amusing to you, perhaps. We have information that a Russian agent has gone to the same area. We find neither the KGB nor the CIA especially amusing."

"I'm sorry," Lia said. "But in view of nuclear annihilation—which we in this group take very seriously—it's difficult to be alarmed by these psychic warriors."

The lama had grown a little testy in this interchange. "So was it difficult to take you physicists seriously until 1945. Now you are gods. Effective control of mental energy can be just as dangerous in the wrong hands," the lama said.

"None of us can take that prospect seriously, I'm afraid."

"Neither did you take the exchange of matter and energy seriously, although it was known in the East for millennia. But in the West you always need proof. Your bomb gave you proof, but look at the consequences. It was Mr. Einstein's mind that released this energy. People forget that mind is the source. This capacity to forget makes the lama's task difficult. When the way off the wheel is so obvious, we keep the wheel turning."

Suddenly, Lia was no longer whimsical. The latest demonstration of Bell's theorem had thrust them squarely into mind itself as the answer to the conundrums of quantum theory. Now Lama Z's presence made Jack's absence especially vivid, and sipping her tea with this man in orange robes, who had brought his suspicions all the way from Nepal to her house, she began to wonder whether Jack might actually be involved in a plot of some sort, and whether his paranoid ramblings in the last letter might have some basis in fact.

The garden gate opened and shut. Voices carried up the walkway.

"My colleagues are arriving," she said and stood up. But Lama Z remained seated as the physicists entered the house.

23

Three butter lamps burned, but the bright moon made the interior seem dark, and Jack blindly prostrated himself beside Gonpo. When he raised his head, he shuddered. Dorje's skin had shrunk over his skull, the tips of his teeth showed in a grimace, and his body was impossibly skeletal. The smell of ancient seabed and rattlesnakes exploded in Jack's nostrils.

"Quickly!" Gonpo pushed Jack by the shoulders. "You must meditate as if your life depends on it. There is one chance to receive Dorje. One moment before all is lost."

Jack turned a pleading face toward Gonpo, but the lama was retreating to the rear wall. Fear froze him like ice; his breath was shallow. And only the last remnants of his will allowed him to fold his legs awkwardly on the coarse blanket before Dorje. He had to force his gaze up from the stone floor and over the crude wooden poles of the crib to the awful figure there. Rising from the dry grass was a naked torso which might have been amputated from its lower body. The emaciated belly was drawn against the backbone. He could not bear to look higher.

Gonpo rang the bell once, and Jack's mind shrank from the sound, pulling down inside him like a candle in a wind. He focused on this spark of light. But the ghastly figure of Dorje before him, the gunfire and flashbulbs and terror of the cave below, had gathered around him like mist. As the mist thickened, the flame drew down smaller, and when it went out, he screamed. But the sound of his voice was thin, a familiar scratching sound that tore through his body like a spike being driven from the top of his head down his spine.

He vibrated with each stroke, whimpering with pain and swaying from side to side. A strange fluorescent light grew in the darkness, became a vast plain of white light. In the white emptiness a single dark line appeared, thin and sinuous, swaying in a wind. It was the sound in his head, writhing on the plain of white light, and it was all that was left of himself.

Shadows appeared and flickered about like bats, as if his own shadow had splintered and were dancing around him. He turned frantically from side to side, trying to catch the shadows in the act of forming, but always they evaded his sight, quick as hummingbirds. And when he reached, trying to stop their movement, the smooth quick shapes slipped away; at the end of his extended arms, his hands opened like leaves and drew him to his feet.

These splinters of darkness flickering just beyond his fingertips spun him in the moonlight; reaching and spinning, he whirled faster, watching his own movement transform the shadows. As his whirling spun shadow filaments, his reaching braided them, and his dance wove them into a familiar tapestry. But at the moment of recognition, the figures in the tapestry unraveled like the whirl of particles in high-energy collisions. They wove and rewove in spirals and exotic loops. Hadrons, leptons or quarks? He tried to mimic their shapes with his own body but only accelerated their movement, driving them wildly against one another until they exploded into still more fragments and combinations. His pursuit created the dance.

Or did the dance create him? He must test the hypothesis. The dancer lifted his right arm. A leg moved in the tapestry. He raised his head, but an arm moved. Or else the arm moved and his leg bent. Time reversed, cause and effect vanished. There was no dancer, only the dance.

"You see." It was Gonpo's voice.

Jack opened his hand and Gonpo's face vanished.

201

"Now you may be empowered."

He sprinkled Gonpo with charmed particles, arranging them in dramatic swirls, enjoying the effect.

"Sit now and prepare yourself."

Jack was so engrossed that he even dared to include Dorje in the dance, spinning him into the tapestry—where he became a many-legged animal nipping at Gonpo's headless torso.

"He risks all to empower you."

The animal and human torso joined into a tusked figure dangling skulls from a necklace. One of its muscular arms swung a great curved sword. Schrödinger's sword! It could cut into infinite possibility and slice out a single particle. By collapsing the wave function, it could cut the shape of reality from the formless void.

Jack reached for the sword.

"A true bodhisattva takes responsibility for all others. You must prepare yourself."

But there were no others. He had made this mistake in the cave below—believing in others and trying to communicate his joy. Now there were no others. He created all. He seized the sword.

"You create only illusion," Gonpo said. "You must cut through it with a single stroke."

He swung Schrödinger's sword and Gonpo vanished. Only his voice remained.

"Dorje risked enlightenment to give you this key. It was a mistake. You are too ignorant."

But Jack was not ignorant. His mind blazed with sudden light. Heisenberg had assumed separation between the observer and the thing observed. But Jack had become both. He had entered the quantum Bardo forbidden by Heisenberg's uncertainty principle. There was no uncertainty because there was only one mind. This was the hidden variable Einstein had sought. The mathematics of understanding flashed before his eyes, symbols arranging themselves neatly as if on a chalkboard.

"Delusion," Gonpo said. "You must cut through it. Now!"

But if he stopped his dance, he would lose the equation. It was

Gonpo and Dorje who were ignorant. They knew nothing of mathematics, which was the key. He had been summoned because of his knowledge. He had brought the key to Dolpo, and this dance was his triumph. He swung the sword at the Tantric demons blocking his path, slashing arms and torsos and hideous writhing appendages. Just when he had waked from a lifetime's sleep, Gonpo was asking him to sleep. Gonpo was ignorant but very cunning.

He must resist the hypnotic influence of this demon who would draw him back into centuries of superstition and darkness. He slashed wildly with Schrödinger's sword, finally raising it above Dorje's head. He whirled and created the dance. And the dance created the dancer.

Gonpo rang the bell—once, twice—and the dance slowed. The equation faded before his eyes. The white plain on which he danced shrank to the moonlit floor of a Himalayan cave; he smelled again the odor of rancid butter burning.

He looked down on this ignorant lama who had destroyed the equation that would have unified physics. Gonpo had stopped the dance. He had called the equation an illusion and torn the tapestry. Jack turned toward the terrible figure of Dorje—the master of black arts who had subverted Gonpo. Together, they had destroyed all hope of unity. The chance had vanished forever and he was lost. The many-armed figure of Mahakala the destroyer marched toward him with his dangling skulls. And now it was he who carried the sword.

The cursed bell rang at slow hypnotic intervals while Mahakala slashed Jack's tapestry into writhing wormlike fragments. Universal death reduced all knowledge. All hope became despair. The traitors had thrown him into a pit so deep that he did not even feel himself sitting down obediently on the blanket, facing away from Dorje, but so close to the crib that in the dim light he seemed to be emerging from between the knees of the guru.

Helpless, Jack's hands unfolded like flowers, and his back straightened as though Dorje were forcing a sliver down his spine. He was impaled. Frozen. While beside him Gonpo's face glazed with sweat.

When the others arrived, Jack was sitting absolutely still, his face blank.

24

Do you mind, Sergeant, not smoking. It aggravates my allergies."

"Sorry, sir. This last film is so exciting, I forgot myself."

"So let's get on with it."

"Well, you see, we've pinpointed the cave complex, you can see the animals here, yak, sir, and the horses and tent. Well, now if you'll look to the north, you'll notice the airstrip?"

"So?"

"You'll notice the road leading here, sir, less than ten miles from the cave complex, sir."

"So?"

"We have reason to suspect, if you'll note these trucks and earthmovers, that a considerable construction project is being completed by the Chinese, sir."

"And?"

"We find it curious that there is little surface activity. We believe the Chinese may be constructing a large underground complex and moving some nuclear facilities to the Himalayas, sir."

"I see." Sergeant Muldoon was such an enthusiast of high-technology espionage that it was necessary to temper him at all times.

But if he had stumbled on a shift of Chinese nuclear capacity, almost by accident, Colonel Yanker had to give him his due.

"And how would this concern our friends in Dolpo?"

"Well, that's precisely the question. It seems a bit coincidental, don't you think, that we discovered this development while tracking Mr. Wilson? Perhaps the physicist knows about these facilities. It is a discovery of some magnitude. We think a higher-level operation may be justified."

"Do we suppose Nepal is privy to these developments?"

"Unlikely. In any case, Nepal is in no position to object. But the Indians are. If they found out about this they'd make a real fuss. Since they've gone nuclear at just this same time, there seems to be, if I may say so, a nexus here."

"Nexus?"

"I've been reading Mr. Miller, sir, his trilogy. Nexus is the middle volume. Fascinating reading if you care for his use of language. And a most bizarre imagination, I must say."

"So we have a nexus?"

"Yes. A nexus of events which could be coincidence, of course. But the very first rule in the surveillance game, sir, is to suspect coincidence. We find it very curious that these events should be occurring at the same time."

"A nuclear nexus, in other words."

"Well said, sir. And it makes the activities of this physicist of no small interest."

"Do you propose we drop operatives into this region?"

"That would be difficult, in our opinion, but may be worth considering. Certainly, if this man emerges alive, he is worth intense scrutiny. Traveling with him is a Tibetan collaborator who acts as interpreter."

"Collaborator?"

"Yes, sir, she was trained by the Chinese and worked for them until 1969. She is part of the Tibetan community in Kathmandu and under surveillance by the Nepalese because of her activity in Lhasa."

"She?"

205

"Precisely. He is cohabiting with this woman."

"Oh?"

"There is also a Russian agent in the same vicinity."

At last Colonel Yanker sat up straight. "Is Wilson aware of these things?"

"Unlikely, since we only discovered the Chinese construction this week. I expect he's pretty well aware of the physicist's personal relations with the woman."

"And you think some action is required."

"Required to be considered if I may put it that way."

"An airdrop would be very difficult without Indian and Nepali assistance. Mrs. Gandhi is not very cooperative since the Pakistani affair."

"Then we might prepare an overland expedition."

"This would require more support from the Nepalis than we now command. Despite this fascinating scenario, I believe we had best rely on Mr. Wilson for the time being. Nothing from him yet?"

"No. We suspect his radio may be malfunctioning."

"Let's wait a week," Colonel Yanker said. "I will bring these matters to council tomorrow."

"Thank you, sir."

"And Sergeant?"

"Yes, sir."

"You really ought to quit smoking. The evidence is quite conclusive."

"That's what my wife says. But it's harder to break than a heroin habit."

"Is that a fact?"

"I'm thinking of hypnotism."

"Really? Well, let me know how it goes."

25

He must have slept. The moonlight was milky. Tsering and the two monks stood silhouetted at the mouth of the cave, and the Onion lay on his side watching. The Chinese woman had been moaning since the firing stopped. Wilson sat up clasping the Hi-Power—something was wrong, he could feel it. They were standing in the cave entrance, perfect targets, and Tsering was speaking. Voices answered in Tibetan. She came to the Chinese woman and shook her gently. The moaning stopped. The Russian was smoking that stinking pipe again. Wilson would give anything to know what the KGB was thinking about recent events. He'd had a bellyful, from the look on his face. Tsering, too. But so had Wilson. There were only a couple of possibilities, he figured, either a drug in the food—but who could have done that?—or else some kind of mass hysteria or psychosis hypnotically induced by the chanting and music. That sort of thing was well documented.

Or the one other possibility—that Gonpo was right about Tibet. That up here these lamas *could* do some of the weird shit attributed to them. Like project those demonic holograms he and the Russian had shot up. A pity he'd wasted two clips in the Browning instead of a couple of rolls of film in the Nikon. Amazing no one was hurt. And somehow, in the middle of it, Malloy and Gonpo had vanished, leaving

Boris and Tsering behind. So much for conspiracy. Malloy was the one. Who would have thought it? He was up to something all right. This lama, too. Right up to their ears.

"We'll go now," Tsering said.

"Those assholes will let us go?"

Her face was drawn, haggard with lack of sleep, whatever had happened to her in the cave, and yesterday with the Khampa; nothing of Kathmandu remained. But he felt the same way.

She managed a weary smile. "They won't let us go *down*, only up."

"So we're still in a trap."

"Yes."

It was amazing what this kind of predicament would do. After what they'd been through, he felt no animosity toward her. Even Boris was a kind of ally. More firepower. They were all in the same boat. Except Malloy.

"Malloy's up there?"

"Yes."

"Then let's go."

"We can't leave Li here alone," Tsering said.

"You sure as hell can't get her up there."

She knelt beside the woman and talked to her at some length. There was no question she was in bad shape. She was injured and could barely sit up, and emotionally she was a mess. Completely loony. Of course, this cave episode would have deranged anyone. Tsering's voice was calming her, but how in the hell could they get her up to that cave without a rope?

"Can I help?" Wilson asked, surprised at his offer. But what the hell, it was the only way out of here. He stood over the two women, looking expectant.

Tsering was as surprised as he. "What can you do?" she asked.

"Maybe Boris and I can carry her."

She considered that a moment. "Impossible. Only one person can climb at a time. And she can't stand for anyone to touch her—not a man."

208

That annoyed him, but apparently gave Tsering an idea, because she jumped up and went to the cave entrance, calling out in Tibetan. A familiar voice answered. He thought Angmo would have fled by now, or been seized by the Khampa, but damned if she didn't climb up and appear in the entrance, that strong chunky little body with the admirable high firm breasts. If she just wouldn't smile, but seeing him, she did—a visible cavity in the dim moonlight. And he couldn't help himself, he grinned back at her. Another ally.

She and Tsering approached the Chinese woman and knelt beside her. As Tsering translated between Chinese and Tibetan, Wilson followed their gesticulations. Since the woman would not be touched by a man, Angmo was going to carry her up the cliff. And Li was agreeing rather than remain alone in the cave with the Khampa on the loose below. Tsering helped the Chinese woman sit up, and Angmo squatted in front of her, giving directions. The woman put her arms around Angmo's neck. More discussion, and Wilson saw the problem. Li was too weak to hold on to Angmo. He pulled off his belt and stepped forward while Li looked at him wide-eyed and moaning. But Angmo grinned approval, and Tsering was silent. He crossed the woman's wrists over Angmo's breasts—feeling them firm and alive beneath his hands—and drew his belt tight. It would hurt her wrists a little, but the alternative, falling down the cliff, was not attractive. Now Angmo was holding out her own hands to him. He took them, callused little wads of bone and tendon, and pulled her to her feet. The surge of her powerful thighs sent an electric quiver back through his arms and down into his own thighs. The Chinese woman dangled moaning from Angmo's neck. She had to get the weight off her arms, and Wilson stepped forward. But he was afraid to touch her. It was Tsering who took her legs and wrapped them around Angmo's waist. Wearing this Chinese woman instead of her porter's basket, Angmo moved effortlessly toward the moonlight.

She had carried eighty-pound loads over the mountains, and he knew the power of those thighs well enough. They'd just about thrown out his lower back and left bruises on his hips. She was nothing but one big muscle. Planting her bare feet solidly, she stepped outside the cave, pivoted with what must be nearly one hundred pounds of dead weight and began to ascend. The Chinese woman moaned as Angmo planted one bare foot in the first chiseled step, reached for the next, and straining, almost slipping back, stretched her body up along the stone face. She had made the first foot of a twenty-foot climb. Wilson paused a moment, then—what the hell, somebody had to do it—he stepped up behind her and spoke to Angmo, without even considering the interpreter. "Tell her to put her feet on my shoulders when you need a rest."

Angmo glanced down at him. He gestured at his shoulders, pointing at Li, and Angmo managed a strained grimace of understanding as she raised her leg for the next step, paused concentrating, and then heaved, the weight of both women suspended on one straining leg. Wilson reached up, put his palm on the familiar muscular buttocks and pushed. Her body straightened along the wall.

"Ready?" Wilson called out. He felt the weight shift from one buttock to the next as she prepared the next step. He felt her leg lift, felt the Chinese woman's thigh against his hand as he pushed. This time, coordinating her effort with his, Angmo made the step more easily. At the fourth step, the Chinese woman helped; she put her feet down on Wilson's shoulders and took the weight off Angmo for a moment. He could smell her feet in canvas shoes and feel her legs trembling against his face, while he clung to the rock.

"Ho!" Angmo said, and the woman raised her legs to Angmo's waist. This time, just at the right moment, Wilson shoved Angmo's buttocks forcefully so that she moved in one smooth motion up the rock.

From below, Tsering and Boris watched the ascent of this human caterpillar. And from below them, the Khampa stood watching and commenting. What they were saying surprised Tsering and made her look more closely at Wilson. One of the Khampa had seen him and Angmo together—she on top, his skinny white legs thrashing under her like a mouse hare. The men laughed at the story, imitating his love yelps as she banged him down against the sharp gravel. They sounded

210

like a pack of dogs in the moonlight. But Wilson, clinging to the cliff beneath the two women, was oblivious to this obscene chorus. She glanced at Boris. He was oblivious, too, studying the cliff above with great seriousness. She had never seen so much hair on a man. He was matted with fur like an animal, from his chest to his thighs. But when he began to move like a single erotic muscle, all that fur had made electricity on her skin. Now, bulky and rigid, he was only an observer for the KGB.

Thick cloud cover obscured the moon, casting a fluorescent, shadowless light. The air was still and smelled of snow.

Whatever she expected in the upper cave, it was not what met her eyes. Angmo and Li sat exhausted against one wall, Wilson beside them. The two monks and Gonpo sat to one side of the meditation crib. Jack sat in front of it, uninjured but looking awful. His parka hung from bony shoulders, heavy beard and uncombed hair obscured his gaunt face, and the shaman sat so close behind him that only his face showed over Jack's shoulder, as if Jack had grown another head or the shaman had grown Jack's body. Looking at this two-headed figure, she felt the fear of the middle cave return. A two-headed demon had towered over her and the others, and she had groveled beneath it. Now the demon reappeared in this human form.

She had seen these crazy hermits in Lhasa often enough. She had seen them buried alive for weeks at a time, she had seen them sit out in winter along the frozen river; she had seen them crossing Tibet on their bellies. They sat alone in dark caves for years. But what such asceticism showed her was precisely the opposite of what they intended. Instead of the possibility of nirvana, it demonstrated the truth of socialism: if these spiritual parasites could do it, so could the workers. A new man was possible.

But she was so shaken by her visions below that it was difficult to look at this one. His death's mask hung on Jack's shoulder, while Jack's own face was so far away, so deep within himself, and so filled with

211

some awful presence, that she felt herself go rigid again with a fear worse than she had felt the night the Red Guards burned Samye monastery and killed the monks; even worse than the night she nearly froze on the pass. Because this fear came from inside—like the demons of the middle cave—and not from outside like Red Guards or blizzards. It was the fear of madness. But when she looked to Gonpo for help, he was explaining to Wilson that he must sit in front of Jack and continue his meditation.

"No," she cried. "Stop it!"

Gonpo looked at her severely. "It is too late. You must be brave now."

All these years she had pitied Gonpo but now would cling to him like a child. She wanted to put her head in his lap and feel his hand stroking her hair.

"You must sit. As if your life depends upon it. Jack's life does depend upon it. You must let these things happen that need to happen. Look at him."

She couldn't look at him. But she did. The mannequin sitting before her was only a shell of the American physicist. And the awful mask hanging from his shoulder cast a familiar shadow. It rose over her, skulls dangling, bloody sword raised.

"I can't."

"You must consider others before yourself. Tell the Russian to sit with us," Gonpo said calmly. "The Chinese woman must sit too."

Impossible. Li could not move. When Tsering turned frantically to Boris, he asked: "This is the magician?"

"Yes," she said.

"Did he cause those things below?"

The answer tore out of her throat like broken glass. She was back on the Chang Tang in the tent, listening to stories of demons and possession and how the great lamas had flown across the countryside and sent their thoughts visibly, like television pictures, to remote places. The famous lamas spoke to their disciples at great distance, and described events all over Tibet as if they were present. These were lamas who, out of love, sentenced their disciples to horrible mental

and physical tortures, tormenting them with demons and physical pain
and denial. She was a little girl again. And she was sinking into fears
left behind so long ago.

He was happy enough to be in the cave, leaving those cackling bastards down below. He'd expected a bullet up his ass the whole time.
But here they were, Angmo beaded with sweat, Li flat on her back. As
he strung his belt back through the loops of his trousers, he looked at
the famous guru. Hard to see much in this light, but if he was still alive
and looked like that, he was capable of miracles all right.

Malloy looked like one of those plaster Buddhas with a faint smile
at the edge of his lips. A smile! After what he'd done to them. Actually
he looked less a Buddha than a survivor of the Donner party or
Auschwitz. But Wilson probably looked no better. His own beard had
quit itching at least, but every time he moved, a variety of odors
wafted up through his clothes. Almost as bad as the Russian. Not that
it made any difference up here, because whatever was rotting in this
cave made him dizzy.

He sat as Gonpo told him, but arranged the Browning, two cam-
eras and tape recorder in front of him. Right out in the open. And
Gonpo didn't say a word. Tsering was a mess, almost as bad as the
Chinese woman, but that didn't please him as much as it might have.
They were in deep shit here, and she had come through pretty well.
Even the Onion was holding up. They weren't the problem any more.
Other than those assholes with the M-16s, the only real problem now
was Malloy. He'd give anything to see inside that head. Because if
Malloy had some sort of control over all that weird shit in the lower
cave, he'd have a report for Denver that would knock their socks off.
He needed evidence. He'd like to get Malloy out of here and debrief
his ass off.

This time, by God, he'd reach for the cameras before the Browning, because any more bullets flying around in a cave this size would
sure as hell do some damage. It would take some willpower, but he'd
get the evidence. Eagerly, Wilson began to breathe, counting each

breath, while Gonpo argued with Tsering. Nothing distracted him. Not even the Onion arranging himself so close beside him that their knees touched. He could see the orange Denver Bronco cap out of the corner of his eye and felt the fur cap sitting on his own head like an electric heater. He grinned. A hell of a swap.

Somehow the Chinese woman got off her back and joined them— anything not to be left alone. He felt her feet on his shoulders and her trembling knees against his face. He began to wheeze like an engine, forcing his breath in and out, trying to drown out his thoughts and get back to that moment when the demons appeared. He must be getting the knack because his mind quieted, and when the monks and Gonpo began making that racket, he almost felt comforted. Except that he could do without the trumpet. It sounded like somebody blowing through a thighbone. With the marrow still in it. There was some other instrument he hadn't heard before, a single string being plucked, and he glanced up. Gonpo and the monks were chanting. But when they paused, the sound grew loud in his mind. Not an instrument but a human voice. But Malloy had his mouth closed. That left the skull behind him. Its mouth was open, but the sound wasn't coming from there. Irritating, like a power saw on Sunday morning, when he was lying in bed with Mudra at the cabin. Now his breathing grew raspy, and he was rising and falling with the sound.

Outside the cave, silence thickened as clouds pressed down on the mountains; the wail of the trumpet stopped, the drum stopped, the bell rang at greater and greater intervals. And slowly the outer silence entered the cave like a palpable substance, absorbent and soothing. Jack sat effortlessly, focused, his limbs so fluid. A thousand years of yoga sat before Tsering. As clouds dimmed the moon, she watched him through a kind of brightening haze. Only gradually did she recognize the source of light.

The four of them were seated in a row before Jack like spectators at a play. Angmo had retreated to the rear of the cave. On one side, Tsering could feel Li relax. On the other side, she felt Boris's body heat, smelled his sweat and fur. Beside him sat Wilson. Inside her mind was this strange phosphorescent glow like dawn, when objects appear but it is not clear at precisely what point they become recognizable. Then she saw the source of light.

Jack's palms rested open in his lap, as though he were holding a bowl. From within the bowl came light. And as she watched, from within the light came a dark cloud, roiling up from his hands. Flickering with internal light, it rose and opened into a dark flower on a thick stem. At the base of the stem, a delicate ring of cloud appeared . . . like a vulva from which this monstrous shape was emerging. As the demons in the cave below had towered over her, this cloud towered over her, but there were no skulls or bloody swords or bulging eyes or grinning fangs. It was absolutely nothing but itself—an elemental shape she had never seen, but recognized. The boiling cloud turned yellow, scarlet, green; lightning flashed from within. She shielded her eyes, but too late, the sound enveloped her like deep water, and a tremendous pressure crushed the breath from her lungs.

As the steel doors opened and the shape emerged, the flash exploded. It was all he could do to keep his finger depressed, clicking off exposures at one-second intervals. Fire blossomed from the silo as this monster emerged from the earth. Slow and ponderous, almost reptilian, it came out streaming hot gases and hung over the cornfields. Then slowly, as if breathing in freedom after long confinement, it rose on its tail and arched into the sky. Blindly he reached for the other camera, fingers fumbling, eyes closed against the blast.

The light was reflected against the far wall, and instinctively he pushed Anna and Vanka to the floor, counting the seconds. Airburst or ground? She was screaming and the boy struggled in his arms. One, two, three, four, five, six . . . two kilometers. Far enough if it were a megaton or less. The wallpaper blistered and smoked. Then glass sprayed into the room like water from the hose in summer, when the children arced the spray over one another's naked bodies.

The rock shook and from far back toward the dormitories came a sound like the roof collapsing. She heard Commander Wu calling for auxiliary power. They had armed all the missiles when the steel doors vaporized, and the cave was brilliantly lit. Commander Wu's body grew transparent, and his ribs cast dark lines across her retina—like waves on the carp pond at home. At dusk.

She was prostrating herself before the foreigner who burned like a funeral pyre, sliding the length of her body along the stone and raising her clasped palms. She stood and knelt again, extending her body toward him and chanting, "The guru is great. The guru is great."

26

After the second round of tea, just when they had all begun to adjust to a Tibetan lama's presence in her living room, Lia said, "We've been trying to contact Jack. But it's hard to judge our success."

"Lia!" Mukerjee said. "Is this appropriate?"

The lama looked patient. "Contact him? No one can contact him right now."

"We're using certain methods for remote viewing developed at a university near here."

"Ah," the lama said. "Remote viewing. I see. Does this have something to do with physics?"

"Perhaps," she said. "If it works, then it's physics. We're dating and recording all our procedures, which we'll compare with his account when he returns."

The lama clasped his fingers under his chin. One of these people had gone to Dolpo in search of a naljorpa. Now this woman was trying to make a science of inner vision. Astounding. These people, who had mastered technology, sought the simplest things as though they were miracles. Still, he had an odd inclination to help. The man with the pipe gave off quite remarkable emanations. And the woman Lia had an attractive compassion and awareness. She was probably older than she looked, living here alone so far as he could ascertain. But beneath a shapeless shirt and loose trousers her body gave notice. She hid herself, probably from the nature of her work and the sort of mind drawn to physics. It made her angular and forthright. But, yes, he was inclined to help these people. They had an interesting link with Malloy, and if there were anything to discover here, this was a good way to penetrate their inner heart.

"Perhaps you can give us some guidance," Lia said.

"I don't understand."

"Jack feels that this lama in Dolpo has psychic powers and has spoken highly of you. Perhaps you can give us some additional insight into the process."

"What is the process exactly?"

"You explain," Lia said to Browny. "I'll bring the materials." She returned with the drawing pad and pencils and tape recorder as Browny explained how one of them served as viewer while another asked questions and the third looked for flaws in the procedure: leading questions, answers that were reasoned rather than seen, or assumptions of any kind.

The lama looked bemused, but after a series of questions clarifying the process, he agreed to serve as interviewer.

Lia immediately volunteered as viewer. She closed her eyes, clearing her mind as she did near sleep, letting the white screen appear. "Mountains," she said finally.

"Why?" the lama asked.

She opened her eyes. "Why?"

"You know he went to the mountains. Try again."

She closed her eyes for a while, and then reached for the drawing pad. She drew a conical shape.

"Are you near or far?" the lama asked.

She thought a moment. "Near."

"What else?"

"Stands by itself. Dark-colored."

"Walk around it."

218

"Walk?"

"Try."

She modified the drawing, making the shape squatter.

"Touch it," the lama said.

"What?"

"Touch it."

"It's soft," she said with surprise. "Resilient. All alone on a flat area."

"What do you see beyond the flatness?"

"Walls."

"Why do you say walls?"

"It's like camping in the mountains, you know, when you pitch your tent in a meadow but all around are mountains."

Lama Z saw the black tent quite clearly, contoured in the Tibetan style against the winds of the high plateau. But it was clear that she had no idea what she was seeing.

"Now walk away," the lama said.

Lia frowned with concentration. "How far?"

"Keep walking."

"There are echoes. We're inside . . ."—she drew a circle on the paper—"this shape . . . well, more ellipsoid than that."

"How did you enter?" the lama asked.

Without hesitation, she marked a place on the drawing. "Here, there is only one way in."

And then the Hindu, Mukerjee, said excitedly, "But it's not so dark, there are lights."

Such spontaneous comments were a violation of their protocol, but when the lama turned to Mukerjee none of them thought to object.

"Can you count the lights?" he asked.

"No, two or three and . . . I think there are people in this space."

"A woman," Lia said.

"Alone?"

"No. Others," she said. "Another woman." She looked surprised. "And another."

The cave and butter lamps were clear in Lama Z's mind now, as he reinforced their vision and let them see through him. The image inside the cave sharpened. Tsering was alive and well. There was indeed another woman, cloudy, but, yes, this woman scientist in Berkeley was seeing truly. There were two women. And yet another woman.

Then the older man with the pipe, to whom the others deferred, spoke. "Jack is present, but . . . what? He is very sick."

"How do you know this?"

"I see a shape."

"Can you sketch it?"

"Perhaps a storm."

He drew a large circle, paused, put a stem on it like a flower.

"Is that a flower?" Mukerjee asked.

"Flower-shaped, but not a flower," Browny said. He drew a face on the blossom, mouth, nose, eyes.

"A person?" Lia asked.

The lama was silent. It was not a person.

"It's like a head turning and watching, but that's not it."

This old man with the pipe could see with his heart, and Lama Z watched him carefully. There was something to be learned here. The shape rose in Lama Z's mind, too, like one of the wrathful deities. But that was not correct. It was not a shape from the Tibetan pantheon. He looked at the notepad. "Can you see it from above?"

The man called Browny was silent a long while, concentrating as the others focused their energy behind him. Browny blew a cloud of smoke that hung in the still room, and all eyes followed the smoke, as if the answer to events in Tibet lay in this palpable smoke in Berkeley.

Lia gave a small groan: "There is pain, people are hurt."

And still Browny was silent. Then, suddenly, he filled in the shape on the page, obliterating the face and expanding it. He sloped the stem carefully up into a roiling, cloudlike base. Gradually the mushroom shape became clear. No one said a word.

For a moment, Lama Z was paralyzed. The wrathful deities had all vanished. They had been sucked into this mushroom cloud that was rising in each of their minds. The naljorpa was dead. He was dead but had left this ominous presence behind. It rose out of Malloy while figures lay around him like corpses.

Suddenly cups on the tea tray began to rattle. A book fell from the shelf; curtains swayed as if a wind had entered the closed room. The lamp beside the couch began to swing in circles. All the objects inside the room came alive, and they were all on their feet, except for the lama. Mukerjee opened the front door, while Browny stood indecisive at the center of the room. "A quake," he said.

Mukerjee stepped outside and Browny followed him. Lia remained standing beside the seated lama, who was watching the shape rise in his mind, obliterating all the wrathful and benign deities, leaving nothing. This naljorpa was a man of remarkable power, and Lama Z stiffened. Dorje was dead. Malloy was alone. And now Lama Z was condemned to help these people.

The house quieted with a faint creaking sound. Tears ran down Lia's face. "Jack's dying," she said. "He's dying. What can we do?"

"Not dying," the lama said. "Yet." He focused carefully. He had not expected to be drawn in this way. But the shape still loomed in his mind. He must help.

The others stood in the garden yelling for Lia and the lama to come out. "What can we do?" she said. "We're responsible for him."

What indeed! Dorje had left Malloy with this thing that obliterated all the wrathful and benign deities, ate them at a gulp like a huge mouth. Why would he do that to any man? The burden was too much. The next sharp shock drove them out of the house, into the wan late October light.

"One of the many advantages of living in California," Browny said. "These little episodes. This was sharper than most."

Lama Z would never have believed it possible without more training, but these scientists had reached Malloy, and their vision had allowed Lama Z himself to see into Malloy's heart. Lia was too desirous of seeing, blurred by some deep emotion, and Mukerjee could not relax fully, but the man with the pipe had great power. He had seen the shape inside Malloy. The shape that Malloy now carried like a huge seed. Were they prepared to receive it?

221

The air was chill beneath a gloomy overcast. They went back into the house but were silent, shaken by the quake, as if the visions inside their minds had been connected to the shaking earth. Such a possibility, Lama Z understood, must make scientists very nervous. They had reached the limit of their experience with psychic energy, and now their science blocked them from further progress. Mukerjee quickly excused himself and jogged off into the dusk, adding another three miles to his total. Browny, Lia and the lama sat down.

"Are we deceiving ourselves?" Browny said at last. "Is there anything true in what we're seeing?"

The lama said nothing.

"We've been obsessed with this thing for years." Browny's pipe was dead in his hands. The earthquake had put it out. "But why has it destroyed our gathering now? Why do I feel the presence?"

This man was worthy of deep respect. He was open to experience, and he had deep insight. But Lama Z had no answer for him. The naljorpa was dead on the border of Tibet, and Malloy had been left with this modern demon. But why in Dolpo, when this awful cloud was far more present here in Berkeley, or in Denver, or Tokyo?

"This I don't know," the lama said. "But I am prepared to find out."

The shape on the pad lay open on the coffee table. Suddenly Lia tore off the sheet of paper and crumpled it up. "I hate that," she said. "Will you stay to dinner? I make a fine vegetable curry."

Browny's wife expected him home, and he declined. But when Lia offered to take the lama back to his hotel afterward, he agreed to stay to dinner.

"If I may use your phone?" he asked.

"Of course," she said. "It's in the bedroom."

27

Jack stumbled toward the cave entrance and a strangely luminescent sky. Shadows swirled beyond the mouth of the cave and when he reached for them, rested docilely on his outstretched palms. They brushed his upturned face and stuck to his tongue. Ash! They were flakes of radioactive ash: the gamma rays were blasting his marrow, blood, liver. Lesions and blindness would follow.

"Can you walk on your own?" Gonpo asked.

"Why?"

"The seed has been cast. You must find fertile ground."

"Nothing will grow."

"It will if you go where you must."

"Don't you understand, in a few days or even hours we begin to vomit, the brain swells, diarrhea, infection . . ."

Gonpo looked at him with concern. "I do not understand this transmission you have received, but the direction is clear. You have the seed syllables of a new mantra."

Jack was not really annoyed at Gonpo's stupidity since he could not be expected to understand the details of radiation sickness. There was no need to alarm him further, nor was there any need for them to walk through the radioactive wasteland of Dolpo. It was pointless in the time remaining. They would stay here and wait for the end.

"You must go very far if you wish to strengthen this sunyata experience. As the arrow to the target, you must not look back."

"Gonpo, there is nowhere to go. Time has ended."

"You are still obscured by illusion."

No illusion. The radioactive glow cast a marvelous clarity. He looked down at a man standing with an automatic rifle. Jack smiled. Bullets would be no use. Didn't this man understand that the ash falling on his upturned face was burning his synapses, that beta and gamma radiation were destroying his corpuscles? He had the illusion of life, but his future was determined by a simple graph: radiation intensity plotted against time of exposure.

"It is useless," he called down to the man. "Guns are useless. Do you want to kill me?" He waved his arms. "It'll be a favor. You'll want to kill yourself soon."

The man raised his weapon toward Jack.

"Have you no idea of the importance of what has happened?" Gonpo said.

Jack laughed at him. After all these years of dread, all these years of guilt and waiting, did he not understand the importance of what had happened? What had happened excised the meaning of words like *importance*.

"Look at that poor bastard down there, ready to shoot me," Jack said, waving his arms. He shouted down, "Make it a good one."

"You cannot expect him to understand. Are you able to walk?"

"The weakness is only beginning."

"I will accompany you."

"Where? There is no place to walk, nor any reason to go. We have truly arrived at the country which is nowhere."

"This is admirable," Gonpo said. "But you must reach the pass before the storm closes it."

Jack did not reply. All his thoughts had been reversed. Once, it had been so important to cross the pass and reach Dolpo. Once, he had worried about doing harm to others. But none of it made the slightest difference. He was free. The guerrilla standing with a rifle was no more dangerous than one of the Tantric demons conjured by the mind.

"Why bother with the pass?" he said finally. "We might as well walk toward Crystal Monastery or Tibet. Or remain here at Twilight Mountain. All directions are the same now."

"This is true," Gonpo said, a little puzzled. "It is a sign of the white light of liberation. But in order to further the Dharma, Dorje has condemned you to *this* world. You're needed here."

"Then he and I ought to have a little chat about what remains of this world."

"You must leave."

"Must?" Jack looked up from the blasted landscape of Dolpo, stretching in the radioactive glow. "Must? This word has no meaning. I will speak with Dorje."

"No!" There was desperation in Gonpo's voice.

"And you will translate. He told me the world would end if I misstepped. So I misstepped and it did. I want to know how, even though the answer no longer makes a difference. This question is as good as any other."

"I see," Gonpo said. "You truly do not understand yet. Come." He turned back into the cave. It was a risk he would have to take as the only way to force Jack's departure.

The Russian, the American, the two Tibetan women and the Chinese lay sprawled on the stone like those bodies Jack had seen in the televised jungles of Bangladesh and Vietnam, at the charred fringe of Hiroshima and Nagasaki. The maimed, the dead.

"They are blessed," Jack said, "and free from the final hours of sickness."

But these last hours were also a blessing because they allowed him to pierce illusion. Tsering lay before him, a momentary shape risen from the void, a quantum resonance which had flickered through existence. The other human shapes had as much meaning as the random flux of particles in the bubble chamber. They came into being and vanished. He had failed them. But how? He had a dim memory of a dance, an equation on a blackboard, and a certainty of the way. But instead of the way he had killed all of them. Now he turned toward the man who had done this awful thing.

Dorje lay facedown across the edge of the crib, and the odor Jack had been smelling for days was not an ancient rattlesnake den: it was the smell of a man being butchered for vultures; it was waking to blood slick and bone fragments; it was the odor of death reaching the nostrils of the still living.

Jack pulled the dorje from his parka, the ugly bronze spider that had spun this lethal web, and he flung it down on the stone. The scepter ricocheted into the dead man's face, jolting his body, and then it fell back to the stone with a dull sound. Jack stared at this stupid object.

"You do not know the meaning of this word *alone*," Dorje had told him. "But you will." Jack had groveled on the bottom of a primordial seabed. Now he stood alone in the wreckage of what he could have prevented.

The trumpet blew a single forlorn yowl, answered by the drum. So, even waiting for the end, the monks persisted.

"Now you see." Gonpo's voice came from the edge of consciousness.

Jack was silent. In the simple, shadowless light that leveled all before it, he knelt in grief, among the corpses. Knelt beside the woman who had given him another kind of life. He touched her face. Put his own face near hers and smelled her breath. The odor of smoke and sweat, food and excrement enveloped him.

Gonpo watched. The power of Dorje's transmission hung in the balance. If Jack clung to Tsering, he would never leave, and Gonpo did not have the means to force him. Dorje had held his consciousness three days after death, waiting for the moment of transmission. Only the greatest Siddha could accomplish so much. And now the man who carried the spark clung to human love. Gonpo watched him struggle, kneeling with his face next to hers, stroking her hair, pressing his lips to her face. Gonpo's heart sank. All was lost.

Jack touched her hand, and her fingers closed around his thumb as his daughter's fingers had once dumbly taken his thumb to her toothless mouth. Sucking. Beside her lay another woman who must have been loved. Her face, too, was warm. And the thick chest of the Russian with the strong odor was elastic beneath his palm. Wilson lay gently curled in upon himself.

He must not wake them. A dim memory of an equation came into his mind but his physics had vanished along with all other meaning. He clasped his head in agony. What was he doing here in Dolpo?

"Now," Gonpo said. "Let us leave."

Gonpo stopped breathing. Would Jack leave this woman? The picture came to him of a familiar landscape, a river beneath willows, and Jack—quite white-haired but still lean and angular—stooping over Tsering lying in the grass. They were in Lhasa. He, too, wished to remain here where he had found peace after so many years. Neither did he want to struggle through the cold predawn toward a snow-bound pass. Yet he must do this last thing for Dorje, into whose face Jack had flung the scepter that symbolized the means of enlightenment. Gonpo picked up the familiar comforting weight and held it before Jack's dazed eyes. An offering. Jack reached for it with feeble hands, and Gonpo let him take the dorje, watching anxiously as he raised it to his face, eyes widening with recognition. Then his fingers opened and the metal object fell back to the stone with a dull ringing, and Gonpo was overcome by sudden weakness. Dorje's attempt to reach out of Twilight Mountain had failed.

Jack staggered to the cave entrance, balancing precariously, and looked up at the falling snow. He held out his hand, examining the melting flakes on his palm. He stared up at the moon-luminous clouds from which the snow fell, as if trying to understand the connection. He was turning back into the cave, and Gonpo cried out in protest but managed only a groan. Jack was on his knees. He was stretching one leg below the entrance, groping for the first step.

Gonpo rushed to the cave edge and stared straight down at the crown of Jack's head. The scepter was meaningless—a bit of metal rubbish—it was this descending skull that carried the entire universe. Gonpo quickly followed Jack down the granite face of Twilight Mountain.

The man with the rifle stood shivering in the snow, watching Jack stumble as though he were very ill, or very old. Gonpo followed him into the lower cave and directed his movements as he would direct a small child. He helped Jack pack his sleeping bag and tent and a little food. Each act seemed new. It was near dawn and time was short, but Jack needed to discover the truth of each act for himself. When at last they emerged into the deepening snow, he stopped, befuddled, staring at the snow as if it were some novel substance. He knelt to examine their footprints, tracing the shapes with his fingers.

Gonpo waited.

The Khampa guard, who was watching the odd behavior of the foreigner, said, "Why?"

"Dorje sends us back into the world," Gonpo replied quickly.

"The blessed one still lives?" the guard asked, blowing on his hands.

"Yes. But he wishes for you and the others to remain here."

"For how long?"

"There will be a sign."

An awful sign: Chinese soldiers destroying the ghompa. But Jack must carry Dorje's mantra to the world, Gonpo must escort him, and these warriors must live out their karma. Gonpo said nothing more to this man who was as good as dead.

At last they left the valley, and it took all Gonpo's strength not to look back at the ghompa. But he would not risk Jack's glancing back, so he forced himself to look ahead, and what he saw frightened him. Beyond the pass was nothing. His inner vision was void.

Whenever Jack paused, Gonpo urged him on. Dawn replaced moonlight. If they were lucky, they would reach the base of the pass by dusk. But would it be possible to cross? Snow rode on Jack's pack, on his shoulders and uncovered head. When they entered the village late that afternoon, Gonpo would have stopped to rest, but Jack walked straight through, looking neither left nor right as the villagers appeared. This man they had captured five months earlier was impervious to their presence. He walked in a trance. And as he passed, they began to chant: *Ommmmm* . . . Women appeared with prayer wheels. *Mani*. Men clasped their hands together. *Padme*. Children stared in silence. *Hummmmm* . . . One after another, they dropped to their knees, prostrating themselves in the snow as they might have done before Dorje himself.

Gonpo watched the voices energize Jack's body and lengthen his stride, accelerating his departure from Dolpo. Gonpo was no longer necessary, he was only an encumbrance, exhausted, ringing his bell and lurching drunkenly through the snow with numb feet. But he couldn't turn back because Jack would turn back with him. When they reached the base of the pass, it was dark, and the snow was deep, but a yak caravan had broken a trail some hours before. This was propitious. Even now, three days after his death, Dorje was watching over their progress. If Gonpo could only conceal his weakness through this night, all might yet be well.

28

"It's snowing," Wilson said, his voice flat and hopeless. He was feeling so goddamned bleak that even snow made no difference. It was the least of their troubles. They could always wait until spring . . . as corpses.

"They'll come back," Tsering said.

But he saw them walking out through the snow, Jack and his orange pack, Gonpo in his red robes, leaving them prisoners in Dolpo. The sonofabitch was a lot trickier than he'd ever given him credit for.

"No, they won't," Wilson said.

He and Tsering had almost become friends since being blasted by visions and abandoned by Malloy. Even Boris was kind of chummy, huddled under the one blanket against the cold. Jack and Gonpo had swung some sort of deal with the Khampa and left the rest of them with a couple of ratty monks banging bones and a dead guru stinking to high heaven. He was dead the whole time, propped up behind Malloy. So what the hell was going on and what had caused the visions? Malloy and Gonpo were the prime suspects, and three rolls of film were the evidence. If there were images, the visions had been projected like holograms, and he would feel a good deal more secure about his own sanity. The trouble with the hologram theory was that

230

everybody saw something different. Tsering told him what the others had seen: some kind of light rising from Malloy's hands. She agreed. Boris agreed. Even the Chinese woman agreed. Something real, outside their own minds, had appeared in the cave. That was crucial. And that something had better show on film. If it did, and he got out of here in one piece, he'd make bureau chief in one leap. But the sonofabitch had gotten clean away, leaving the rest of them trapped by the Khampa, without porters or Sherpas, in a blizzard that was the beginning of winter.

Angmo huddled against him and he had no complaints. She was warm. On the other side under the blanket, the Chinese woman, Tsering and Boris were all jammed against him. They waited for dawn in a Himalayan cave where people had probably huddled since the Neanderthals. Left with a dead guru and a couple of monks banging away and chanting. It was like being sucked back down his brainstem into another region. Only two months ago he'd been playing tennis on top of a five-story garage in Denver and drinking mai tais.

He felt a hand on his crotch. Impossible! Only hours after she'd been prostrating herself frantically before Malloy, as though he were the Buddha incarnate, and she was rummaging around in his trousers. He shifted slightly to give her a better angle, and she grabbed his cock with a cold hand. She exposed her rotted teeth in a grin.

"*Om* . . . ," the monks chanted.

"*Mani* . . . ," she echoed, wiggling her fingers.

Under the circumstances, it was about as likely as an armed Minuteman rising out of a silo, but damned if he wasn't getting a hard-on. There you were, anything could happen in this place.

Her hand was warming up, but the angle still wasn't great, so he rolled toward her and threw the mass of bodies on the other side of him into commotion. They'd been doing this for hours under the small blanket, moving as one body in order to stay warm. None of them would guess the reason for this latest disruption. Or would they? Come to think of it, Boris had been shifting around a lot over there. You don't suppose—with women on either side of him . . . Angmo started licking his ear. Her breath smelled like sardines.

≈

After the past twenty-four hours, this new thing was scarcely alarming. Could have been in his mind, could have been outside—made little difference. Huddled against Tserosha, he felt Anna's body and Vanka's trembling beneath his own as the building collapsed. Now the sound of automatic weapons. Not the M-16s that had kept them pinned in the cave for two days, but Kalashnikov assault rifles. For a moment he thought troops had come to rescue him from the collapsed building. But he knew better. Rising quickly from the pile of bodies, pushing the Chinese woman and Tserosha back to the floor, as he'd pushed his own wife and son to safety, he drew the Tokarev and slithered on his belly toward the entrance. These damned monks making their infernal noise had become intertwined with his hallucinations and the sound of weapons, a constant texture around him, like one of those straw baskets Baba Grusha made on the commune. She was so old and gnarled and half blind that none of the communal affairs touched her, weaving baskets that would hold onions and squash and potatoes in the brief Leningrad fall, and muttering her prayers. And now, listening to the methodical chant of the monks, her grandson felt the comfort of her fingers weaving the rough texture of events around him.

The volume of fire was surprising—a dozen weapons firing and only four bandits left. At last the Kalashnikovs were answered by the American M-16s. So even before he looked down from the cave, he saw what he would see. And his mind was such a curious mixture of hallucinations, unexpected memories, and what should have passed for real events, that he was almost tranquil as he looked out of the cave.

It was dawn of course.

In order to stay out of the line of fire, Wilson had crawled clear around in back of the crib—a stinking mess of straw—and gagged. Actually gagged. How could he ever have thought the man was alive?

232

At the cave mouth, he looked across at the orange Denver Bronco cap and saw himself with drawn pistol peering down from the cave. He shook his head, too exhausted to resist this new illusion, too exhausted even to dread the sight below: the cluster of green uniforms surrounding one of the Khampa, two others stretched out in the snow. The Chinese had struck at dawn in the storm, and the Khampa had had no chance. A voice called out. It was the surviving Tibetan, prompted by a rifle in his back.

Tsering's voice answered. And then she appeared in the cave entrance, a wild figure of tangled hair, sooty blue parka, scuffed boots. She spoke in Chinese. The Chinese soldier spoke to her. Wilson looked at Boris. They were trapped: they might have escaped the Khampa but not the Chinese. Now it was hopeless.

The snow was continuous and slow, falling indifferently from a gray dawn sky. The landscape was coated and transformed into a new bleakness. The black tent had turned white. The surviving Khampa warrior stood, head down. From behind snow-shrouded boulders came more green Chinese soldiers.

Li appeared beside Tsering, smiling for the first time, waving her arms and speaking to the man below. She began to scramble down the stone wall but stopped and spoke to Tsering. Then she continued down to join her colleagues.

"Leave your weapon," Tsering told Wilson. She spoke briefly to the Russian, and then to the two monks at the rear of the cave. They looked at her, but did not move. Again she spoke. Again they watched indifferently. It was clear they would remain with Dorje. If the Chinese wanted them, they could come up to the cave.

"All right," she said to Wilson. "Are you ready?"

"What will they do?"

"This depends on what Li tells them, on what I tell them. Since they are in Nepal, there may be some restraint. You will have to trust me now."

"And her?" He meant Angmo.

"They care nothing for her or the monks. They will believe nothing that happened here. Only that you and Boris are spies. They can understand that. But if your criminal president has made a good accommodation, you may be spared embarrassment. Boris I am not so sure."

Descending, she thought quickly. The last living Khampa, Aten, was doomed. He'd either be executed or taken back to prison. Li knew nothing about Wilson and Boris and Jack except what Tsering had told her, but what would she tell the Chinese? Tsering's own story would have to match, and she would have to find a convincing reason to have crossed the border, and a reason why the Khampa had followed and taken Li captive.

She stepped down into the snow and walked toward the familiar Chinese soldiers, who at one time had protected her and other Tibetans from the Red Guards, until all order broke in 1966. She greeted the one with pockets sewn all over his jacket and a pen conspicuously displayed—the subtle symbols of authority in the people's army.

"You are Tibetan?"

"Yes."

"Why do you speak Chinese?"

She glanced at Li. What had she already told them? The answer to this question would seal her fate. But no easy lie came to her lips.

"I learned at the Beijing Institute for National Minorities."

"You are a Chinese citizen."

"No."

"Why did you cross the border into China with these bandits?"

These were the things that could never be explained to a soldier ten years younger than herself. He looked at her severely, and she knew this was only the beginning of questioning. She must not contradict what Li said, or there was no chance for her. Why had she gone into Tibet? Jack thought she had been sent by Dorje to bring back the Chinese woman. But that was preposterous. And, furthermore, if true, it had been a serious miscalculation, since Li's arrival had destroyed Dorje's ghompa once and for all.

"I don't know why."

He shook his head at her. "Very well, we will find out why later. Who are these foreigners?"

"They are scientists."

"What science?"

"They have come to study Tibetan religion."

"Why are they with these bandits?"

Now she must make a choice. There was no way to know what Aten or Li would say, but only one possible way to disentangle them.

"We are prisoners."

"Prisoners? What nationality are these men?"

Again, there was no point in lying. "American and Russian."

"Why are an American and Russian here together?"

Now Li intervened. "There was another American."

The officer waited for Tsering to confirm this. "Yes. He escaped with a lama."

"Escaped?"

"I told you, we were held by the Khampa."

"Not Khampa. The men from Kham are loyal citizens of China. These bandits are criminals and will be treated as such."

"Then you ask Aten whether we were prisoners or not." She was risking everything on this ploy. Aten must speak before they killed him.

"He will be interrogated in China."

Her heart sank. She had to confirm the Tibetans' function as armed guards for Dorje. Quickly, she asked Aten, "Why did you keep us prisoner?"

He looked at her dull-eyed. "You were not prisoners. You could leave when the lama gave permission."

The officer swung his rifle on Aten, driving him down into the snow. "There will be no talk between the criminals," he said. "Now, foreigners and spies go into the cave."

She turned and saw Wilson and Boris standing in a group of soldiers. Li was watching her with a sympathetic expression. "Where did the other American go?" she asked.

"To join a large expedition nearby," Tsering told her, thinking rapidly. "They will return with other Americans in a day."

The officer looked at her. "There are more Americans?"

"Yes. The American who escaped is bringing help."

It was the best she could do on their behalf. Nothing Li had seen disproved this story, and Li herself could certainly testify to the hostility of the Khampa. But there remained the question of why she had descended into Tibet and been brought back, apparently against her will. The officer was young, her fictional group of Americans near the border had him worried, and the falling snow forced him to make decisions quickly. If Jack and Gonpo returned now, alone, all of them were doomed. But they would not return. Wilson was right. They had taken the visions from the caves and discarded the rest of them like debris.

The officer pushed her down. She sat, waiting for her fate to be decided.

29

She looked down at the round brown belly and soft breasts. He had the skin of a thirty-year-old, quite remarkable, and even now his face was benign, almost meditative. That was terribly exciting.

"So the purpose is to *conserve* sexual energy?" she asked.

"Correct."

"This is true of women too?" she asked.

"Correct."

"Then I am failing badly."

"It takes many years to master."

"I think," she said, "that I am about to fail once again." The idea of *not* coming was producing remarkable results.

"This will pass in time. However, if you move your leg, so, and turn, so, there are possibilities for delay and perhaps transcendence."

But she ignored him, canting her hips forward and jamming him down into the bed, jiggling all the Buddha fat into quivering ripples.

"Just hold still," she said, as the ripples started in her own belly. "I'll transcend later."

Since she wasn't supposed to be coming, she could simply let her head fall back and stare up at the ceiling while a warm feeling rose up her body to her head. And then the buzzing sensation moved back *down* her spine. She might get the hang of this yet.

"Better," he said. "Now let us try a simple reversal."

She found herself bent over staring at his feet—which *did* show his age, the nails were like yellow claws—while his fingers traced the route of kundalini energy from her brainstem to her tailbone.

"In this way," he said, shifting his cute, pudgy little cock inside her, "apparent opposites take strength from one another."

She was so cavernous by now that she was like a huge mouth sitting over him. "I see," she said as the most recent orgasm dwindled.

"The discharge of vital fluids is avoided and transferred instead into kundalini. Often in the West, I believe, correct me if I am wrong, the yin and yang are taken as entirely separate, and the discharge of sexual fluid becomes, how to say it, the end in itself."

"An accurate assessment," she replied, flexing her thighs to get a better grip. "Sex does become an object." She slid back an inch. "Not a means of sacred union."

"Precisely. For this reason erotic sculpture is sacred to us."

There would come a point, she supposed, when emulating erotic sculptures might demand more than a forty-five-year-old body could manage. So far, so good, however. When she got a chance, she'd take a pair of nail clippers to work on those feet. But just now the delicate finger was moving up her spine again. Except this time the tingling appeared in her feet, which were pressed up on either side of his belly.

An orgasm in her feet?

"The feet," he said, touching the back of her head, "are especially erotic because all energy channels end there. Can you feel this?" He tapped the top of her head.

She had never had an orgasm in her feet, but at the same moment that he tapped the top of her head, his hand touched the sole of her right foot, and she jumped like a rabbit, rose off him with a loud sucking sound.

"I see," she said, clasping his feet like the handles of a wheelbarrow, her hair hanging over her eyes. Whatever was happening in her foot was moving up her leg. "I see. Very interesting."

"Tantric practice is generally not revealed to the uninitiated; there is so much unhealthy interest; however, it is apparent to me that a woman such as yourself . . ."

She sank back cautiously, engulfing him. Now her left foot was beginning to tingle. "I'll be damned," she said, hanging on for dear life.

30

They slept in the tent, both of them crammed in Jack's sleeping bag, Gonpo shivering uncontrollably. "We must return to the village in the morning," Jack had told him, alarmed at Gonpo's weakness. Everything depended upon overcoming this weakness, this numbing lassitude, but warming himself against Jack was not the way to do it. He must set an example for Jack to follow. Twenty years ago, on a moonlit night like this with a wind blowing, he had sat naked beside a frozen stream and dried three wet sheets placed around his shoulders. He had sat in the snow all night. But that was twenty years ago when he had burned with the pure force of Tantric discipline. Now he was soft.

Gonpo unzipped the bag. "I am comfortable now," he said. "I will sleep in my robes."

Jack protested, but Gonpo pointed out that both of them could not sleep in the single bag. The closed tent had warmed, and he would be quite comfortable. "I wish to meditate," he said.

Tum-mo, the practice of his youth, drew heat from the void itself. Now he brought Vajra Yogini into his mind, and she appeared ruby-red, holding the curved knife and the blood-filled skull, wearing her tiara of skulls, necklace of freshly cut human heads, and mirror of karma. Slowly Gonpo's body warmed as energy began to circulate through the psychic nerve channels. He shrank Vajra Yogini to the size of a pea, and began the calm breathing, letting the syllable *hum* radiate from his mind. The moonlight seemed to brighten, as if the cloud cover were thinning. If the snow were not too heavy during the night, if the trail broken by the yak caravan were still open, then Jack would go ahead. But he wouldn't leave if Gonpo were weak.

At dawn, Gonpo was sitting with the tent flaps open, watching the snow. It was sporadic now and the temperature was dropping. His hands and feet were numb, but he was still warm at the center of his body. He considered Sonam and Gyatsu chanting the Bardo Thodol over a human husk in the cave, but his mind would not rest there for long. The distance grew. And only slowly did he understand the reason.

He had become attached to the ghompa and Dorje; he had become attached to this life. And now as the moon and dawn mixed somewhere above the cloud cover, as the lifeless landscape appeared from the mist, his heart rose with certainty. *This* was what he had come to Dolpo for—these final hours in which to witness the clear light and achieve dharmakaya. Here at the base of the pass, where Jack had once killed a man and a dog and fought with the Russian, here under a stone overhang out of the worst of the snow, he studied the violent emanations of the region. He could escape the wheel or he could purge these hungry ghosts that sucked in human life: refugees, bandits, warriors, foreigners. If he failed, the wheel would spin him into rebirth and another lifetime of struggle and suffering.

Jack prepared tea and oatmeal on his small stove. To please him, Gonpo ate. Delicately. He drank the tea English-style with milk and sugar, remembering his many years in Kathmandu. The oatmeal was soft and bland as his life had been. The clouds appeared to be lifting. Jack's eyes were clear, and he radiated energy. A few hours' break in the snow would see him safely beyond the pass.

Jack was speaking of Tsering and Gonpo as if he thought he would see them again soon. Although he carried a message from Dorje that must reach the outer world, he did not yet understand the message and spoke of equations. Either Dorje had chosen a worthy vehicle or not. Time would tell. Gonpo could only guide Jack into the world and make certain that he understood his obligation.

"The others will be following you," Gonpo said.

"Then why am I leaving?"

"Please . . . ," Gonpo said wearily. "You know the reason."

Jack's eyes glazed with concentration. "The equation," he said. "Of course, I must discover the equation."

Gonpo did not dispute this interpretation. Equations were as mysterious to him as the world of Tantra to Jack. Perhaps an equation could guide men to the great liberation as well as a lama's words. "You must cherish their pursuit because they empower you. They will help to spread the teaching," Gonpo said.

This seemed to make sense to Jack. Wilson and the Russian would naturally want to discover what powers had been released in the cave, and if the Chinese woman returned to China, she, too, would spread strange stories of the American physicist. But it was Tsering who most interested him, and about whom he could not ask Gonpo directly, because he was afraid of the answer.

He wiped his cup and put it away in his pack as if he were returning to Berkeley from a Sierra jaunt. He pulled a wool cap over his ears. The idea that pursuit would spread the teaching appealed to him and gave purpose to his flight. He would lead a merry chase.

Gonpo helped him fold and pack the tent. They were ready for departure, and Gonpo must give no sign of weakness. Perhaps, he told Jack, he would replace Dorje in the cave and become a devoted lama attended by the two monks and thus remain near his beloved Tibet.

Jack liked the idea. "Yes, this is the best for you. And I will return to see you."

"Of course."

"I will know where to find you."

"Of course."

They embraced. Gonpo welcomed this last human touch, standing beneath the rock overhang on the bare spot where the tent had stood. The ground was almost dry. The transmission had occurred, and the messenger was on the way. The rest must await circumstance.

"Tell Tsering I will meet her in Kathmandu."

Gonpo nodded at this absurdity.

"Tell her I understand love at last. She was right. The other was a sticky residue."

"There is a fine line between human and divine love," Gonpo said. But it was not true. His love for this man who had brought him from Kathmandu was human. And this love had led him back to the path. There was no distinction, only a difference of intent.

"They won't catch me," Jack said.

"Catching you is not important. It is the pursuit."

Jack picked up his walking staff. "Good-bye," he said.

Gonpo pressed his hands together in silent recognition of Jack's task.

"You have taught me everything," Jack said.

"No, my friend, we have both taught and learned."

The orange pack started up through the snow, turned, and Jack waved. Gonpo raised his clasped hands. The clouds were dropping again, but the track left by the yaks was clear. This evening Jack should reach Tsharka and Weaver Yondon's house. In a week, if his strength held and he continued this day's pace, he would reach Kathmandu.

When Jack had vanished into the snow flurries, Gonpo lowered himself onto the bare ground, still warm from their bodies, and arranged his robes. The wind began to blow snow under the ledge. He felt it strike his face.

"*Om*," he began, as the wind entered his lungs.

"*Mani*," as the flakes stuck to his eyes.

"*Padme*," as his mind emptied.

"*Hum*."

Wind wuthered on the stone ledge above him. Swirling snow closed around him like a garment. He was alone. He felt the earth sinking into water, the water into fire, the fire into air, and air into consciousness—it was the moment of death come to him. "Recognize the clear light of the Bardo as dharmakaya." The Bardo Thodol's

243

words came to him. "Your mind is now empty of illusion and attachment; your mind is the Buddha-mind; use the clear light of death for the good of all beings."

The compassionate one rose before him, and the sacred mantra began to glow. The wheel was slowing. Each of the guardian deities passed before his eyes in a slow dance as his breathing slowed. His robe flapped in the wind. Snow drifted against his legs; it settled on his shoulders and caught in the folds of his robe. Ice crusted his eyelashes. But at the corners of his mouth a smile appeared like the upturning of his fingers in the snow. Like the unfolding of the lotus.

The snow was heavy, and warm. The wind spoke to him.

31

A cold rain had been falling all afternoon, washing excrement from the streets of Tsharka into the roiling Barbung Khola below the village. At first the villagers did not recognize the lone figure stumbling toward the village. Except for the orange pack and rain slicker, he might have been one of the hairy ones who left tracks on the high snowfields and sometimes carried off children. When he came straight to Weaver Yondon's house, the villagers remembered the foreigners of two weeks before—the smelly one, the one with the big eyes, and this one with the walking stick. Weaver Yondon welcomed him into the smoky upper room and poured salt and butter tea, which the American cupped eagerly in his hands. His face was hairy and chapped; his hair hung in long strands from under a wool cap, and although Weaver Yondon did not notice, his clothes were filthy with grease, smoke and charcoal. The man tried to smile, but his face seemed frozen, and he grimaced. For just a moment Weaver Yondon feared he was a hungry ghost, one of the restless dead wandering the land.

"Eeezup," Yondon said, trying his English. "Godom. Biopiss."

The American replied, possibly in Tibetan.

"Wooo car," Yondon said, determined to master English.

He poured more tea and made eating gestures. The American grimaced and nodded. Yondon called out, and from the animal shed below a woman climbed up carrying a small bundle of sticks. She crouched over the fire. Yondon pointed to the filthy blanket by the wall, where the Russian had recuperated, and Jack dragged his pack there. He was still dazed by the cold and wind of the pass where, except for the yak caravan the evening before, he might have lost his way in the blowing snow. Gratefully, he spread out his sleeping bag, wanting to lie down and forget the oppression in his mind of walking alone into a world he did not wish to reenter.

Smoke inside the room thickened as the woman stirred the fire. Perhaps he would rest just a moment, he thought, and stretched out with a sigh. But when he closed his eyes, he saw himself returning to Dolpo, laboring back through waist-deep snow. On the other side of the pass, the familiar vistas of Inner Dolpo had been replaced by a painted backdrop of mountains and human figures like a crude stage set, or like a thanka of Tantric demons and saints. On the backdrop, a man was striking another man with a walking staff; a dog's throat was slit; a band of Tibetan horsemen circled two men fighting on the ground; and a nuclear plume rose from the dun-colored peak of Twilight Mountain. Beyond the painted backdrop, like faces looking over the top of a shower curtain, were three giant figures: Tsering, Wilson, Boris, looming against the Tibetan sky. His pursuers.

Then the curtains of snow closed, and he was asleep.

"The bandits brought you back against your will?" her interrogator asked.

"Yes."

"They struck you?"

Impulsively, she pulled off her parka and pulled back her shirt. Bruises were visible on her arm and back, and on her breast where the Russian's teeth had left a dark mark.

"You were returning to your country?"

She lowered her head. "I don't know," she said, knowing she was trapped.

"This is not satisfactory."

She looked at the smooth, arrogant face of the Han radiating superiority. She had lived with this arrogance for years in Lhasa.

"I was walking."

"Across these mountains? Across a closed frontier? Please explain yourself."

"I considered returning."

"This you can do legally at official entry points. You are suspected of spying."

"Then why did these Khampa force me back?"

"The bandit will tell us the reason."

The snow was heavier now; she felt it blanketing her heart as her fate was decided by this child.

"In what village is the American expedition?"

She named the nearest village.

"You are with this expedition?"

"Yes."

"In what capacity?"

"Interpreter."

"Why is the Russian with them?"

"You are familiar with the word *detente*?"

"I see."

He did not see, of course. The young Chinese officer was concealing his own ignorance. The real interrogation would be much more subtle. She would be subjected to self-confession, *thamzin*, and much would depend upon what Li and Aten told the Chinese, and what had happened in Tibet since Deng's return.

Wilson, Boris and Angmo stood dutifully to one side of the cave amid all the strewn baggage.

"I have some questions for the American and Russian."

Tsering nodded.

"Why are they carrying these weapons?"

"Listen," she said to Wilson. "I am going to ask you some questions now. You are with a large expedition. Jack has escaped to bring help. Make your answers seem convincing. Wave your arms about—"

"Please," the Chinese said, his boyish face very cross. "I asked a very brief question."

"I am trying to explain."

"The answer?"

"Why are you armed?" she asked Wilson. "Now be outraged."

Wilson waved one arm. "To protect ourselves."

"It is perfectly obvious why," she told the Chinese. "They regret not having more weapons."

"Why does he carry a radio?"

"It's the first I've heard of this," she told Wilson. "What's the radio for?"

Wilson waved his other hand. "For emergencies. But it's not working."

"To stay in contact with the main expedition," she translated. "It is not working."

"Why did they come to this forbidden border?"

"I told you."

"Ask."

"Why are you here?" she asked Wilson. "And for God's sake look more annoyed. You need to frighten them with possible repercussions."

"We came here because your friend Malloy knew about this guru," he shouted at her, this time managing to wave both hands and frown at the same time. "You know why we came."

"He is very annoyed," she translated, "at this questioning in a neutral country. He refuses to answer any more questions."

The officer stared at Wilson, who stared back from behind thick glasses, clenching both fists. "What about the Russian? I wish to know these same questions."

"You and Wilson are with a large American expedition," she told Boris. "Jack escaped to bring help. Look friendly with Wilson and annoyed at these questions."

"I am with the Americans?"

"Yes. Show it."

He put his arm around Wilson's shoulders. "Comrade," he yelled in Wilson's ear. Wilson looked pained, but managed a thin smile, putting his arm around the Russian's shoulder. "International solidarity, very important," Boris yelled.

"What's that?" Wilson asked.

"International solidarity," she told him. "You're the best of friends. Detente. The arms race has ended. Peace and tranquillity reign."

"Really?" Wilson said. Since the Russian was shouting and stamping his feet, Wilson banged his own chest indignantly, managing to pound on Boris's shoulder at the same time. "International solidarity. Very important. Now winter. We leave."

"Better," she said.

"Comrade international brotherhood," the Russian said. "You barbarian monkeys are the curse of the civilized world."

At all the arm-waving, the Chinese looked alarmed. "What is happening?"

"Your questions have annoyed them; you have no right to search their belongings on this side of the border. They are both intending to report your behavior. Embassies will be notified. There will be trouble."

Wilson and Boris continued to slap each other on the back and shout while the Chinese looked baffled. He had not counted on this kind of resistance and didn't know how to behave. She was depending on his youth, on the fact that he had illegally crossed an international border, and on the snow itself, which would hasten a decision.

Sensing the Chinese officer's indecision, Boris and Wilson redoubled their efforts, stamping about the cave and shouting at one another and the officer and Tsering. She no longer made any sense out of their rantings, but cautioned them against overacting.

"You can stop now," she said in English and Russian.

"What have you said?" the Chinese asked.

"That they must contain their anger, that you mean well and do not intend any harm."

249

The officer thought a while. Then, with a sudden cunning look, he said, "If they remain here, you must come with us."

"I would prefer to finish my duties with the foreigners."

"But you were trying to escape them."

"I did not know that I had crossed the border."

"This is a lie. It will be necessary to detain all of you."

"What is he saying?" Wilson demanded.

"They want me to go with them."

"Do you want to go?"

"No. But if I stay, they'll detain you and Boris."

The Chinese interrupted. "There has been enough talk. What are you saying?"

"I am explaining my decision," she said to him and then quickly to Wilson: "Tell Jack what has happened."

"You're going back? What will they do to you?"

"It's not possible to know with the Chinese. Long interrogation, some form of public confession. Perhaps prison, perhaps menial labor. Or, who knows, they may want to demonstrate tolerance of minorities since the Cultural Revolution. Perhaps I will become a showpiece."

Wilson held out his hand to her.

"I'd keep your distance," she said.

"No more talk," the Chinese said. "You have a decision."

"I have a decision," she replied.

He woke to moonlight on this side of the Himalayas. The storm had passed, but he woke thinking of those left behind. "Cherish them," Gonpo had said. So why leave them in the first place?

He saw his footprints and Gonpo's, like the tracks of mesons or pions created by collision with a target in a bubble chamber, Dorje's bubble chamber. Leading away from the collision were the tracks of new particles linked by their common moment of creation. But human beings were not linked by a wave equation. People were not particles, and what happened to him on this side of the Himalayas could not affect Tsering on the other side. Twin-state photons were forever correlated at any distance, the spin of one forever dependent on the spin of the other. But that was the subatomic world. He must stop this insane speculation.

When he woke again, it was dawn; there was smoke in the air. "Eeezup," Yondon greeted him.

"Eeezup," Jack replied.

The nightmare doubts had passed, and he felt stronger and more focused. Quickly he stuffed his sleeping bag and prepared his pack while Yondon pantomimed that he must stay and eat. Jack looked out the low doorway. Roofs and stone streets glittered with ice. The temperature had dropped, and the passes between here and the Kali Gandaki would be icebound. He and Yondon and the woman mixed ground barley with salt tea in a mush and ate, staring at one another across the gap of language without comprehension but with good intentions. Stripped of language, he sat, like the dumb lens through which Dorje had projected visions into the minds of others. Jack, the quantum lama, the mute.

"Minus-h-bar squared over two-m . . ." He began to recite Schrödinger's wave equation. He'd used this empty formula all his life. "Del squared psi plus v equals i-h-bar partial of psi with respect to time." He completed the litany of Schrödinger's wave function, to Weaver Yondon's delight.

"Abar," Yondon echoed, mangling Planck's constant. "Delswear veequal." He began to giggle. These syllables had no more meaning for Yondon than the Buddhist mantras had for Jack. But the sound had magical properties. He jumped up, and to the delight of Yondon and his gap-toothed wife, banged his head on the low beam. "Minus-h-bar squared over two-m . . . ," he said rubbing his head, stunned by the blow.

The echo came back: *"Mindachbaar overto om."*

Repeating the empty quantum syllables, now echoed by Yondon and his wife, who clapped their hands at this peculiar stranger, Jack shouted and ducked beams. He saw his footprints rejoin Gonpo's, like a Feynman diagram of particle creation and decay, reversing time. He saw other human tracks from their collision in Dorje's bubble chamber, joining one another and separating, all of them spreading meaning they could not understand—creating new particles that would exist only briefly before decaying into still more particles. Energized by Dorje, the lama-magician, this cascade of particles was spreading from Dolpo into the world. The dancer could never be separated from the dance. So Jack created his pursuers by fleeing, and they created his flight by pursuit. They must cherish one another. That's what Gonpo meant.

And now in Weaver Yondon's hut, flapping his arms and legs, rubbing his head and chanting Schrödinger's equation, Jack felt he was not the one dancing. He felt as if all the shadow fragments that had escaped his grasp inside the cave had now aligned themselves into a palpable presence that was guiding his hands and legs. As he spun in Yondon's hut, as Yondon and his wife clapped their hands and jumped from foot to foot, howling Tibetan syllables at him, Jack remembered his dance in the cave and that moment when he remembered the lost equation and lost it again. He heard again the chants and ringing bells and howling thighbone trumpets streaming out into the vast silence of Inner Dolpo—the puny sounds that were supposed to reconcile human consciousness with the void. Now other lips were forming the sounds from his throat, and the familiar equation of the mathematician Schrödinger was being shaped into something new—a quantum mantra containing the clear light of one mind.

He seized his walking staff and strode to the door, stepping into the frozen dawn. A flood of unintelligible Tibetan mixed with quantum syllables followed him.

"*I-h*-bar partial of psi with respect to time," he replied. Ahead, the icebound passes glittered like highways.

The four dead Tibetans were stacked like cordwood in the snow. Aten, his face swollen where he had been struck by the rifle barrel, stood like a man already dead.

The officer spoke curtly to Tsering and she replied. She stepped toward Boris bundled in his furs and orange cap. His eyes streamed tears that were freezing in his beard. As they embraced, the Russian kissed her roughly, passionately, while the Chinese officer stood waiting.

She came to Wilson, who held out his hand.

"Please," she said, extending her arms. "Take this back to Jack." Her body was more slender and sinewy than Angmo's; he felt her heart beating, her blood pulsing, as she raised her face and kissed him full on the lips.

"Yes," he said.

When she kissed him again, his glasses fogged. It was a promise he would keep. But to deliver it, he would need to be a different man than the one who had entered Dolpo.

She stepped back, her eyes dark and certain, and picked up her blue pack. Then she followed the officer whose rifle was slung over his shoulder, and began her return to a country that had vanished, the country which is nowhere. The snow fell steadily, filling her tracks, and Boris made snuffling noises. Wilson watched her blue speck disappear in his fogged glasses.

When it was clear the Chinese would not return, Wilson and Boris began stuffing supplies into their packs, and Angmo prepared her basket. Wilson held out his tennis shoes. She looked at them. He made tying gestures. She grinned. Then he held out a pair of wool socks, wool trousers, a wool shirt. She accepted each item with a grin and a sucking sound. Then he held out the fur cap to the Russian, who looked tempted before shaking his head and pulling the orange cap down firmly over his bushy hair. When he thought the others weren't watching, Wilson stuffed the rolls of exposed film into his pack. He left the cameras, the tape recorder and radio in the cave.

As they descended the valley, the sound of the monks chanting in the upper cave came to them on flurries of wind and snow. Only Angmo could understand the words of the Bardo Thodol being said over Dorje's corpse, a lama who instead of leaving the wheel of birth and death had returned. But instead of being reborn in the future, he had entered a still living soul that was clouded by personal consciousness and accumulated karma. Only the very greatest yogis could do such a thing. And it was a great risk, but he was riding out of Dolpo like a burr stuck to an animal's fur. Contained in this prickly seed, which at any moment might fall from Jack onto sterile ground, were thousands of years of wisdom, passed from one master to the next.

32

Snow had piled against Gonpo's legs, filled his cupped hands and sat as a mantle over his shoulders. Eyes closed, a faint smile frozen on his lips, Gonpo sat guarding the pass to the outer world; his red robes were the one spot of color. Angmo threw herself into the snow and raised her clasped hands in obeisance. The ghostly sound of drums and bells and trumpets rang in Wilson's ears.

He looked at Boris. This was the only level spot for a tent, but what could they do about the frozen lama? Burial was impractical, to move him unthinkable. Boris shrugged his shoulders and began tramping down snow beside the lama, making a small firm platform. While Angmo continued her prostrations in the growing dusk, the two men erected the tent with one nylon wall pressed up against Gonpo. They ate and slept crowded inside—Angmo jammed between the Russian and American in their sleeping bags. The tent flapped and fluttered as wind drove powdery snow across the stone land, and the temperature dropped, hardening the frozen presence outside. Why had Gonpo been left to freeze? Wilson remained awake, watching the moon cast Gonpo's shadow on the tent wall.

He had only his nose sticking out of the sleeping bag, but at some point during the night he smelled the unmistakable odor of sardines and felt a tongue licking his face. He shifted, embracing the bulky woolen figure, who buried her face in his neck and began to nibble at him. The Russian grunted and turned against her from behind, forcing her tight against Wilson. The sudden pressure reminded him of Tsering's final embrace and her passionate kiss. Was she even now sitting in some Chinese encampment, awaiting judgment? He was sufficiently dazed by events and lack of sleep that the woman lying against him seemed, for a moment, to *be* Tsering. And then he became the woman pressed up against the Russian, yearning for his translator, with tears in his own eyes. Were they the Russian's tears, or Tsering's, or his own? No matter. On this high plateau, it did not seem a particularly remarkable feat—drifting off to sleep inside the mind of a Tibetan and a Russian.

If it snowed all night they would be unable to cross the pass. But that no longer mattered to Wilson. In fact it was difficult to remember *why* he wished to leave Dolpo. He supposed that it was important to catch up with Malloy . . . ah, yes, because he had tapped into some kind of psychic energy. But so had they all.

Angmo's freezing hand slipped inside his bag and began to pinch him gently. When Wilson moved his hand down her body, he met another hand . . . the Russian's.

"Tserosha," the Russian muttered softly, as if in his sleep.

Neither man moved but remained touching under Wilson's wool shirt brought all the way from Denver and given to Angmo. So even the KGB had forgotten Malloy. If mind control were possible, it could be used. In the morning, that might seem more significant. But for now, there was only this warmth of three humans tangled together beside a frozen lama.

They slept like drowsy animals in a den, petting one another sleepily in a way quite familiar to Angmo, who in another night or two would be sleeping with two brothers, her husbands. Their mingled and fetid breath condensed on the inside of the tent, where it froze. Clouds cleared and a waning moon, near full, cast a pure white light over the snowscape. Light fell on the blue tent and on the frozen figure seated beside it. The same moonlight fell on the filthy village of Tsharka, perched on the Barbung Khola, where Weaver Yondon slept in a sweatshirt with a man's head printed on the front. It was the benign face of Albert Einstein, looking over the twentieth century like a sad buddha. The same moon was shining on the iced lakes of the high plateau and the tepid rivers of India.

Over the Rockies where this moon was setting, a Coors beer truck driver snored in his sleep. Beside him, Mudra watched the moon, wondering why she did these things. The man was gross. When they had come into the apartment near two, the child in the next room woke looking sullen and resentful. There had to be a better way, she thought, rolling carefully to the edge of the bed. As a distant peak cut into the soft belly of the moon, she wrapped her arms protectively over her breasts. There simply had to be a better way.

"I see he's back," the little Hindu said. He was catching the last afternoon sun in the garden.

"Who?"

"The American at the institute."

"Are you quite sure?"

"Of course, look at the walking stick."

"What do you suppose happened to him?"

"Well," the little Hindu said, "at least he's still walking. Some of them are missing toes and fingers or don't come back at all. He doesn't look so bad."

"He looks terrible. Do you still think he's CIA?"

The Hindu sipped his tea reflectively.

"Another biscuit?"

"Please."

"No," he said finally. "I suppose not. The CIA wouldn't do this sort of thing to themselves. Aren't these people amazing?"

"Indeed. When they aren't blowing us up, they're punishing themselves for it. More tea?"

"Just a dollop. And perhaps one more biscuit."

257

≈

"He'll be arriving this week," the lama said on the phone.

"How do you know?" Lia asked.

"I meditated."

Lia accepted this prophecy docilely enough, because, since the lama's visit to California, her critical faculties had gone on vacation. Improbable events had taken over her life, and at her age, the surprise was quite pleasurable. Her decision to go to Nepal had left a trail of concern and envy among her friends. That, too, was pleasurable. Lia had become so unpredictable, they said.

"Nepal?" Mukerjee asked.

"Why not?" she replied.

Then Browny tuned in: "You *really* expect to meet Jack there?"

In the past weeks, Browny had become obsessed with Jack's whereabouts, which had become tangled up in his mind with the recent experiments at Berkeley substantiating Bell's theorem. "If, after Bell's theorem, there's no hidden variable behind quantum theory," he had said, "then quantum reality is crazy. But why aren't we crazy? Something's wrong."

Now he looked at Lia as if she were crazy. "You're going to Nepal?"

"Yup."

"To see Jack?"

"Yup."

"Do you want company?"

She was stunned. Browny rarely left his house, much less Berkeley, and in recent years wouldn't fly anywhere, which limited his range a good deal. He couldn't be serious, yet his face told her that he was. He'd become so consumed by Jack's whereabouts, by Bell's theorem and by the possibilities of consciousness since their remote viewing experiments, that she was reminded of his earlier days at the university. When Browny became focused on an issue, students and colleagues were aligned with his vision, almost against their will. Now these myopic obsessed eyes stopped her practical objections—that he

258

couldn't take a train to Nepal, that he would miss Thanksgiving with his wife, that he had angina and high blood pressure. His proposition was so absurd that it made sense to her.

"Why not?" she said.

Now it was Mukerjee's turn to be stunned. For weeks he'd been worried that their psychic experiments would discredit the Consciousness Group even more than Jack had already done. Even though the remote viewing with the lama had shaken him, like the earthquake, he couldn't let himself go back to the superstition he'd grown up with. Lia said, "If we can't explore consciousness freely, then let's disband and go back to being quantum drones." That was easy for her, since she no longer seemed to care about her reputation at the lab and university. And since Browny had retired, it made little difference to him. But a wrong turn now could ruin Mukerjee's career. He'd even considered dropping the group since an astronomer and a number of graduate students had expressed interest this fall. Lia even wanted to begin a newsletter. Now, when she turned to him and asked, "Krishna, what about you?" he was actually trembling.

"Oh, no," he replied quickly. "I couldn't. There are so many obligations at this time of year. My relations are coming from England." Then he stopped. There was no need to defend himself from this ridiculous proposition. He wasn't the crazy one. And yet as they went their separate ways, he was envious of Lia and Browny going halfway around the world because of a few cloudy visions and intuitions, and because of a lama of considerable personal charm. And because Jack, whatever he was doing, had infected their minds.

Out of Jack's gaunt, hairy face peered feverish eyes.

"My God, Jack," Lia said.

The walking stick dropped clattering to the concrete floor of the institute as they embraced. Jack's voice was scratchy and dry. "I dreamed about you," he said. "I was hitchhiking from Bombay, and you and Browny picked me up in a limousine."

"He's here, too," she said.

"Browny's here?"

"At the hotel. Come and clean up. Are you all right?"

"What are you doing here?"

"I came to see you."

"How did you know . . . ?"

"Lama Z invited me."

Jack looked at Lama Z, who bowed his head modestly.

"Why?"

"We were worried about you. I have plenty of vacation time."

"But how . . . ?"

"We've been watching you." She meant to be amusing, but he looked stricken.

"Lama Z was good enough to help us locate you," she said.

It was heartbreaking to see him in such a state. She wanted to wash his clothes and scrub him down and shave off that awful gray beard that made him look like an old man. In the foyer of the institute, he stood feebly like some bearded hermit with his pilgrim's staff who had stumbled out of the mountains, bewildered, into the twentieth century.

Lia's presence struck him like stone. He had been searching frantically for a course of action as he raced down from the Himalayas, wondering what he would do when he reached Kathmandu. Last night he dreamed of Lia and Browny. Now their appearance and the dream had become part of the invisible tissue of connections that had infiltrated his consciousness these past months. Even after his death, Dorje was orchestrating events. Browny was the one theoretician who might be able, mathematically, to reconcile Jack's intuition with physics.

"Browny *insisted* on coming," Lia was saying. "He's talked incessantly of seeing you since he had the vision."

The mushroom cloud boiled up from his hands. Bodies sprawled on the cave floor, and he stepped into the radioactive glow of universal death.

He stared at Lia.

She and Browny had been drawn across the Pacific to Nepal as he had been drawn to Inner Dolpo. A human bridge now stretched from one world to another, and the thousands of years of mystic teaching behind Dorje had sparked across time into the quantum community. Dorje had tried to reach from the edge of Tibet, where Buddhism had been reduced to ashes. He had tried to reach this strange new science that was also exploring the interface of consciousness and the void. But his desperate experiment made sense only if physics were also leading toward enlightenment and the quantum masters working toward becoming quantum bodhisattvas. In which case, he had made Jack the trigger, the quantum agent. Lia and Browny would fire the gun.

"We're being followed," he said to Lia. "We must act quickly."

"Followed?" she asked.

"CIA, KGB, whatever the Chinese call it. Spies," he said. "The spies know about us."

"Jack, you need rest. Let's go to the hotel. Browny is waiting."

"But they give us legitimacy, don't you see? As long as they think we have a secret, we'll be taken seriously. Their paranoia is necessary."

Lia's hand was on his arm, her face concerned and wavering as though underwater. Lama Z, uncertain whether to intervene or not, took one step forward and stopped.

"Otherwise," Jack said, "Dorje is simply another crazy mystic. But they give him legitimacy. They're also contaminated. They're like ants carrying poison back to the nest. We're the poison, Lia. Enlightenment is poison to any military exploitation of quantum knowledge."

Her face continued to waver, and Lama Z, in his orange robes, continued to approach like a curious fish.

"They'll help us spread the enlightenment equation," Jack said, and once again felt other lips shaping the sounds from his throat.

The longer they threw off the pursuit, the more important their secret would become, and the better their chance to find the equation. But in the interim, they needed Lama Z's help. Both Lia and Lama Z flinched when Jack threw himself down on the concrete floor, prostrating himself before Lama Z and raising his clasped hands over his head in the manner of devout Tibetan Buddhists before a great teacher.

Lama Z was not as gratified as he might have been. Dorje was very bold to come here in the guise of this filthy and half-demented American. "That is not necessary," the lama said gruffly. "Please."

"Jack, are you all right?" Lia was saying. But the gaunt figure on the floor would not look up. In the manner of believers who circumambulate sacred Mount Kailas on their bellies, or are seen creeping beside the roads of Tibet toward the holy city of Lhasa, Jack was moving across the floor in a series of prostrations, and Lama Z was following him, flustered and embarrassed for Lia to see such a thing.

"We must hide until the equation is found," Jack was saying. "The longer the pursuit, the more they'll spread the conditions of enlightenment, like a contagious disease, from within the establishment itself."

As Jack rose repeatedly and extended himself full length on the hallway floor, hands raised above his head, they followed him toward Lama Z's chamber. Once the door was closed, and Jack had reached the meditation mat and sat up in a lotus, a greater certainty came to Lama Z. He sat opposite Jack, while Lia sat stiffly to one side, rubbing her hands together and watching her friend with an expression somewhere between horror and elation.

"You must stay here," Lama Z said. "Of course."

"Too obvious," Jack said. "The first place they'll look."

Of course that was true. At the moment, Lama Z lacked the inner vision to unravel this conundrum posed by Jack's appearance in Kathmandu. He'd simply have to stall. "If Kathmandu is too small a pond, perhaps you had better hide in the ocean. We could arrange for you to enter India, unofficially."

Jack frowned.

"We have many contacts there. A man could disappear into India for years without a trace."

"Years?" Lia looked alarmed.

"It depends on what Mr. Malloy wishes."

"You and Browny must come with me," Jack said.

Lia's heart pounded frantically. The husk of Jack's body seemed to have been inflated by another presence and his face stretched like leather over a shoemaker's last. She was terrified.

"We're due back home after Christmas," she said.

"Due back?"

"At the lab."

"Ah, yes. The lab."

She looked pleadingly at Lama Z for some way to handle this situation, but he was no help. He knew only too well that Jack was beyond their control. They could help him or he would go his way alone. There was no other choice. The awful sight of Jack prostrating himself across the concrete floor of the institute, like a gangly caterpillar, had shriven Lama Z. Dorje would stop at nothing.

"Why don't you rest," Lama Z said solicitously to Jack. "Your mind will be clearer tomorrow. We can make plans then."

Jack looked dazed.

"See me in the morning," Lama Z said. "By then I will have made a plan."

Jack paused, as if listening to a distant voice, and Lia quickly interjected, "Come to the hotel and clean up, Jack. Eat a good dinner and talk with Browny."

Browny's name produced results. Jack snatched his staff off the floor and started for the door. Lia called after him, "Jack, you're exhausted, it's miles from here." But he did not look back.

When Lama Z's car reached him a mile down the road, and Lia ordered the driver to stop, Jack seemed surprised to see her looking out of the tinted window of a black Mercedes. He seemed to have forgotten their meeting minutes earlier at the institute, and like an obedient child, he got into the backseat with his walking staff.

Now she was truly alarmed by his emaciated face. She had the distinct impression that someone else was sitting in the car with her. And reaching for his hand was no consolation. It was cold, bony and alien, and he did not look at her, but kept his eyes fixed on the road ahead, as if commanding the bullock carts and bicycles and cows to move out of the way. As the driver plunged with appalling speed through the unfamiliar mayhem of an Asian city, Lia clung to the seat back, bracing against imminent collision, and trying to avoid looking at the presence beside her. Her body was rigid.

33

Angmo accompanied Wilson and Boris to the rim of the great Kali Gandaki gorge. She arranged food in villages along the way and guided them down the trails. During the night, she listened to them sleeping on either side of her, murmuring in strange languages. Now trying to make it clear that she must return to her village and husbands, and that from here on they could find their way alone, she pantomimed and shouted. The bushy one was the first to understand. He embraced her with a powerful hug and started down the trail, his orange cap bobbing down through the snow. Wilson remained with her for a moment, making a series of interesting sounds, which gave her an idea. Where they stood was sheltered and sunny, almost warm. The snow had melted. In a final effort to communicate what these weeks with him had meant to her, she threw herself on him. When she stopped, he was drenched with sweat and whimpering. She pulled at his peculiar, skinless thing, batting it playfully like a cat. But there was nothing left. They must be born without skin on the lingam, she decided. Most peculiar. Otherwise·it worked fine. It occurred to her that a child with a fair skin would not be a bad thing in the village. But would a boy have skin down there or not?

Wilson stood up, naked, preparing to dress, and she studied his body. It gave her great pleasure to look at his pale skin and to recognize with affection certain bruises and scratches, and it made her sad to see him cover it up. She would never see it again unless there was a pale child with a funny lingam.

As he descended into the gorge, she stood in his tennis shoes, wool trousers, shirt and wool socks, with a pair of polka-dot undershorts stuffed in one pocket and five thousand rupees, many times more than the agreed sum, stuffed in the other pocket. When he turned and waved from beneath his fur cap, she grinned at him, blowing good wishes through her rotted teeth. Then she turned and started home. At the first pass, she circumambulated the stone chorten ten times, chanting Om, mani, padme, hum. Her husbands would be very pleased with the clothes. And the five thousand rupees was a sum too great for her to comprehend. Her life would never be the same again.

"Something has happened, sir." Muldoon was disheveled with excitement.

Colonel Yanker looked at him patiently. Despite Muldoon's exotic scenarios, Yanker had lost interest in this extravagant and expensive surveillance of the physicist Malloy. There had been little enthusiasm upstairs, and it was generally agreed that Wilson's report would suffice.

"That facility in the Himalayas, sir?" Muldoon insisted.

"Yes."

"Remember the earthmoving equipment I told you about?"

"I remember, Sergeant."

"There's been an incident."

"Incident?"

"We're not certain. Emergency vehicles and a general exodus from the area have occurred. We'll have the report later today."

"An accident at this presumed nuclear facility?"

"We think so."

"And our friends are in the vicinity?"

"We presume so, but we can't be certain until we hear from Wilson."

"Are you suggesting a connection?"

"The first rule of—"

"Yes, I know, Muldoon, the first rule of intelligence is to look for connections before accepting coincidence."

"Well, there are known guerrilla elements in the area. Sabotage is a possibility."

"Sergeant, you have an admirably fertile mind. But why on earth would a man like Malloy work with Tibetan guerrillas to sabotage a Chinese facility? This is absurd. The guerrillas are virtually exterminated, and they never had the capacity for more than minor mischief."

Muldoon was silent.

"Personally, I've never subscribed to the view that Malloy is anything but what he seems—another of these Californians wigged out on too much LSD. If word ever leaks out that we're tracking some hallucinating psychic, we'll be laughed across the river. Do me a favor, Sergeant. First, let's be certain there *is* a facility. Second, let's be sure there *has* been an accident. Third, let's debrief Wilson."

Muldoon drooped. "You still want the report and photos?"

"Of course. Just hold the theorizing."

Muldoon turned away.

"Oh, Sergeant . . ."

Muldoon turned back, eager. "Sir?"

"How did the hypnotism work on your smoking?"

"Well, sir, it's actually a form of meditation, it turns out. By stilling your mind, you know, the noise of everyday life that crowds our waking hours . . . ?"

"Yes."

"Well, by stilling our mind and focusing on the moment, we see such desires for what they are."

"Which is what?"

"Just ripples on the pond, sir, distorting life the way ripples distort the surface of water."

267

"Ripples, Muldoon?"

"Yes, sir. Once you see that you're causing the ripples, they go away."

"And along with them your smoking habit?"

"That's correct."

"And is it working?"

Muldoon coughed. "In a way. I've cut back to ten a day."

"That's good news."

"You might try it, sir, it's very restful."

"Perhaps your example will inspire me. Until then, let's not blow Malloy out of proportion, all right?"

"Yes, sir. But wait until you see these photos, just ten miles from that hermit's cave—"

"Thank you, Sergeant."

Lama Z meditated. If Dorje had focused all his spiritual force on Malloy, and the physicist had drawn the American agent, Wilson, and these other physicists, then the linkage was certainly worth monitoring. But what did Dorje hope to accomplish by casting himself into this form? Answers depended on Tsering, and her absence was troubling. He needed her to guide his actions with the Nepalese in case of political repercussions. Why had Jack left her and the others?

And where could he hide a physicist? Kathmandu was too small. But India—the possibilities were limitless. In Dharmsala there were too many Westerners, and Wilson might think to look there. In the countryside, Jack couldn't help but attract unwelcome interest among peasants. But in a city such as Bombay, where foreigners who looked as demented as Jack were common fare and attracted little interest, there was a possibility.

Lama Z began to see the bright side of this affair. By risking this expedition to the border, he had gained some interesting new connections in the world. Now Malloy was dependent on him. So was Lia. Tsering would provide any missing clues. And out of this peculiar mélange might come some interesting advancement of the Dharma in

America. The more he thought about it, the better he liked this linkage with physics. It was a pragmatic opening to the West.

Browny sat on the toilet smoking, while Lia scrubbed Jack's back. "Jesus, you're filthy," she said.

He had his head down on his knees while Browny questioned him. "So you saw a unified theory."

"I saw unity, Browny."

"You think there's a mathematical formulation?"

"Yes. I saw an equation and lost it. We simply need to start from a new place to find it. I keep asking myself, what is the fundamental postulate of quantum theory?"

"Hard to say. Wave/particle duality?"

"And what creates the duality?"

"Come on, Jack! What kind of a question is that?" Browny asked.

"We create duality by observing, right? We look for waves, we see waves. We look for particles, we see particles."

"That's one way to look at it, yes."

"Don't you see the flaw?" Jack asked, looking up from his knees. "No."

"The problem lies in observation. We assume the observer exists outside a closed system, and then quantum theory has to compensate for the resulting paradox. What if we start with another assumption?"

"Raise your arm," Lia said. "Yuck! When was the last time you had a bath, Jack?"

"I don't remember."

"I need a wire brush to get this off."

"Oddly enough," Browny said, blowing out a huge cloud into the already fogged bathroom, "this is precisely where Bell's theorem has driven us."

Lia lathered a washrag furiously. "We've been into Bell ever since you left," she said, "and getting nowhere. It's like watching your eye watching itself."

"Precisely," Jack said, snatching the washrag and running it over

269

his face. "Precisely. What if, rather than a detached observer, we start with the assumption of unity?"

"You'll need to define unity," Browny said. "Is physics even possible without an observer?"

Lia had seized the washrag back and was working on Jack's feet.

"Maybe the unified theory *is* enlightenment," Jack said. "And it's eluded us because we've been looking for proof outside the mind."

The others were silent.

Finally Lia said, "No proof, no science."

She was washing his muscular calves and was once again startled by the sensation of another person occupying the bathtub, a ghostly figure. But the flesh beneath her hands was not ghostly, nor was the morsel floating between his legs. She remembered her last exercise in Tantric sexual yoga with Lama Z, and for a moment saw Lama Z's Buddha belly floating in the tub.

"Perhaps," Jack replied, "proof is the problem."

Mukerjee woke with a wail.

"Krishna, what is it?" his wife said.

"I want to go home," he said.

"Good lord," she said, sitting up in bed and turning on the light. "Not Bombay!"

"No, I can't remember where."

"Is it a place, a country?"

He wailed again. "It's nowhere."

"You're dreaming," she comforted him.

"I don't know," Krishna whimpered. "Am I still asleep?"

"There, there," she said, stroking his forehead. "Why don't you go to the bathroom. You know what happens when your bladder is full. Then I'll fix some hot milk."

Krishna's head was swimming with confused images of battle and flight, as if he were Arjuna, riddled with "the doubt born of ignorance" and fighting his own kinsmen in the Mahabharata.

When his wife returned with the hot milk, she was astonished to see the physicist reading the Bhagavad Gita, looking for his dream. And even more astonished when, a little later, he pulled off his pajamas dramatically and threw himself on her with more fervor than she remembered him showing in years. She even had a sense that, on this particular night, the body of her husband, newly muscular from jogging, was occupied by some other person. And she responded with such unexpected enthusiasm that he was reminded of a night in Cambridge when a young Indian physicist first met this pale English girl whose father had once commanded troops in Bombay.

Browny looked through smoke and steam at his two friends. Jack's eyes were bloodshot, his lips chapped, his chest a map of ribs, and his gray beard floated in the water. Lying in the tub was no one Browny had ever seen before. But Browny didn't care, because he was relishing the possibilities that lay ahead, and enjoying this surge of energy he was feeling. Just when his mind had become sluggish near retirement, something tremendous had happened. He felt clear and vibrant, as if the summer fog were burning off the Berkeley hills.

He puffed enthusiastically on his pipe, watching Lia kneel over Jack's skeletal body, and he began to focus on the problem of unity. What could it mean to say there was no observer? He felt that wonderful sense of power that had once come when he pitted himself against the most difficult mathematical problems. Once or twice in his lifetime, this sure expectation of a breakthrough had occurred to him. But then he was a young man. Now, well, now he was in another country.

"Let's rinse you off and tackle that beard," Lia said.

But Jack was asleep, dreaming. Tsering lay on a metal-frame bed in a cavernous space, like a sheet-metal Quonset hut. The Himalayas that stood between them were a mere whimsical wrinkle in consciousness, and since the observer and observed were never separated, the two of them could not be rejoined. "I'll see you here one day," she

271

was saying. *"Tashi shok."* *Tashi shok*: May these blessings prevail. As he reached toward her, he woke up sputtering, soapy water up his nose.

Lia had draped the washrag over his erection. "Really, Jack," she said, "whatever were you dreaming?"

"I was dreaming of you," he said.

"I'm flattered," she replied. "Hand me a towel, Browny."

"Perhaps there *is* a way," Browny was saying. "Unity. What an odd notion."

Jack modestly wrapped the towel around his waist before stepping from the tub.

"Aren't you starved?" she asked.

"I could eat something."

"Browny?"

"What?"

"Do you want to eat?"

"No, I want to take a stroll around the campus and do some thinking."

"Browny?"

"What?"

"You're in Nepal."

"Really?" He looked bewildered. "Ah, yes," he said. "Well, what of it? I'll take a walk around the campus anyway."

Browny opened the bathroom door and Lia followed. And then Jack followed his two friends into the luxuriously carpeted bedroom of the hotel. Together with their pursuers, they were stepping into the void. And with any luck at all, the quantum masters spread all over the world would follow them.

Tashi shok

GOSHEN PUBLIC LIBRARY
601 SOUTH FIFTH STREET
GOSHEN, IN 46526-3994

272